I0451718

Just a Scream at Twilight

Hugo Miller Mysteries 6

Joseph Allen

Published by Rogue Phoenix Press, LLP
Copyright © 2022

ISBN: 978-1-62420-659-7

Credits
Cover Artist: Designs by Ms G
Editor: Kitty Carlisle

Dedication

For Angus, Isabelle and Xixi, and for all my Miller relatives in Texas, especially Gus and Jane.

Chapter One

My friend and colleague, Gabriele Cortese, and I were sitting in my living room on a fine late spring day having an afternoon glass of Cabernet Sauvignon when we heard a scream—a blood-curdling screeching yell that sounded like someone was being killed—from somewhere outdoors. The sliding glass door to the balcony was open because the outdoor temperature was perfect. Not hot and humid, not chilly. We both ran out on the balcony to see if we could see the screamer.

While we were standing there, with the Chrysler Building in front of us, there was another scream that must have been from the same woman, and this time, since we were outside, we could tell the direction it came from. It sounded like it was probably from the front of the building I live in.

I'm Hugo Miller. My friend, Gabriele, and I spend a lot of time together—almost always during the daytime, because Gabriele is a partner in a hugely successful Italian restaurant in the SoHo section of Manhattan. He works the dinner and late-night shift with his cousin/partner, Dante di Benedetto, who is the chef at the restaurant, so Gabriele's almost always busy evenings. He grew up on the Isle of Capri off the west coast of Italy, and Dante grew up in Naples. They're both gay, but neither one has a significant other, as far as I know.

I'm mostly retired from the sports PR company I founded, although I still maintain my position on the Board of Directors, since my name is still on the door. The company has been successful and allows me to maintain a lifestyle for myself about the way it was when I was working every day, and traveling fairly constantly, staying in good hotels, flying in the front cabin more often than not.

Anyway, the scream was all we could think about right then, and we went downstairs to see if we could find out what was happening. Jimmy, the day concierge, was standing on the sidewalk in front of the building, with his hands on his hips, staring at the building across the street, which opened onto the cross-street, and not onto the avenue that our building opens onto. Translation: we had to walk about twenty feet from the front door before we could see a small crowd of people on the sidewalk, looking up at a balcony on that building and pointing at something.

Gabriele and I hustled ourselves down toward the dozen or so people who were on the sidewalk, and then we could see a woman on the balcony covered with blood. It was all over her clothes, her face, her surgical mask and hair. Like she had been dipped in a vat of blood head-first.

She screamed again. Same scream, but this time it was words. "Help me, somebody! Help me!"

Just about that time, an NYPD car with lights flashing and siren blaring, came racing down the avenue and around the corner, stopping in front of the building where the woman was standing on the balcony.

I live in Long Island City, which is a part of Queens that is on the East River, and is gentrifying with people who really can't cope with the sky-rocketing high rents in Manhattan. I had lived in the Manhattan Theater District for a decade or so, but finally the latest annual rent hike was too much for me, and I found an apartment that was approximately the equivalent of my place for about a third of the rent—and this one had a washer and dryer in the apartment. The building I live in is directly across the East River from the United Nations, which is why I can see the Chrysler Building big as life from my living room couch—right over the television, and all lighted up at night. The street in front of my building looks for all the world like it might run right into 42nd Street if the river weren't there. But my street is 50th Avenue, not 42nd Street. There is no Manhattan-like street grid in Queens, although the street-numbering system makes it sound like there might be.

Best of all, where I live on Long Island City is one subway stop from Grand Central Terminal, about a four-minute ride under the river, so the attractions of Manhattan are no more distant than they were when I lived in the Theater District. Still and all, it's not Manhattan, so people who live on that blessed isle usually decline to visit simply because it's Queens and not "The City."

The cop car pulled over to the curb so as not to block the narrow street from traffic, but left the lights blinking as they hustled themselves into the building.

My cellphone, which I keep in the left back pocket of my jeans when I'm not in my apartment, vibrated. It was my friend and sometime "boss," Mike di Saronno, a highly respected NYPD detective who had been on the cases of several headliner homicides. In fact, I met Mike when I was snooping around the edges of the death of a famous harpsichordist, who fell—splat—onto the pavement of 7th Avenue from an apartment that used to be on top of Carnegie Hall (later demolished and replaced with something else).

"What's up, Mike?" I asked.

"You're probably going to be hearing sirens, because there's been a death in your neighborhood. My chief wants me to be on the team looking into this one, because the woman who admits to having committed it was someone I collared years back for drug smuggling. She was a flight attendant and spoke several languages, but was caught smuggling cocaine tied up inside condoms, inside her vagina and anus. One of them had started to leak, and made her high as a kite when she tried to go through customs and immigration. Her name is Maggie Landover, but she has used a lot of aliases. She apparently slit the throat of a man she said she met on the subway. He was trying to rape her, or so he told the cops who are in her apartment right now.

"I am looking at her standing on her balcony right now," I said. "She's covered with blood from her head on down, as far as I can tell. I heard some screaming, and Gabriele and I went downstairs and followed the noise to find a crowd of people staring at her, while she was yelling for help."

"She apparently grabbed a kitchen knife while he was trying to get her clothes off," Mike said, "and accidentally—so she says—cut his neck. Must have cut a big artery in the side of his neck, like the carotid where we feel for a pulse, because his blood sprayed all over the room, the Queens cops told me. By the way, I wouldn't be inclined to believe much of what she says. She makes it up as she goes along, and very little of what she said to me turned out to be the truth."

"So, this guy who was molesting her," I asked. "He lives in the same neighborhood? The building she is in is across the street from the building where I live. I think it's high-end condos. My building's all rentals. Her building was an empty lot when I moved in."

"No idea," Mike answered. "He apparently had no ID on him, and of course dead men don't talk. Maybe his prints will help us. Maggie apparently told the cops there that she had no idea who he was, just that he had his hands inside her bra, and the buttons ripped off her blouse. I wonder if she's still a flight attendant. I doubt it, since her drug incident would sour any airline that wanted to hire her. She was a pretty thing, as I recall, but that's been a while back. I probably wouldn't even recognize her these days if she sat next to me on the subway."

"Do I take it correctly that you might want me to help out somehow on this case? Is that why you called me?"

"Sorry, yeah, I think you and your merry crew might be able to think outside the box on this one. I have a feeling that will come in handy. Besides, the guys at the 108th there on your street don't have a lot of experience with homicides, and I'm obviously not close either. I may need eyes and ears."

Mike lives in Hell's Kitchen in Manhattan, and he can walk to work because his office is in the West Midtown North precinct on West 54th Street between 8th and 9th Avenues.

"L-A-N-D-O-V-E-R?" I asked. "Margaret?"

"You got it," he said. "Except maybe her legal name is Maggie, not Margaret. Keep track of your expenses on this one, because they'll be reimbursable, which means I have to approve anything expensive in advance."

He told me there would be a flat fee on this assignment, too. I usually don't get paid at all, btw. Volunteer civilian criminalists usually work *pro bono.*

"Gabriele? Ruth?" I asked him.

"Yup, sure. No trans-Atlantic flights, and no first class either."

"Nobody's ever asked you or the PD to pay for airplane fares for us—or hotel or food costs," I said, "and by the way, we fly business, not first. I'm too tall for the main cabin; can't get my legs to fit in a coach seat—my knees get hung up on the back of the seat in front of me, and I can't get my feet on the floor. And Ruth still has a gazillion airline miles from when her husband used to travel all over the world while he was still alive."

Ruth's husband, Murray, had died about five years earlier, and Ruth had been using his miles all that time, so we could fly business round trip to anyplace in Europe, for instance, for a cost of about seventy-five dollars per person.

This was happening during the coronavirus pandemic, so New Yorkers were wearing surgical masks, which can make it difficult to recognize even people you know pretty well. Voice recognition comes in handy, and of course the way certain people walk or act identifies them if you keep your eyes open. Some tall people are easy to recognize, maybe some short people. But the average people—unless they're talking—can walk right by you without you ever realizing they are there.

There were a lot of twists and turns ahead.

Chapter Two

The man Maggie Landover killed had been wearing a surgical mask on the subway. It was in the lockdown times of the COVID-19 pandemic, which had come down on New York City like a ton of bricks. There was a Navy hospital ship in the harbor to handle overflows, and the Javits Convention Center in Manhattan had been transformed into a huge Covid-19 makeshift hospital. As a result, a lot of New Yorkers were constantly masked, constantly staying six feet from other people when possible, and constantly washing our hands, especially since Purell dispensers appeared like bugs in the summer—everywhere you looked. Subway cars were a sea of light-blue surgical masks, which were about the only type of face covering that was readily available. The N95 masks were only for front-line healthcare workers—and they're harder to breathe in anyway.

It turned out that the victim's name was Manuel (manWELL) Acosta-Gonzalez, born in Calexico (on the Mexican side of the California border), but a US citizen after naturalizing in his early twenties. He was a resident of Rancho Mirage, an affluent area near Palm Springs, and had a long list of arrests for drug-related transactions and probably drug dealing—with an apparent connection to the dangerous and super-rich Guadalajara drug cartel.

Mike di Saronno called me and told me that most surprisingly, the guy she killed had been married to Maggie Landover briefly a couple of decades earlier. She had said he was a stranger, that she didn't know him. He was still wearing his mask when the EMTs hauled his body to the nearest trauma center where he was declared dead. She killed him without ever seeing his face unmasked.

I called Gabriele and Ruth on a conference call, to bring them up to date, and to tell them that we apparently had a new case.

"That's going to put a different color on what happened, if they really were married," Ruth said. "Hard for the woman to say she had no idea who he was."

"Can you please see what you can find out about Miss Maggie?" I asked. "She apparently lives across the street from me. Her address would be on 2nd Street, but I'd guess her apartment opens on the side of her building that faces where I live."

Gabriele was interested in the victim, thought he might have been in Ora di Pranzo, Gabriele's highly successful Italian restaurant in the SoHo district of Manhattan. It's the kind of place where you can't get a reservation for months if you call up. I've known Ruth and Gabriele for years and years, so we can waltz in and sit down just like we belonged there.

"He is drug dealer?" Gabriele asked.

"No idea," I said, "but I'll see what Mike knows and send you a text."

"Is his *cognome* (the Italian word for 'surname'). Maybe I hear it before."

"You mean you've seen his last name someplace? It's unusual, with two Hispanic family names connected with a hyphen. Looks more upper-class."

Although Gabriele Cortese has been in the United States for many years, he tends to scatter Italian words and phrases in his speech. He can speak with no discernible accent if he wants to, but as the major-domo of his restaurant, his foreign way of talking is probably a plus. Local color, you know.

Gabriele is startlingly good-looking, with a clearly Mediterranean ethnicity—black hair, slightly swarthy skin tone. People stare at him— men and women. He looks like a movie star, and he lives on the Promenade in Brooklyn Heights, probably the most beautiful place to live in all of New York City—with spectacular views of downtown Manhattan and the Brooklyn Bridge. When I first met him, he was tangentially involved in a murder that I was helping Mike di Saronno with. He was a sex worker at that point, and lived—or worked—in my general neighborhood, which was then in the Theater District. I moved to Long Island City in the Great Recession, when Manhattan rents kept skyrocketing for no obvious reason each and every year.

Ruth "the Sleuth" Jensen and I have been friends for decades. We met when we were introduced to each other by a now-deceased mentor of mine, who was a financial analyst for an old and respected New York stock brokerage. She is a fashion-plate, well-connected, a big opera fan and member of the Opera League. She is a widow and super-attractive to me. I'm twice divorced and not looking for the third strike in that arena, but if I were, I'd be chasing after Ruth. She lives on Park Avenue in a Classic Eight apartment that her husband owned and left to her in his will. She invented her moniker, by the way. It wasn't me.

Both Ruth and Gabriele pitch in with me when I am working as a civilian criminalist for the NYPD, and particularly for Mike di Saronno, a high-ranking detective in the Midtown North of Manhattan, not far from a place I used to live in the Theater District.

Ruth is a whiz on her computer doing research. Her husband, Murray, had a ladies' clothing business—and was what they call a "*garmento*." He travelled all over the world finding little companies that could turn out large quantities of fine, well-tailored clothing on a tight schedule. Vietnam, China, Mexico, Brazil, and other "emerging" economies. Lots of air miles, which has kept Ruth (and us) in first class for almost no cost over the last many years.

I couldn't get the picture out of my head of that woman, Maggie, standing on her balcony covered with blood, looking like Medea fresh from killing Jason's children. There is something about blood that makes me want to run and throw up at the same time. I couldn't see her face for the blood, which was also clotted all over her hair. Like she had been dipped in a vat of it, head-first. I guess when she sliced his neck, he spurted like a fire-hose, but the mask never came off, so she had no idea who he was. Maybe that was a blessing.

My phone vibrated. It was Mike's number. "Can you and the gang come over to my office tomorrow?" he asked without an introduction.

"Probably, depends on timing, but Gabriele and Ruth are always ready to comply, you know."

"Apparently Maggie is being held at the local precinct there," he said, "but they're bringing her, all cleaned up, to my office tomorrow, so I can interrogate her. I want the three of you to watch from the observation room."

"Good. I can't do the covered-with-blood thing. Makes me want to puke, and I know the smell makes it worse. Had a few minutes years back with a woman who'd been stabbed in the arm, bleeding like a stuck pig. Smelled like something I could never have imagined."

"Around eleven in the AM," he said.

I told him I'd do my best to get all three of us there ahead of time. Gabriele was up for it immediately. Ruth started to quibble, and then just agreed. We decided to meet at Mike's office about ten forty-five AM so Maggie wouldn't see us. I wondered if she would be cuffed. Probably. If she was cuffed and in custody, there would probably be a lawyer with her, too.

Gabriele asked if he could just stay overnight. That's always okay with me. He doesn't snore, and he makes a good breakfast every time he stays over—great French toast with cinnamon and nice strong coffee. I turned on the TV to one of the local network channels. There had been another in a series of seemingly pointless attacks on elderly Asians—this time a woman over seventy was punched in the face and knocked to the ground. Some palooka was blaming her for COVID-19, which seems to have originated in China, but which came to New York City from Europe. There are always jerks ready to slap or sucker-punch or even stab somebody innocent in times like these, just for something as irrelevant as looking Asian.

And the "Black Lives Matter" protests were making virtually daily appearances as well. Pandemic lockdown seemed to fracture society into political splinters. There were far-right people, too. White supremacists and whatnot. Everybody demanding their fifteen minutes of fame. This kind of protest kicks up quickly when a black or brown person is victimized by the police, no matter where it happens. And of course there are time after time mass shootings in schools, work places—frequently for no discernible reason. Automatic weapons that can kill tens of people per second. Assault weapons created for battlefields.

For some reason, the pandemic "lockdowns" are seen by some people as incursions against their constitutional liberties and rights. Sometimes that includes mask mandates to help prevent the spread of COVID-19. Fortunately for me, I'm what they call "fully vaccinated," meaning I have had the two Pfizer shots that are supposed to provide something like ninety-five percent protection against the coronavirus that causes COVID-19. I still wear masks though, and try to stay at least six feet away from other people. I've taken to wearing double masks a lot of the time—they say it is safer than just wearing one. For some reason, many urban areas are more receptive to mask mandates and social distancing.

We wandered over to Tuk-Tuk, a local Thai eatery that makes excellent food, and makes it fast. We took it home and ate watching the news. They would've delivered it, but we wanted to look at the full menu. I like their "fake duck" salad, probably mostly soy-based, but delicious.

Chapter Three

We agreed to rendezvous at Grand Central and then walk to Mike's office. We all took the subway to get to Grand Central from home, but the walk from 42nd Street to 54th Street and 8th Avenue was a treat; good for the lungs and good for the legs and body core. I was a little sweaty by the time we got there.

Mike brought us up to date about the dead man. He had in fact been briefly married to Maggie Landover, so she had been Maggie Acosta-Gonzalez for a while. Later on, she had married again; a medical doctor named Horace Landover. But she had been pregnant when she and Manuel divorced; she carried the baby to term and gave birth, and then assigned her parental rights to her ex-husband, so that he could raise the little boy at his home in California.

"As far as we can tell, her birth name was Maggie Gaston, which is probably an Anglo-Norman name since she was born in Ireland, near Dublin, where there were a lot of Anglo-Norman families."

The boy was named Jesus Emmanuele Acosta-Gonzalez, and was called by the familiar nickname of Chuy (pronounced like "chewy" in English, a common moniker for boys named Jesus, at least in Mexico and southern California).

As usual, Mike had coffee for each of us, right out of the police vending machine; not tasting much like coffee, but with milk and sugar, it was okay.

Maggie was wearing tight jeans and a flowered shirt tucked in. Not unattractive, probably late forties or early fifties. Nice figure, and a distinctively Asian cast to the eyes, which was all of her face we could see above the blue surgical mask. We three were standing in the observation room behind a two-way mirror, so we could see her but she couldn't see us, although she clearly knew she was being observed. We had full audio of the session.

"Thanks for coming over," Mike said, and they elbow-bumped to avoid touching one another. Mike was wearing a navy blue suit, so there was plenty of cloth between their elbows when they bumped. "I notice that you checked 'Other' on the questionnaire answer about 'ethnicity.' Do you mind telling me more? You look Asian to my eye."

She took her mask off, and he could see that the rest of her face was mixed, too, with a low bridge on her nose, and a mouth that looked European, accented with pink lipstick. "I am mixed European and Chinese," she said. "My parents were missionaries in China. Dad was a Catholic priest, so they weren't married in church, but they were a couple. They wanted a child, but she couldn't conceive, so he bonked the Chinese girl who was the maid, and she was my birth mother. Then she went home to her parents, and I was given to my mom to raise with my priest-dad. I guess I was a bastard under strict legal guidelines. Can't ever be a nun." She laughed.

"Birth name on birth certificate is Maggie Gaston, which was my dad's last name, though Orangeman was my birth mother's name, which is what I preferred to go by. Both Dad and 'Mom' were Irish, so I guess I'm half Irish and half Chinese.

"The cops in Queens told me that the man I killed was Manuel Acosta-Gonzalez," she said. "If that's true, I was married to him—in church—for a few months when I was about twenty-two. I was pretty then, and he wanted me in his bed, so we got married. I got pregnant and then we got a divorce. The boy was a baby, and I had no way to raise him, so I agreed to sign over my rights to Manny, who said he had a nice big house in California. He was a drug dealer, and had lots of money. Like a lot of Mexicans, he was off-and-on super-Catholic, so the boy was baptized in a church that was called Our Lady Queen of Peace, which sounded like a joke to me, because Manny could shoot a guy in the face as easy as shake his hand. He made me a drug mule, pushing condoms full of coke or whatever into my ass and vagina so I could smuggle them into the United States for him. Whatever his flavor of the week was. Anyway, not for sale, but for him to take."

"Yes, I remember arresting you at JFK a long time ago. You were a flight attendant coming in from Colombia," Mike said. "I'm fairly sure you were full of oxy that trip, and you were high as a kite, and only semi-conscious. We squirted some Narcan in your nose, and that woke you up. Then I think we got you to Elmhurst Hospital in Queens, and they took care of you for a few days until you were okay. Then I think you were in the slammer for a few weeks, but I don't remember exactly."

"Oh, that was you, was it?" she commented. "In that case, I wish he'd shot you in the face. Then he woulda been in prison and I woulda never met him on the subway and ended up with blood all over me and my apartment. And I wouldn't be here talking to you either. I was in the klink for a while after that happened when you arrested me."

Mike smiled and responded, "What happened to the baby?"

"His father named him Jesus Emmanuele Acosta-Gonzalez, and he's probably living in Manny's big house in California. He'd be in his twenties by now. Really, I had no idea that guy that followed me home was Manny. Masks make it hard to recognize people, even the father of my only baby." She added quickly that she hadn't seen him or heard from him in over twenty years. "He used to send me pictures of Chuy, so I could follow him getting bigger and always happy, like he was being tickled. But then he stopped, and I never heard from him again."

"And Landover?" Mike asked. "Who was he?"

"He was the doc that delivered my baby Jesus—my son Chuy, not the original Jesus—and he wanted to get in my pants, too, so I married him, but he was a lot older than me and he died—dropped dead from a heart attack at work -- and left me some money and an apartment, which I sold, and moved to Long Island City. And all of a sudden I was respectable, for the first time in my life. A widow. We got along okay, Horace and me, but I was okay when he had that heart attack, because I knew he would leave me better off. He was a good guy."

"Have you ever made contact with your son after he grew up?"

She shook her head to say no.

"Could you please answer with your voice? We're being recorded."

"No, never. But they call him Chuy, which for Mexicans is a nickname for Jesus. Don't ask me why, because I don't have any idea. No speaka Spanish. Got a little bit of Mandarin from some people in Taiwan who claimed to be relations of my birth mother, but no Spic."

Mike showed her a photo. "This is, I am told, a high school photo of your son. He looks a good deal like you, but you have curly hair and his is straight, like a lot of Asians."

"Even I can see he's my son, and most people don't see any family genes in themselves," she said, sounding pleased. "We're almost twins, and my curly hair is out of a bottle. It would be totally straight if I didn't have a smelly permanent fairly often. Good for the Chinese girl. Her name was Li-Li, but Dad always called her Lily, like the flower. I guess he thought she was pretty. I don't remember her. I'd like to meet Jesus if he's still alive. Anybody living with Manny is likely to die young. He hangs with a bunch of Mexicans that like to cut off people's heads. I used to hear from him every once in a while, but other than the subway with a mask on, never saw him again. Too bad, he was a good-looking stud when I met him and married him. Good sex. He popped my cherry the first time, or at least that's what I told him."

She looked around the room and focused on the mirror we were standing behind. "Who's watching us?" she asked.

"Nobody you know," Mike answered. "They work for the NYPD. You know you're being held pending the Medical Examiner's report on how Mr. Acosta-Gonzalez died, so don't expect privacy. And if you want your lawyer, just say so. I believe your Miranda rights were read to you when you were arrested," he said. "Right?"

"Yup, right," she said out loud. "Am I headed back to Long Island City? Food ain't no good in that police station. Pizza or pizza, that's the choice. Don't matter what time of day. Oh, there's always bitter black coffee, but not even a donut, which you'd think would be all over a cop station like that one. Fat cops everywhere you look."

"I think you'll be heading to Riker's Island pending arraignment," Mike said. "Up to the judge whether you stay there or go home to wait for the trial.

"Have you been abused or harassed because you look Asian?"

"Why you asking me that?"

"Because we've had a rash of Asian Hate problems since the COVID-19 virus got here. A lot of people seem to want to blame Asians for it. Like the so-called 'Spanish Flu' in 1918. It originated in Kansas, but a lot of Americans wanted to take it out on Hispanics because of the name. It was the American dough-boys who spread it all over Europe, not the other way around. I think it killed something like sixty million people. Anyway, any anti-Asian experiences in your life recently?"

"Not that I remember," she said. "I don't take that kind of shit sitting down either. I punch them in the face until they bleed." She made a fist and brandished it in the air like she was punching somebody.

Mike picked up his smart phone and punched in a code, and two uniformed cops stepped in and ushered Maggie out to go to Riker's and await her first day in court and a bail hearing.

"Good luck, Maggie," Mike said as she left, handcuffed behind her back.

Mike wanted to hear what we thought.

"Tough broad," Ruth offered. "But not holding anything back. I think she's giving it to you straight about not knowing who the guy was."

"Same here," I said.

"Is tell truth," Gabriele added quickly. "She want see son."

"I have a feeling she'll get to see her son, since he's also the son of the decedent."

"Great cop word, 'decedent,'" Ruth said, but slightly under her breath. "I'd say 'dead guy.'"

We left Mike there and headed for Thalia for a drink, even though it was the middle of the day. "It's five o'clock someplace," I said, echoing my dad when he wanted a drink in the afternoon. Like on Derby Day, the first Saturday in May.

"She's like a Damon Runyon character, somebody from 'Guys

and Dolls,' don't you think?" Ruth said as we sat down at the bar.

Gabriele looked confused.

"It's an old Broadway musical," Ruth said. "A classic, full of tough characters like racetrack touts and other kinds of lowlifes. Here she is a day or so after she kills a man in her kitchen with a knife, and the subject never came up."

Never do I recall a day when my dirty vodka with olives tasted better. I was frankly confused by Maggie, who didn't seem to have any fondness for anyone she mentioned. She killed her own husband, the father of her only child, and never said she regretted it. Of course, she thought he was trying to rape her, which was probably a lot of her attitude. But it seemed to me that she was aping some hard-ass women in film noir movies. Like The Maltese Falcon maybe.

"I wonder about the boy, her son, who'd be a young man by now. I wonder if he's a carbon copy of his mom," Ruth said, looking at Gabriele and then at me.

Gabriele said he would like to meet the young man one day. "Hard way to grow up, but not so different from growing up in Napoli or Sicilia with 'Ndrangheta and Cosa Nostra everywhere—even killing judges in the streets."

Chapter Four

Sure enough, Mike told us later, Maggie ran face first into a bunch of women who yelled things like, "Go home where you belong, bitch," as soon as she got to Riker's and into the General Population of the Women's part of the notorious prison.

She fought back, but those women didn't give in easy. Maggie was bruised all over, including two black eyes. Actually more purple than black. Painful looking. She looked like she'd been dragged behind a horse for a mile or so, at least that's what Mike said.

Luckily, Maggie didn't spend much time at all behind bars. She avoided prosecution because the police who'd been called to the scene of the attack in Maggie's apartment were witnesses to the actual accidental killing. At the arraignment, the cops who'd been on scene testified that Maggie hadn't actually stabbed Manuel at all. She didn't swipe the knife at him. She was holding the knife when he lurched his head and the blood spurted from his neck. He did it to himself. It wasn't her fault.

It's difficult to describe life around the time of the pandemic. People were getting deadly sick in waves that choked hospitals, and there were no meds that had much effect on it. People would die from lack of oxygen in their lungs, with tubes down their throats to pump more oxygen in—to little or no avail. Once you were on one of those breathing machines, you seldom came off of it alive.

And at the same time there were other plagues like the plagues of ancient Egypt in the Bible. For some reason there were strings of mass shootings, where for no discernible reason, mostly young people would lay hands on automatic weapons and just walk into a Walmart or a FedEx terminal and start killing everybody they saw. Several of those were in schools, taking down kids and teenagers.

And at the same time, there were a bunch of situations where police officers found themselves in conflict with youngish Black men and boys, and the Black folks got shot, of course. Some of those names became famous, like Eric Garner, who was killed in a chokehold on Staten Island for selling cigarettes on the sidewalk. You sell cigarettes; you get killed. He was remembered for saying, "I can't breathe, I can't breathe," as he died. Then later there was a shockingly similar death in Minneapolis when a tall strapping Black man named George Floyd died in police custody after he allegedly passed a counterfeit twenty dollar bill in a little store. He was saying "I can't breathe" too, and he died, like Eric Garner before him. Only big difference was that there were peaceful demonstrations all over the USA after George Floyd died in custody. One of the cops was convicted of homicide, which would never have happened years earlier—remember Rodney King in Los Angeles. As far as I'm concerned, things were heading in the right direction, Liberal, you know. New Yorker.

For some reason, some people blamed the Black victims for what happened to them. And then they blamed the pandemic and surgical masks for making it happen. Didn't make sense, but that didn't stop it.

Manuel and Maggie grew up in the Eisenhower years, after World War II. Some kinds of segregation were just a fact of life. Different ethnic and color groups lived in their own parts of town. So Black people lived in Black areas, and White people lived in White areas. Schools were segregated by color, and so were water fountains and park benches, not to mention rest rooms.

Then there was Brown vs Board of Education, and the law of the land was that schools had to be integrated. They almost never were, to tell the truth, but the law was that they should be integrated. Then Jackie Robinson integrated Major League Baseball in Brooklyn. Basketball came to be dominated by very tall African-Americans like Kareem Abdul Jabbar and Magic Johnson. A lot of prominent Black people became Muslim, like Cassius Clay, who changed his name to Muhammad Ali—

for years he was the most famous person in the world; handsome and funny and always a provocateur-hero.

Then when the police vs. Black men thing started to take place at the time of the pandemic, there was a social movement that was called BLM, for Black Lives Matter. It became an odd combination of peaceful protests during the daytimes and riotous lootings at night in many places. In Portland, Oregon, there was a federal courthouse that was besieged by BLM protesters for weeks, which went on until the National Guard was called out.

It was a perfect storm. Black people were standing up for themselves more, and White people were blaming them for all the trouble. Clash-bang-scream-loot-destroy.

During the protest-and-riot time, Maggie managed to get released from Riker's Island and went home to her condo in Long Island City. I would see her in the grocery store sometimes, and once even invited her over to my apartment for a snack and a cocktail. The magic of New York City kept the grocery stores and liquor stores well stocked, and the restaurants packed to the gills with couples and families living the high life.

She wanted to meet her son, Chuy, face to face. That was all she really talked about, according to a conversation she had with Ruth (she really didn't think Maggie had any close relationships with men). That, and the fact that she had killed her ex-husband—accidentally, she insisted over and over—without knowing who he was, because he was wearing a surgical mask and didn't talk to her, so there was no way to recognize his voice. She was going through the rigors of Hell for that. She told me she wished they had never broken up, that he was good to her, and she was such a dodo for giving up her son to him to take to California.

Then all of a sudden, Chuy just showed up. Kind of a spindly, thin, young guy; nice-looking in a way that Eurasians can be. Exotic, you know, like his mother, but with a blank look on his face that might be a hint that he has no moral compass, in spite of appearing to be a devout, church-going Catholic. He apparently just walked into the downstairs lobby of his mother's building and asked the concierge to buzz her and see if it was okay for him to go upstairs to meet her. Floated into town like a breeze smelling of forest fires from the West Coast.

Oddly enough, Maggie called me when she found out he was downstairs in her building. I called Ruth and Gabriele and invited them to come over to take in this odd home-coming or whatever it was. Then I suggested that Maggie and Chuy might come over for a drink and maybe some chips and salsa.

"According to Maggie, Chuy really is a baseball fan, mostly the Dodgers, but open-minded. And one of the things he seems to remember most fondly about his father is playing catch," Ruth said. "He takes his baseball mitt with him wherever he goes. Maybe worth knowing?"

"I have to admit that although I am also a fan, I don't have a mitt, and if I had saved my old one, it wouldn't come anywhere near fitting. Maybe I'll ask Gabriele to stop at Dick's Sporting Goods to get a couple of grown-up mitts. That way we can throw the ball around with Chuy if he feels like it."

"I bet he'd like to go to Cooperstown if he's really a fan. Baseball Hall of Fame and all, you know," she said. "I'm a Mets fan myself, but I like the Yanks, and of course when I was a kid, the Dodgers were in LA, but we still thought they were our own team forever. Duke Snyder and Jackie Robinson, Pee Wee Reese, after all."

My phone rang and Jimmy the concierge told me that Mr. Cortese was on his way up.

When the doorbell rang and I opened the door, Gabriele was carrying two large paper bags, one of which had the Dick's Sporting Goods logo on it, and the other apparently was full of groceries. I was about to ask him what he had brought when he blurted out, "Surprise for you, and surprise for Chuy." In spite of his normal cool demeanor, he looked unsure of himself.

"I bet you've never played baseball," I said to him.

He nodded.

"So, you're right-handed?" I asked.

Another nod.

"Then you're going to wear the mitt on your left hand," I said.

"You're going to catch with your left hand and throw with your right hand." *He's normally so athletic,* I thought. *Why would he be worried about a baseball?*

"Is very hard, yes?" he asked. "Baseball? Hit head, break bones?"

"It's a ball, and it's called a hard-ball, but it's not heavy and it's not dangerous," I said. "And nobody's going to throw it at your head. What we're talking about, it's called 'catch' not 'hit.'"

He handed me the Dick's bag, with a tentative look. There were two outfielders' gloves, both fitted for left hands. I smiled and told him he had done good. Then I looked in the grocery bag. Rapini and sausage. "For me?"

He beamed at me.

"My favorite," I said. "You're the best. There's nobody as wonderful as you. Never will be."

About then the doorbell rang again. It was Maggie and Chuy, both wearing blue surgical masks and jeans and t-shirts; Dodgers for Chuy, Mets for Maggie.

"Look," I said to Chuy. "Look what Gabriele brought," I said, brandishing the two new mitts. "We can play catch now. I used to have a mitt, but it got lost years back; no idea where it might be. We just have to remember that Gabriele has never thrown or caught a baseball in his life, so we have to teach him how to do it."

Chuy was wearing an old, much-used backpack. He took it off and produced an old mitt and a major-league baseball. I smiled at him, and told him that Gabriele was going to make some lunch for us before we went outside to try a game of catch.

Chuy looked tentative, especially when he saw the rapini.

"My favorite," I said. "Best Italian dish there is, says me. Lots of sausages and garlic. Delicious. And Gabriele is one of the best cooks I've ever known."

Gabriele produced a bottle of Cannonau di Sardegna, a deep red wine very popular in southern Italy and on the islands like Sardinia (English spelling of Italian Sardegna—and pronounced the same way), which has some of the most beautiful beaches in the whole freaking world. He retrieved the bottle from my hand and popped the cork quickly with a French waiter's knife. Then he poured a taste into a lowball glass and handed it to me.

"*Perfetto*," I said, swilling the tannin-rich wine around in my mouth and savoring the taste on the back of my tongue. I looked at Chuy and swallowed, then said, "We're going to have to teach Gabriele how to play catch. Would you believe this is the first time he's had a mitt on his hand?"

Chapter Five

First of all, Chuy and I tossed the baseball back and forth in the green area behind the building I live in. Gabriele watched. Then we started standing close together and tossed the ball to each other, taking a step or two back after each round.

Before long, Gabriele made his first catch, and then he was totally into it. Good hand-eye skills, which is half of playing baseball, like it's half of playing golf. He was throwing to Chuy and Chuy was throwing to me. I was throwing to Gabriele. Big smiles all around. What is it about playing catch? It makes me feel like the blue sky will be here forever.

"My dad and I used to play catch every day when I was a kid," I said, throwing the ball overhand to Gabriele so that it made a smacking noise when it hit the mitt. "I miss him, but he's been dead for a long time, and we hadn't played catch for a long time when he died. He'd taken to playing catch with my two sons of two different marriages." It's a little like beach volleyball; makes you feel like you and the warm day are both made of the same things.

It was a mistake. Chuy's face looked like a black cloud was passing overhead. "She killed my dad," he said in measured speech, like he was reading a billboard slogan out loud in a moving car. "My dad was always good to me," he said in a normal voice.

"But from what I understand, he was not particularly good to her—your mom," Ruth blurted out. "It's your mom who carried you in her belly and nursed you when you were hungry."

"I know," he said, "but I don't remember that, and then she left me. And she roots for the Dodgers because I do, but she's a Yankee fan.

I know it. And I don't have a dad anymore."

"You can still be a Dodger fan without your dad. Everybody's dad dies at some point," I said softly. "Mine did, too, but that's different because I was grown. And as I understand it, your dad didn't want your mother around. It wasn't all her idea."

"I was grown when she killed him," Chuy said. Í was just not grown enough." He was tearing up.

"One of the hardest things in life is learning how to live on when people you love die. And it kinda doesn't matter whether they die from a heart attack or a bullet. Once they're dead, they're dead, and you have to do your grieving. If you don't, you'll get sick or depressed and have to take anti-depressants to be able to cope—and the worst part of that is you still have to do the grieving you didn't do, or you may end up doing something you'll regret bigtime."

He looked like he was going to cry. I put my arms out for a hug and he ran to me.

"I don't know what to do," he said between sobs. "I miss him. I need to talk to him and I can't," he sobbed into my chest.

I responded like a father because I was thinking about my own children, whom I hadn't seen in a long time because that's what they preferred. I grieved for the kids, but I kept my part of the unspoken bargain, though I did contact them on birthdays, Christmas, and some other holidays like Independence Day. I sent them all back-to-school cards and gifts every year, but I never played catch with them again, like a Dad should. Or dolls or whatever. I'm also not paying child support anymore because they're all either college graduates or married.

Then Maggie showed up at the game of catch. "I heard that snap-bang noise of a baseball being caught," she said. She was wearing a mitt herself. "Mind if I join in?" she asked, as though she expected an answer. "I know I'm just a damn Yankee, not as good as a Dodger, but I can catch a ball. Did you ever see that movie with Madonna about a girl's baseball team? I think it was called 'A League of Our Own,' or something like that. Well, that's me. I always wanted to be a catcher and tag out some poor bastard trying to steal home."

Just then Chuy spread his arms, probably to welcome Maggie, but we never found out. Gabriele extended his left arm with the mitt on it, and grabbed Chuy's left arm with his own right hand, and pulled him close. Before we could say Jack Robinson, Gabriele was holding Chuy like a toddler holds a teddy bear. That's to say it looked like Chuy might not be able to breathe, but there didn't seem to be any problem in that department. Chuy looked like he was enjoying the whole thing like a teddy bear likes being hugged and squeezed.

About the same time, a voice from across the little parklike area where we were doing a three-way game of catch, called out. "Chuy?" it asked the whole area. It was a thirty-ish Eurasian guy. I looked at him and thought he was around five-seven, short by most American standards, but clearly very fit, with muscles bulging from the arms of his t-shirt: big biceps, triceps and deltoids. Looked like big pecs, too.

"Chuy?" he queried us again, and Chuy raised his hand tentatively.

"I'm Chuy," he said, looking a little puzzled.

"I'm Morgan Michael Wong," the newcomer said. "I was a friend of your dad. I heard what happened, wanted to come and tell you I'm here for you. Looks like you've got some friends already, though," he said. He held out his hand to Gabriele, who still had the young man in what looked like a wrestling hold.

Chuy was beaming. "My mom lives right near here," he said, "and these guys are my friends. This is Gabriele. The tall guy is Hugo, and that pretty lady is Ruth. She's a good catch," he said reassuringly. "We were playing catch, like I used to do with my dad. These guys are Yankees though, not Dodgers."

"Now wait a minute," I said. "I grew up in Los Angeles, always a Dodger fan. I admit I'm a Yankee these days, but look where I live." I held out my hand and asked if I could call him Morgan. "I'm Hugo." He took my hand with a smile. "You here just to see Chuy, or are you in New York on business?"

"Well," he said, "My sister is looking for a dependable private adoption service. She's been having a fling with an American soldier-boy back in South Korea, and now she's pregnant, which is the cue to find out that Mr. Wonderful has a cute little wife back home, and has zero interest in a baby. So, Julie plans to give the baby up for adoption when it's born." He looked like he knew he had said too much. "There's a lot of people adopting Korean babies these days. Our name sounds Chinese to Americans, but we're Korean Baptists, and want to do the best thing for the child." He changed the subject. "I worked with Manuel for years. He was a well-known go-between in adoptions, so I'm trying to tap into his network."

He said that Julie would be coming over to New York from Seoul before she was too far advanced in her pregnancy to fly. "She's around four months now. I told her she can stay with me and I'll keep an eye on her." He said he had a short-term rental in Manhattan.

"We're gonna be taking Chuy off to Cooperstown," I said to Morgan. "Baseball Hall of Fame, you know. Lots of Dodgers there." I paused and looked down, then back up. "Happy to help however I can with your sister's predicament."

I didn't go into what we were going to treat Chuy to, but Cooperstown is also a matchless country village on a sky-blue lake. It looks like a nineteenth-century Hudson River School painting wherever your gaze falls.

I had made reservations for two rooms (one for the two girls, the other for the three boys) at the Otesaga Hotel, a spectacular old hotel with a portico that looks like it was ripped off the front of the White House in Washington, DC. There's also a summer music festival there in the Glimmerglass Opera House at the northern end of the hopelessly beautiful mirror-like lake. Not all opera, in spite of the name, but I've always been an opera fan of the most crazed type. Brava! to the soprano! Standing O! They were doing Mozart's "Die Zauberflöte" ("The Magic Flute" in English), Verdi's "Il Trovatore," and two modern pieces I'd never heard of. I felt good about all four of them. Usually very strong young singers, some of them with beautiful voices making their debuts, it seemed to me from having been there several times in the past. Not as outstanding as the Santa Fe Opera in the summers, but a bit more daring, and good productions, too.

Odds are he's going to be bringing a bunch of young girls over here, not just his sister—if she's his sister at all—and we'll start seeing store-front "spas" where customers can get "happy endings" to massages.

"You wondering about what Morgan's up to?" Ruth asked me in a whisper. "I'll give you two to one he's got a line of young girls waiting to be put on a plane in Korea. He's going to market the hell out of them, and they're all gonna end up pregnant, so he can sell the babies. See what Mike di Saronno thinks."

Gabriele and Chuy were standing close by, and they were nodding at what Ruth was saying. "Your neighborhood is going to get very sexy," Gabriele said to me. "Pretty Asian girls, lots of them. Near the subway stations. Convenient."

"Look, I'm thinking about Cooperstown," I said to them both, feeling like I was on the high road for sure. "Not brothels."

I told them about one year when I accidentally ended up in Cooperstown on Induction Day. Like Times Square on New Year's Eve, and old-timers lined up behind folding tables autographing baseballs for a fee to benefit the Hall of Fame. I saw some players I never dreamed I'd see. Whitey Ford, Willie Mays—even Don Drysdale, one of my own heroes from when I was a preteen and teenager. Never mind there were no hotel rooms to be had anywhere. I had to sleep in my car and use the restrooms at gas stations. AOK as long as I was surrounded by baseball players I knew from the headlines of my dad's morning newspapers that I would see as a kid while he held the papers up and drank his morning coffee. He always read the sports pages first, of course.

My phone vibrated. It was Mike. "You guys still heading for Cooperstown tomorrow morning?"

I explained what had happened with Morgan Wong appearing on the scene.

"Where is he from?"

I told him I didn't know, but he was of Korean descent, and probably lived somewhere near where Manuel Acosta-Gonzalez lived in

California, because Chuy seemed to know him, or know him by name.

Mike was silent for a minute, then came back on the phone with the news that Morgan seemed to be an alternative for a colleague of Manuel's with a long record in California, and with various federal agencies. "If he's the guy I'm looking at on the computer, maybe his specialty is sex trafficking, especially with girls trying to get jobs and residence permits in the United States. No convictions that I can find. Be careful, though. For these guys, the girls are like dry goods. No holds barred. If they don't come through with what they're supposed to earn, they get treated like animals—or worse than animals. Girls have no value. There are always more to replace the ones you don't need any more, or the ones you go overboard with, teaching them lessons. Same if some guy decides to use a girl for a punching bag."

"Sounds like we need to call off our trip to Cooperstown."

"I don't know about that," Mike said slowly. "Chuy's looking forward to that one, and he might be the key to a lot of what we need to know about people like Morgan Wong." He paused and then added, "and believe me there are a lot of Morgan Wongs out there ready to treat a roomful of girls like a roomful of old dogs. Have 'em for dinner if you want—or sell them off to some guy that has rough trade johns. Lots of those around."

"We've seen some pretty nasty things," I said.

"I doubt you've seen the worst of the worst, and I don't want to be the guy who puts you and Ruth and Gabriele in a position to deal with a sadistic son-of-a-bitch who doesn't stop until his girls totally give up. Broken teeth and blood everywhere."

"You're scaring the shit out of me," I said. "I think I should cancel the Cooperstown trip. If Chuy's disappointed, too bad. Hey, I've got granddaughters who're the same general age as a lot of streetwalkers."

Ruth and Gabriele were only hearing my end of the conversation, but they were looking like they wanted to sign off as soon as they could.

"Look," I said to them, "Chuy isn't dangerous, as far as I can tell. He's half kid and half pimp. That's probably a volatile combination, but as far as I can tell, he's happy to be with us going upstate. Mike wants us to keep to the schedule. That means we should take off tomorrow morning fairly early, so we can check into that gorgeous hotel while they still have some prime rooms. Ruth and Maggie will be bunking together—two queen-sized beds in the room. Chuy will be sharing with Gabriele and me, also two queen-sized beds."

"I looked at the website for the Otesaga Hotel. Looks like quite a palace," Ruth said. "But I don't want to skip out of town and let Morgan or someone like him get his little whorehouse all set up."

"On the other hand," I said, "we don't want him to be afraid to get his hand in the game. If that's really his sister that he's talking about, maybe there's a chance that he's not the son of Sam after all. So, let's just rendezvous here tomorrow morning at nine and be ready to make the most of our trip to the Hall of Fame."

I told Ruth and Gabriele that the hotel, as far as I knew, was built in the late nineteenth century. It was what they called at that time a "railroad hotel." Railroad hotels were luxurious and spacious, a US version of a bunch of Canadian Railway hotels like the castle-like palaces at Banff and Lake Louise. Never been to either one, but my Texas grandparents had haunted both of them in their day, and sent me postcards when I was still in short pants. My grandmother thought Lake Louise was surely the most beautiful place on Earth. I've always been a hotel junkie; still remember the first time I stayed at the Savoy in London. Wow. The Otesaga was in that same category as far as I was concerned.

As we broke up, I was thinking to myself about the empty storefronts on the "main drag," Vernon Blvd. There were lots of them, dating back to when a bunch of small businesses abruptly closed their doors when the first pandemic lockdown went into effect. I was thinking particularly of a store that was full of Oriental carpets—two or three of which were mine, since I knew the entrepreneur who opened "Rugland/LICity" in about February 2020—just in time for my friend Betsy to file for bankruptcy. I lost my three rugs (and what they were worth) when the inventory was liquidated. I could visualize that store with opaque glass on the streetside and a sign that read something like "Moonlight Spa and Massage." In my head, there were two pretty Asian girls hanging around outside the door, wearing dresses made from head-scarves that basically covered very little of their bodies, but managed to complement the curves that were there. I had already taken a write-off of about three thousand dollars when my rugs were sold off in an auction for near-zero bucks. I had taken some common stock in exchange for my rugs, so they were right-down to zero when they were sold off and my stock was cancelled out completely. At least I had the write-off, which helped out with my income tax for the year. Not enough, but better than a kick in the ass, or getting poked in the eye with a sharp stick. Those are things my dad used to say; never made sense to me.

Chapter Six

As it turned out, not only did Gabriele stay over at my apartment, but Chuy did, too. He was showing signs of having a crush on Gabriele, which would be easy enough if either of them were so inclined. I doubt Gabriele was interested. He certainly didn't act like he was interested. He made chicken parmigiana for dinner, served on top of a tangle of spaghetti with fresh marinara sauce on it, full of garlic—way full of garlic. The fact that there were three of us meant a change in sleeping venues, too. Usually when Gabriele stays over, he sleeps with me, so he can enjoy the AC and the fact that there is a bathroom that opens inside my bedroom. So he can take a shower without having to wander around the apartment. He slept on the living room couch instead.

Chuy was relegated to the second bedroom, which has a relatively comfortable pull-out queen-sized bed. It also has its own bathroom *en suite*, but opening in the hallway, so not as private as the one in my bedroom. He didn't seem to be disappointed. After all, he was bunking in with the big boys, not the girls. Maggie and Ruth ducked out and probably went to Ruth's super-spacious Park Avenue apartment.

We agreed to meet at my place for an early breakfast, so we could take off for Cooperstown before the rush hour clogged up all the streets. I had rented a four-door sedan so the five of us could fit into the car for a longish ride. I figured we'd stop around New Paltz for a snack and a potty opportunity, and so we could show Chuy the Huguenot Street, which dates back to the early 1700's, and also featured a recently added Native American style "wigwam" (yes, that's the word they use on the sign). New Paltz also has a good college with a specialty in foreign languages and comparative literature. I had studied Italian there some years earlier, which helped me translate Gabriele's Italian and Napolitano inserts in his otherwise broken English. They used to do weekend "immersion" courses, which meant NO English would be allowed after dinner on Friday night until time to bail out and go home on Sunday afternoon. Very frustrating and very helpful at the same time.

Unfortunately for me, most of my day-to-day Italian had gone by the wayside due to lack of use. For years I spent a lot of time in Italy—mostly weekends around client visits. One of my clients was the Italian Stock Exchange in Milano, called Borsa Italiana. It was later acquired by the London Stock Exchange and disappeared. It was in a Mussolini-era building in Piazza degli Affari ("Business Piazza" and in the local parlance "Piazza Affari"). The Palazzo della Borsa was a perfect example of Fascist architecture, built in super-gigantic size to make everyone feel small and inconsequential, which has just the right proportions for me to feel awed. I loved going there just to experience the huge marble-faced buildings, but also because it was not a long walk from the convent where Leonardo painted his famous mural of "The Last Supper." I could usually presume upon my contacts at the Borsa to get me admitted to the convent of Santa Maria delle Grazie, so I could gaze at one of the most famous paintings in the world. I always saw something new every time. Fascinating.

At any rate, when I woke up the next morning, the smell of coffee was already seeping under my door. I thought, *thank God for Gabriele.* He was making a big (maybe ten-eggs) omelet with the leftover marinara sauce from the previous night poured over the top. He was using the largest cast iron skillet in my kitchen—the size my grandmother used to fry a couple of chickens for dinner. The omelet was stuffed with mozzarella and real sheep-cheese Pecorino Romano for good measure; the smell was irresistible, even to Chuy, who had wandered into the living room just by following the smells. Always lots of garlic, natch.

The doorbell rang. It was Ruth and Maggie. They found their way to the dining table right away, and started setting placemats with plates, flatware and coffee mugs.

Long story short, a hearty breakfast was had by all, and within an hour of sitting down to eat, we were on the subway going to the rental car office on East 46th Street near Grand Central and piled into the Ford Explorer that I had rented, and were on our way upstate. There was plenty of room, no crowding at all.

There are few places in the United States that are more beautiful than upstate New York. As late spring turns into summer, the trees are fully loaded with leaves, and the green color begins to turn to a slightly darker forest green, as opposed to the light green of the early days of spring. Forsythia and purple magnolias bloom first, and then there is an ever-changing floral parade, dominated for me by flowering fruit trees (think of the pink cherry blossoms) and the stately dogwoods that look like they've been coated with snow overnight. But of course, there's no snow, just the white or pink blossoms that stand out from everything else. Then bearded iris and rhododendrons. It seems like there is no end to the flowers of spring. Tulips and daffodils in big splotches of color, waving hi to all of us, and then wilting back into their bulbs before you're ready to say good-bye.

In order to get to Cooperstown, we could have driven due west through the Catskills, but I decided to take the big highways up toward Albany, then west for a bit, then southward to the huge agricultural bounty of the farmlands that stretch far and away from Interstate 88 heading toward Pennsylvania. All told, with a pause in New Paltz for some fast sightseeing, gas and snacks, about five hours on the road—a couple of hours longer than the Catskill route, but less likely to induce vertigo or car sickness from driving on hairpin curves. I was looking forward to stopping at Beekman 1802 on the way home; it's a goat ranch in a town called Sharon Springs, not far east from Cooperstown. I wanted to buy a small wheel of yummy pale, almost hard goat cheese rolled in grape pits (sounds a lot less wonderful than it actually is). Heaven on Triscuits or rolled up in a piping hot tortilla with a smidge of melting salted butter. Beekman 1802 is run by a pair of gay guys who left Manhattan and bought an old house, some land and a bunch of goats. Nothing better anywhere. Guaranteed.

"Are we there yet?" Chuy kept asking, like he was programmed to say something, and the same thing over and over worked okay for him.

I kept thinking about my various children asking the same thing as we headed into the Sierra Nevada for some camping years before, and kept wondering what kind of family life Chuy grew up with. Do Mexican drug dealers coach Little League teams?

Ruth smiled like the famous Alice-in-Wonderland Cheshire Cat every time he asked his repetitive query.

Gabriele looked vaguely annoyed at hearing the same thing over and over. Chuy made a show of not noticing any of that.

In the event, we were checking into the venerable and super-impressive Otesaga Hotel just after three o'clock. A good-looking athletic valet took the car and gave me a pink stub to use when getting it back for sightseeing or whatever. The hotel itself is a magnificent late Victorian pile with the distinctive look of a pre-Civil War southern plantation (only it was never a plantation, built by the New York Central Railroad. Great restaurants and bars, and very large high-ceilinged guest rooms. Expensive-looking overstuffed furniture. Short walk to the Baseball Hall of Fame—about the distance of two city blocks in Manhattan).

My cellphone vibrated. It was Mike. "Just wanted to bring you up to date. Two new possibly suspicious day spas with apparently nubile teams of masseuses suddenly opened in Long Island City, both of them on Vernon Boulevard—other end of the street from the subway station. Pics of super-young Asian girls in erotic postures, but no looking inside, due to dark smoked glass on the windows." He paused, then added, "No way to describe the signage except to say it's garish signage. Lots of neon; can't miss 'em."

Then he clicked off, followed by a short text message telling us to have fun over the weekend. Sure, thanks for the update, Mike. Good to know you're thinking about us, and wanted us to know that there were two new brothels near where I live that might be connected to Chuy and/or Maggie.

Gabriele and Chuy were flinging themselves onto the two queen-sized beds and rolling around. Generally messing up the tightly made beds. Kids. Even when they're mostly grown-up, they're still kids.

"So why did they call him Pee Wee? Just because he was a shortstop? He wasn't a little guy, was he?" Chuy wanted an explanation.

"Pee Wee Reese?" I asked, giving myself time to think. "He was a normal-sized guy, and yes, he was a shortstop, although I suppose he was shorter than a lot of the other players. I think he was five foot nine when he started with the Dodgers. Who knows where he got his nickname? Maybe in high school? Maybe when he was a kid? Did you have a nickname when you were a kid?"

"Some of the kids called me Pipsqueak, whatever that means," he said in a soft voice.

"Pipsqueak sounds like an unfriendly nickname for someone who's not as tall or muscled as other guys. Not so different from being called Pee Wee, which I think may have been the name of one of the Little Rascals, if you ever watched them on TV," I said. "Who knows? Could be from anything anytime. I read someplace that it had something to do with his preference for playing marbles, which he started as a little kid. But he never tried to get people to change it, as far as I know.

"There's a famous story about Pee Wee on Jackie Robinson's first day as a Dodger. The crowd started to boo because Jackie was a Black man. Pee Wee walked over to first base, where Jackie was standing, and put his arm over Jackie's shoulder, then started to chat with him." I paused and looked him in the eye, then continued. "The crowd stopped booing immediately and went silent. Tells you something about Pee Wee Reese. A big guy in lots of ways, even though people called him Pee Wee. Spent his whole baseball career with the Dodgers, in Brooklyn and in Los Angeles. We'll find a Pee Wee Reese jersey for you to wear home if you want."

There are souvenir-hawking people all over Cooperstown all summer. They line the streets radiating out from the Hall of Fame, and they aren't bashful, more like carnival barkers. A Brooklyn Dodger jersey with Pee Wee Reese's old numeral one that was retired when he left the team and the name "Reese" should be easy enough to come by. Who cares what it costs? It will be a high point in a young man's life. That's worth any price tag.

He beamed at me, and Gabriele patted him on the back. "You're a good guy, Chuy," he said, so the whole room could hear him. That is, Gabriele himself and me were the only ones in the room, but Gabriele's loudish voice might have been heard in the hallway outside the room.

Chuy felt like he was six feet tall, I thought as I looked at him. He was puffed up like a kid pretending to be a grown-up. Chest out, shoulders back. Exactly what I had hoped would happen. And hyper-oxygenating to boot—probably thinking more clearly than he had in quite a while. Nothing like a dose of oxygen to clear the mind, at least in my experience.

Truth be told, my first impression of Chuy was that he was a little scrawny, maybe skinny and nerdish looking—anything but strong. But as I looked at him right then and there, I realized that his arms were worked out in a gym sense—good biceps, triceps and deltoids. Respectable forearms, too. Probably the years of playing catch and finding pick-up baseball games. He was still a wiry Asian—not an ounce of fat anywhere that was visible, but he might just be a good ball-player, too.

As it turned out, Pee Wee Reese had passed on years earlier, so it was impossible for Chuy to meet him, but there was still the opportunity to see film footage and his display in the Hall of Fame. I knew for sure we'd be able to find a jersey. Every kid in Cooperstown—local or tourist—was wearing some kind of Hall of Fame jersey. I loved the idea of Dodger jersey Number One (Reese), especially if we could get one that fit Chuy. My best guess was that he would be a man's size small. He looked to be about average with thick-soled and heeled shoes that he wore a lot of the time—or maybe just when he was wearing his well-worn and clearly favorite Nike Air sneakers that he probably thought made him look taller. He was physically smaller than Pee Wee, but he was sold on the idea that Pee Wee had been a hero, as a friend of Jackie Robinson, one of the greatest players of all time, and the first Black player in the Major Leagues. Never mind that he wasn't allowed to stay in the same hotels as the White players. He was a hero to absolutely every baseball fan.

We went out to play catch—something Chuy was always ready for—and I led us to a card table where some guy was selling players' jerseys. And wouldn't you know, he had a Dodger One jersey that fit the young man like a glove. He couldn't stop smiling, and neither could Maggie, shining all over with a mother's pride.

Chuy didn't want to stop playing catch, not under any circumstance.

We took a ride up to the northern end of the lake and had a look at the Glimmerglass Opera House, which was roofed, but open on all sides, and built with natural color wood—a very handsome building with louvered blinds keeping any breeze from blowing the ladies' hats off. There was a performance going on, something that looked and sounded like a revue; bits and pieces of arias and well-known groups like the sextet from "Rigoletto." The voices could have been better, but they sounded close to perfect—and, surprisingly, Chuy seemed to be listening closely, and with no interest in cutting short his operatic experience. There was a young woman who sang "quanto rapito in estasi" from "Lucia di Lammermoor." Not a perfect rendition, but way better than average, with really beautiful coloratura runs and high notes. The crowd inside the Opera House gave her a resounding standing ovation—which she entirely deserved. She must have been super-worried, although she sounded like a total pro.

We tossed the ball back and forth while we headed for the car, and made it back to the hotel in time to order a juicy hamburger and a plate of fries with just the proper crunch. I ordered a chocolate shake, and Chuy wanted a Coke.

That night Chuy wanted a steak, which he got (a T-bone) with a baked potato with butter and sour cream. I found myself wondering where the food was going.

"You must have a hollow leg," Ruth said teasingly. "Otherwise I can't imagine where you're putting all that food." She giggled good-heartedly, and I could almost see the little girl in her teasing her brothers.

The next morning as we were driving to Beekman Ranch to buy some cheese, my phone buzzed. It was Mike di Saronno calling from his Manhattan office. "There's been an outbreak of Asian hate," he said. "An eighty-three-year-old woman was pushed onto a subway track on the upper East Side," he said. "She was rescued, but that wasn't the only thing that happened." He paused and continued. "A middle-aged man was punched in the face and knocked down with a bloody nose. Seems to have a connection with what the kid who hit him called the 'Flu Manchu,' a clear reference to the COVID-19 pandemic. Must be people blaming anyone with Asian features for spreading the virus, which apparently someone believed had jumped from Wuhan, China, to New York City with no obvious carrier." He couldn't stop himself, and continued, "Total bullshit, of course. And these poor guys are getting beat up for no reason except their Asian eyes."

"You want us to have a look around when we get back to town?" I asked. "We should be home in Long Island City about sundown. Any chance you can send over some info on what happened?"

"What would help me would be if you and your crew could have dinner someplace in Chinatown, and see if they're having issues there, too," Mike said.

"I've always liked 456 New Shanghai on Mott Street," Ruth volunteered via speakerphone. "Great dim sum, and nice spicy food if you like that."

"Let me know what time and I'll be there," Mike said. "I should have known you'd be an expert, Ruth," he said. "My mom used to say if you want Chinese food, ask a Jew. Ask Mrs. Schlossberg next door. Why don't I remember things like that?"

"Is that a good place for spicy chicken with peanuts, like Kung Pao Chicken?" I asked. "I particularly like Chinese food with shrimps or chicken, or both," I asked Ruth.

She nodded, and said it was a particularly beautiful place, too. "If anyone has sprayed graffiti on it, it'll look like a mortal sin. All red and gold inside, like the palace of a Chinese emperor."

"Hey, see if you can make a reservation for the whole bunch of us. Put it under Mike's name, and copy him on the confirmation," I said.

My phone buzzed again. It was Mike again. "There are three new day spas on Vernon Boulevard, one of them less than a block from the subway station. They look similar, and they seem to have the names of three well-known Chinese sisters. The one closest to the subway is called Soong May Ling, which is the name of Madame Chiang-Kai Shek, who fled China when Mao Zedong took over for the Communists. Chiang had been an ally of the United States and the Europeans during World War II. The other two are named for her two sisters. One was called Ching-ling, who married Sun-Yat-Sen, the first head of the Republic of China, so both of those were first ladies of China. Then there was Ai-ling, who married a super-rich banker or financier. At the time, they said one sister loved money (Ai-Ling), one loved power (May Ling), and one loved China (Ching-ling, who married Sun Yat Sen, and never left China for her entire life). None of them deserves to have their name on a day spa, especially if that spa specializes in 'happy endings' for male clients."

When we got to 456 New Shanghai, it was immediately obvious that it had been spray-painted and tagged in difficult-to-change patterns. I could only imagine that it had said things like "Go back where you came from" or "Get the hell out of our country," or "Take your virus back to China and never come back." It was still beautiful but had clearly been defaced in a big way.

Mike asked the server if somebody had tried to make the walls look bad. She nodded, and tears came to her eyes. "We used to be the most beautiful place in Chinatown, but now it won't be beautiful like it was until the virus is gone, over with, cured." She spoke English as well, it seemed, as she spoke Mandarin to Maggie and Chuy.

There's a reason hate is so vicious, I thought, *and a reason why prostitution is called the oldest profession. It seemed a terrible shame that such an obviously beautiful interior space could have been damaged to the place where it couldn't be restored.*

Mike paused, and said, "I think somebody is capitalizing on being a historic and classy Asian. The real May Ling went to Wellesley College, and ended up living in the United States. She's buried in Westchester County, just north of New York City. Somebody probably thought the names were classy, and made the spas look like they weren't sex stores. But if you look at the smoked glass on them, there's no doubt what was most likely going on inside where you can't see in from the outside." He paused again and said slowly, "Probably if there's a plague of Asian hate going around, these high-class names are intended to make them more respectable-looking."

Ruth wrinkled up her nose, and Maggie made a series of screwed-up faces. Hard to tell whether they were reacting to what had been said, or to the potential for disgusting surprises from behind the smoked glass.

There were several areas of the restaurant interior that looked like they might have been defaced or maybe had paint splashed on them. There were no places where words could have been spray-painted with obscene phrases or words. But it was clear that the original red-and-gold colors had been damaged, and then patched up, rather than being turned back to their original rich coloration, which also spoke of the Chinese flag with its blood red and golden yellow colorations.

"The food is still wonderful," Ruth said. "Take my word for it."

Maggie said that she had told the server in Mandarin that if someone in the kitchen spit in the food, she would know, and would have someone's hide. It was clear that what Maggie said was not only heard, but heeded politely.

We ate quietly with our chopsticks, and had orange sections for dessert before we left, and included a handsome tip on the credit-card slip. It was pitch dark as we left, and the restaurant was mostly empty, except for a few small tables with people who looked Chinese. No round-eyes at all, not even Midwestern tourists with shorts and baseball caps from Chicago or Minneapolis or St Louis.

Chapter Seven

When I woke up the next morning, I was still disgusted, with a terrible taste in my mouth. Chinese people have frequently been mistreated in the United States. Think of the Gold Rush and the terrible labors of building the Transcontinental Railroad during and right after the Civil War, between 1863 and 1869. But it just didn't make sense, people hailing back to the bad old days of Asian hate just because the COVID-19 virus probably originated in China. Lots of influenza viruses had originated in China over the years, including the H1N1 variety that caused a near epidemic in the United States a decade earlier. I never got it, probably because my annual flu shot protected me. Certainly it wasn't wearing a paper mask around pretty Asian girls. My best friend was from Poland, but was married to an Asian girl. I never stopped finding her sexy, although I never made any kind of pass at her. Our children were the same age, which acted as a damper on my hormones.

But the more I thought about the day spas that sprang up like dandelions after a rain, the more obvious it was that the problem was more one of forcing sex trafficking on women and girls, not just slant-eyed people; women and girls with a prominent epicanthic fold in lots of cases, or eyes that look to Europeans like they are almond-shaped, and possibly smaller than Caucasian eyes, not to mention the relatively broad range of eye colors amongst Caucasians. Yes, there are also multi-colored eyes in Arab and North African countries, but they are shaped like Caucasian eyes; no epicanthic fold. Exotic maybe, but not Asian-sexy.

But of course exotic is exotic, and attractive is attractive. A slim Asian or Eurasian girl—Japanese, Chinese, Korean, Vietnamese—will catch the eye of a Caucasian male, almost unfailingly. A slim body with feminine curves, and even Asian-styled clothing, can easily accentuate the girl's attractiveness, especially if the skirt is exaggerated by a slit that exposes one or both upper legs. Smokey eye makeup helps, and so does sexy jewelry like dangling earrings. Add a slightly open neckline, or a boatneck shoulder-to-shoulder slash exposing unblemished skin that continues up the neck and down her arms with shiny fingernails shaped to make the fingers slightly pointed. A splash of Chinese red nail polish never hurts, especially if it echoes the color of her lipstick.

One of the things that a girl can trust in is male sexuality that makes itself obvious quickly, filling the guy's pants with an erection that makes itself as noticeable as the girl's bosom, displayed without need for imagination. Once he is excited, the game is afoot if the girl cooperates, maybe even slips off her underwear a little surreptitiously.

I didn't have sex with anybody, male or female, until I was in my early twenties, but I have to admit that once I'd been there, I was ready for more. I don't recall ever being with a pro girl—I would always have been afraid of a variety of "dirty" diseases. My religious upbringing pushed me into the one-at-a-time group of guys. One girlfriend at a time. I married a pretty Euro girl with reddish brownish hair, and a preference for Pucci dresses. Sexy as all heck, and ready to have fun; also a drug user, which I had no idea about until after we were married, and as you'll see, we were not legally married. It was the 1960s, and everything was okay in those days.

We eloped to Hawaii from southern California on the strength of a newish (and unused) credit card, and hung out there for the better part of a week after having been married by a justice of the peace in a part of Oahu called "Haiku Plantation," which was really an upscale residential development with gates to keep people out. We both forgot to sign the wedding certificates, and were subsequently divorced and annulled when her father stepped into the picture. I didn't have another affair with a girl for nearly five years, at which time I got married again—this time in a church near UCLA, where I went to school. We stayed married for a long time, well over 45 years. I never cheated, although I admit I found out that she did. Also never tried sex with a guy. Didn't appeal to me at all. She had been a singer and went on a State Department-sponsored tour of eight Chinese cities, in the company of a horny tenor. Yes, they did it. I took the whole thing as a more-or-less divorce, and although we never did actually break up the marriage, even though I moved to Manhattan to take over a new office, I didn't feel like the marriage vows mattered much anymore. Still never had an affair. Too fond of the children. And I took care of her until she died of natural causes, well after 45 years of marriage.

I had her cremated, and bought a handsome brass urn, which I gave to our daughter, who was, understandably, very torn up that her mother had died. I had been visiting her in a nursing home for nearly seven years, and was ready for the end. Not happy, you understand, but ready for an end. The failure of our marriage had affected my relationships with the children. I am super-fond of both of them, although our son more or less left the family when he married a woman who was more than a decade older than he was. They say your son's your son until he takes a wife. Your daughter's your daughter for all of your life.

It was true, at least in my case. My son has never spoken to me after he realized that his wife wasn't going to get pregnant. Not ever.

So back to the day spas. Yes, they were fronts for prostitution, which meant that the only real clients were male. Not an LGBTQ+ type of place, at least as far as I ever learned. I wasn't ever a tail-chaser. I admired beautiful, sexy women—never took any time for me to learn to stare at a gorgeous woman, but I seldom made the connection between admiration and sexual desire. I wanted a certain type of woman, not just a sexy woman who wore her clothing well. Probably something lacking inside me. I always connected sex with babies. I wanted babies. We had five; I wanted seven. I had names for the two we didn't have: George Vincent (my grandfather's name) and Rachel, a Tennessee housewife who, after the Civil War, loaded her furniture on a wagon and moved to Texas, where there was reportedly, lots of ranch land for the grabbing. For a land-poor Confederate widow, nothing could have sounded sweeter. Rachel was a wanted woman who had killed a Yankee soldier she caught stealing a side of pork from the smokehouse. She said it was the last bullet she had for the rifle, but maybe it wasn't. She shot some deer on the trip to Texas, and she pushed her way into the Miller ranch, one of the biggest in the area, eventually to be divided among several brothers, one of whom was named Hugo—which is where my name originated. Of course my forebears from that part of the family were Germans (Prussians), and spelled their name Mueller. They changed it to the English spelling, Miller, during the first month of World War I.

I never had a grandson who could have been named Hugo, but I changed my own name to Hugo when I decided to write the memoirs of my work with the NYPD. Seemed right to call the fictional me Hugo, instead of the name that was on my Sports PR firm, which I'll keep to myself for now.

Chapter Eight

But of course the fact that I wasn't personally attracted to the Best Little Whorehouses in Long Island City didn't mean that nobody else was curious and ready to pay the piper for a happy ending. Pretty clearly there was no intention for any of the girls to get pregnant with their young suitors' flooding cum and excess sperms. The girls were careful to insist on the use of condoms, which also started quickly to blanket the sidewalks at night. Somebody seemed to sweep them up in the daytimes. Otherwise they would have been so thick on the ground that they would be impossible to clean up without soap, water, and scrub brushes.

Over the first week or so of the day spas opening, all the lotharios in the neighborhood staked out their stations within a few yards of one or the other spa location. With that came a regular kerfuffle as young toughs started taking over the area—replete with tussles and various kinds of fights with young Asian men, who, under some circumstances, might have been suitable suitors for the female workers at the day spas. In the way of the local toughs, of course the girls were regarded as the property of the teenage toughs who had staked out the area.

That then attracted clusters of uniformed cops who may or may not have been attracted to the girls, but who definitely wanted to be part of cleaning up the neighborhood, which had been largely populated by Latin toughs and some muscle-bound, mixed-race, post-high-school sexy fellows who stood out as potential trouble-causers. As soon as someone then threw a punch, the cops were all over them with batons and handcuffs.

It was obvious from the first night that there would be trouble in the six-block section of Vernon Boulevard that housed the three day spas. We didn't have to wait long. I started hearing what could have been fireworks at night, but fireworks don't blast holes in windows, and I found the telltale bullet holes, called the cops, and watched as they picked bullet metal out of the walls. When bullets fly inside my apartment, that's more than I can tolerate. I could be killed while I was asleep. I may not be young, but I'm not old enough for that. Hey, I may not be a full-fledged cop, but I'm an employee of the NYPD, and I don't want to be shot at. I don't carry a gun, don't have a badge, but I have an ID card as a civil criminalist, and I feel like I deserve protection. Fortunately I live on the tenth floor of my building, so not many bullets make it into my apartment, and the ones that do usually imbed themselves in the ceiling, because they were probably pointed up into the air when the triggers were pulled. I did manage to get a bodyguard—actually three of them on an aggregate of twenty-four hours per day. There was always an armed guard there in uniform, and that made me feel a little bit more secure.

It wasn't the same on the street level. Bullets tore into flesh, especially on or near Vernon Boulevard. No surprises, most of the victims and shooters were black or brown, possibly looking to take advantage of the Asians, most of whom were new to the neighborhood. There had been a few Chinese restaurants and take-outs, and at least two Thai eateries, but the owners and employees probably lived in Asian ghettoes either in Queens or Manhattan. The local police precinct hadn't had a gang war on its turf in years—maybe decades, and where there had been long-lasting gang problems, they had tended to be wings and branches of tough bands of rowdies from other parts of New York City, or other urban areas from across the nation, including West Coast cities like Los Angeles, as well as localities like Compton, Gardena, and Vernon, not to mention heavily segregated areas of Los Angeles like Ladera Heights and Baldwin Hills. Crips and Bloods, now augmented by local brotherhoods of Central American gangs from Nicaragua, Guatemala and El Salvador—mostly undocumented except infants born to undocumented parents.

Most of the US citizens were younger than elementary-school age. Due to the influx of pretty Asian girls in the day spas and free-lancing hookers, the mixture of races was gradually broadening.

There were lots of weapons, including AR-15s and other semi-automatic guns, many with bump-stock add-ons that allowed literally hundreds of bullets to be shot in seconds—like battlefield conditions, not petty crime situations like robberies or drive-by shootings where the victims were frequently children and grandparents.

Due to the evolution of the neighborhood, the people with the biggest targets on their backs tended to be White singles or couples. Not a lot of guns because none of the thieves wanted to be accused of serious gun-toting offenses.

Not surprisingly, Maggie Landover was able to worm her way into the day spa world. The fact was that her son, Chuy, was part of the genesis of the whole idea. Also not surprisingly, Maggie's apartment became a venue for a variety of sexual activities, including a lot of sex groups that tended to grow larger from time to time, verging on orgies. She didn't seem to develop relationships, and I don't recall seeing her with her clothing off, or partially off. She looked and acted more like a hostess, pouring drinks and bringing out potato chips and Fritos

Word had it that Chuy was not enchanted with his mom not only joining an open sex "club," but taking a lead role in bringing in new participants, and probably making enough money to line her pockets in a way she hadn't had for years, maybe decades. Clearly Maggie was not looking to get pregnant or to have sexual experiences in any way—she was too old to want that, or to be happy about finding herself in the family way. She told Chuy she was taking birth-control pills, but that didn't make him friendlier to what his mom was up to.

"Whore," he muttered to me. "And she killed my dad, too." Nonetheless, it seemed she saw this as a career potential. Maybe she was seeing herself as a middle-aged Madame, making good money on a regular basis. Certainly her ex-husband hadn't left her any of his fortune, and her son, while he paid for some things—dinners, drinks—was not born generous.

I played the side of family peace. "My impression of your mother is that she loves you very much. I hope you will try to forget and forgive her for the things about her that you don't like. I know there were things about my mother than I had a hard time with—her politics and mine were very much at loggerheads, for example. You mom probably sees the day spas as somehow connected to you or your dad. I doubt thinking of her as a whore is going to help matters. I am truly sure she loves you. Tell me you'll try to give her a new chance to get in your good graces. Think of how much fun we had when we went to Cooperstown! She really does love you."

As soon as Chuy left, I called Maggie and asked her to come over. Since she lived just across the street, it only took her a few short minutes to be at my door. After welcoming her and offering her some coffee or a glass of wine, I dived into the subject I wanted to explore with her.

"Chuy seems to think you're personally involved with the day spa business," I said bluntly. "Maybe even having some social gatherings at your apartment. He seems to be worried that you may be getting involved sexually with some of the guys."

She put her hands on her hips and made a face of disapproval. "If I wanted a boyfriend, that'd be one thing. But I don't want a boyfriend. And I'm not interested in sex and I'm not interested in men. I've been pouring drinks and acting like a mom at a birthday party a lot. I think it's better for a hostess to be uninvolved. The girls at the spas give me a small cut on every guy they send over to my place. I don't have sex with them. Too old for that," she said with an almost fierce look. "Not even a little. I got married once according to the Church—to Manuel. I had a baby once, and as it happens, I had some surgery that made it unlikely I would ever have another baby. Not that I wanted one. I met my son when he was already grown, and I'm happy with him. He's my kind of man—not for sex, not interested in sex at all. I don't remember having as much fun as we had when we went to Cooperstown—ever. Not ever. It was because you and Ruth and Gabriele were fun to be with, and Chuy was a perfect son. I loved playing catch with him. I was really proud of him when he put on the Dodger Number One jersey. It made me puff up to see him so interested in something wholesome like baseball. I could have hugged him over and over." She shifted her eyes and her stance.

"Don't take this the wrong way, but I think Chuy would be happier with a guy than with a girl. He may have never really thought about it, but I watched him staring at Gabriele. No idea how old Gabriele is, but I'd guess nearly twenty years older than Chuy. Perfect—half father potential, half sexy older man.

"As it happens, Gabriele is gay. Don't know if you knew that, but maybe if you didn't know, you just made a good guess," I said. "He's always said he wanted me, but I'm not attracted to guys, so there was never any future in that. We've been best friends for years, since he was involved with one of the police cases I worked on. I've watched him turn heads for years. He's hugely handsome. Worse things could happen to Chuy. I've seen him turn down some terrifically attractive men, so I don't know what future there might be between the two of them."

She put her tongue in her cheek, and said, "I'll put my mind to it, see what I can do. Chuy is quite a prize, to tell the truth, and like you said, Gabriele is enough to make most gay guys drool. You never know," she said, and ran her thumb and index finger over the sides of her mouth. "I appreciate your help and advice, and I'm going to head home."

She never sipped her wine, a nice Italian pinot noir. But she was smiling like she had just heard something really funny, and had her hands in her side jeans pockets, looking very pleased with herself.

Chapter Nine

There's definitely a yenta inside me somewhere. After that conversation with Maggie, I called Ruth with a full head of energy concentrated on the potential for Gabriele and Chuy to make a couple together, in spite of the fact that the whole idea made me feel like leering like a circus clown. I explained to Ruth my discussion with Maggie, and asked her bluntly, "Any ideas how we might get Gabriele and Chuy to spend more time together?"

As I said it, I knew that I didn't want to palm Gabriele off on anyone, much less a mentally unstable young man like Chuy, who grew up with a schizophrenic father who was half devout Catholic, and the other half Mexican gangster who was never far from running a truckload of cocaine across the US southern border, and even less far from killing someone in the process.

I secretly thought Maggie was the preferable parent—a mom who was willing to live with the son God gave her—her smiling, catch-playing con Jesus, AKA Chuy. Maggie probably had a fairly traditional upbringing before she met Manuel Acosta-Gonzalez, who was, from all I could tell, a born criminal, never more comfortable than when he had a machete in his left hand and a semi-automatic handgun in his right hand. Except when he was praying during Mass, preparing for communion at his parish church in Guadalajara.

I, of course, never met Manuel, who died the night I was first made aware of the fact that he was a human being who was in the process of being murdered with a kitchen knife while I heard his ex-wife scream across the street from my apartment. I was attracted to Chuy's built-in enthusiasm for life and fun, in spite of the fact that he was brought up by a screwed-up father who was raised as part of a Mexican drug cartel. I think I would have adopted Chuy. I was too old to be a dad again, and he was too old to be a kid, even though he acted like a kid a lot of the time. The only straight thing his dad implanted in him was a fervent love of baseball—in particular, baseball as played by the Los Angeles Dodgers, and maybe as typified by Jackie Robinson and Pee Wee Reese. But that was enough for me. Baseball is a personal mania for me. I can watch any game any time—and like it. My own son went to Dodger Summer Camp for two years in a row. I myself was always a little afraid of foul balls hit into the stands, and would duck them rather than stick my hand up to catch them. Chuy was fearless when it came to the potential to catch a "free" ball to take home as a souvenir.

Maggie, his mother, whom he had grown up without, was now willing to take Chuy wherever and however he presented himself. She took him to baseball games, to rock concerts at the Staples Center (the big basketball palace in downtown Los Angeles). She also took him to Sunday Mass after she killed his father, whom she thought was trying to rape her, in spite of the face that they had previously been married. Her ex had refrained from saying anything on the subway as he made a pass at her. He was wearing a paper surgical mask because of the COVID-19 pandemic. She had no idea who he was. He knew her because she wasn't wearing a mask, and she was willing to talk enough to tell him to go to hell when he grabbed her breast, so he knew she had been his wife at some point, but all she knew about him was that he was grabbing at her, and when he followed her home, she accidentally slit his throat while he had his hands in her bra—still without ever saying anything to her at all. I always wondered if he kept thinking it would dawn on her who he was. Then, of course, in his mind, she would give in.

Not.

Also, not a surprise that Chuy might impress his own mother as a young man with the potential to fall in love with another man. Maybe he was gay, she thought. Maybe. Hard to tell from just looking. You can't tell a man's sexual preference from his hair color or the way he ties his tie. You might be able to pick up hints from his behavior, especially if he acts a little like a girl. But at least half the gay men in the world don't act feminine. How else would they attract their mates who are looking for masculine men?

For my purposes, Gabriele is as masculine a guy as exists anywhere. If there's a queer bone in Chuy's body, he should be drooling after Gabriele, whether anybody notices or not. Gabriele would notice for sure. Gabriele and Chuy could play catch day after day after day for the rest of their lives—sex or no sex.

Gabriele and I have spent a lot of time together. We've slept in the same bed at times. In nothing more than skivvies. I find Gabriele very masculine in virtually every way. He made a pass at me once, many years back. I told him "no" and he never came back at me again.

I had a crush on Ruth for years. We were introduced to each other by a rather well-known stock analyst who was conducting a trade show of sorts at the Waldorf-Astoria. Ruth, who had worked for a former mayor of New York, was not only beautiful and a total fashion plate, she was funny, had a smile as big as Texas, and—as I found out—had a secret boyfriend who worked in the music industry. John, the stock analyst, wanted us to be a couple. I liked the idea and the girl herself, but I was still married, and had no intention of getting un-married. I took my marriage vows seriously, even though my wife and I didn't get along well a good bit of the time. She eventually broke up with Mahmoud (the boyfriend), and eventually married a nice Jewish man named Murray, who came to be a friend of mine (since I was a friend of his wife, I think). I considered Murray a close friend, could never have made a pass at his wife.

They weren't married for long. Murray had a heart attack and died, but they were gloriously happy for the few years they had together. Ruth gave up her beautiful apartment on Riverside Drive, and moved in with Murray in his Classic 8 on Park Avenue between 60th and 61st Street. Not the most glamourous address in New York, but plenty posh, and with every bit of the room a house in the suburbs would have had. Murray had been married before, and had a thorny relationship with his former wife, and a closer, more loving relationship with his daughter, Molly, who nevertheless had a difficult time getting along with her dad's new and unusually pretty and well-dressed wife, who had a thing for classic (second-hand) Chanel, and was able to wear Chanel linen suits without ever showing a wrinkle. Ruth also knew everybody worth knowing in Manhattan. She was a longtime volunteer at Carnegie Hall, and a forever member of the Opera League, and went like it was a religion to Monday evening opera performances on the Dress Circle of the Metropolitan Opera House. Black tie to the extreme. I occasionally went with her when Murray was out of town, which was fairly often, since he was a middleman in the garment industry, importing women's wear from small countries with big garment businesses—places like Vietnam, Mexico, most of South America and lots of southeast Asia—places where antsy American buyers went to avoid buying clothing in China, which was the largest market for all kinds of clothing—not just high-fashion women's wear, which is where Murray's interest was.

But, to counteract what I said above about being true to my wife and stuck on Ruth, I found myself very attracted to Maggie, who was a good bit younger than me, but very pretty, with flashing dark eyes, and more of an hourglass figure than most Eurasian women, who tended to be slim and trim with a shape like a runway model—small hips, understated bust (but still noticeable). She dressed well, and had a good tailor, who made her clothing fit like elbow-length calfskin gloves.

I guessed that Maggie didn't seem to need a lot of foreplay, and she was also not above initiating things herself. Maybe she was getting some action from the guys she recruited for the day spas. I didn't want a complicated relationship with a woman. I had two strikes—two swings at the ball, both of which missed by a mile. Like they say, three strikes and you're out. No matter how male fantasies play out, it's usually the guy who initiates intimacy. I always associated sex with wanting to have babies—and I couldn't envision having a few babies at my late middle age. I was going to be eligible to be a grandfather again soon anyway, and didn't fancy having kids and grandkids at the same time. So there was a certain frequency in kissing and hugging, but truthfully Maggie didn't want to have children—and maybe couldn't anyway—she hinted that she couldn't conceive because of problems when Chuy was born. I had never thought of having a mistress, which is what Maggie would have been, since I still considered myself married. Trying to nurse a second relationship so soon after the primary relationship ended when my wife died—it just didn't make sense. And our sizes didn't fit. I'm well over six feet, and Maggie topped out at about five foot two inches. My wife was five foot seven inches, and I had always been attracted to her in those years when we were still young or youngish. When she wore high heels, she was nearly my height, which, even though it was "fake," made a difference, at least when we kissed or danced.

I was fully functional. That wasn't a problem. Just wasn't willing to move ahead. Maybe it was my upbringing. Maybe it was the way my parents raised me with regards to sex. Sex was always, for the most part, a mortal sin, and worth throwing me into Hell. That was always frightening to me—more frightening than the potential for sex was interesting. I think I had PTSD from something that happened when I was still pre-pubescent. My dad went on an extended business trip when we were preparing to move to California from Texas. My dad was looking at neighborhoods to live in all those miles away. My mom didn't want to sleep alone, so she moved me into her bed and out of my bedroom. I knew the phrase "sleeping together," and I found myself really worried that my mom might get pregnant from sleeping with me in the same bed. It tortured me, and I never asked my mom if it was possible. I never asked the priest at Our Lady Queen of Angels. So I think I carried the guilt with me for a long time—maybe even when I was finding myself attracted to Maggie Landover. There's nothing like guilt to dampen a man's interest in sex.

Maybe I was a mental case. Maybe I still am. I'm Episcopalian now, too late for Catholic-style confession. No obvious way to be forgiven, especially for something that never happened. After all, I've been married and had children. I know that "sleeping together" doesn't cause pregnancy. There has to be real sex, which clearly there never was between me and my mother. Not a chance. It would have been too icky-dirty-disgusting by miles and miles.

Chapter Ten

Meanwhile, the Asian Hate activity was getting more and more common—and vicious. More people pushed onto subway tracks. More elderly people knocked to the pavement and kicked without any provocation at all. The only seeming reason why a Black or Brown or White homeless person should attack Asians had to do with the COVID-19 virus, which may or may not have originated in China.

And even if it did originate in China or elsewhere in Asia, why should a New York-born Asian be punished for it?

An unusually large percentage of perpetrators was being apprehended on the site of the crimes. It seemed that many of them were homeless or had been sleeping on the streets or in buses or subway cars. So maybe the attacks were simply matters of lack of knowledge, or simply having no place to run to. If the virus was from China, why not blame Chinese people? How can you tell if someone is Chinese? They have almond-shaped eyes and are generally small in stature. Frequently pretty and with good skin.

Most arrested people were not kept in lock-up for long, because many of them were hapless, incoherent, had no explanation for what happened. Unfortunately, the way laws are written, hate crimes can be punished draconianly. The relatively recent Black Lives Matter demonstrations and parades that sometimes became riotous were powerful reminders of hate crimes being visited on people of dark skin. If Black Lives Matter, why shouldn't Asian Lives Matter?

What are Asians known for? Well, if they're Chinese, the answer is probably food. Like Mexicans, soul food vendors, Cubans, Latinos,

Blacks and Asians. Non-Whites. Asians and Latinas are also known in parts of the city for sex. Hookers are reputed among street people to be brown, black or yellow, to use the colors the way hate crimes frequently use them. Also, occasionally blondes with unknown racial background—mostly bottle blondes, as you might guess. White girls are more likely to be call girls or to work from an "agency" on a computer or phone site, working for telephone agencies—White girls are seldom streetwalkers.

My exposure to prostitutes has been almost nil over the years. Not that I've never sat next to a professional girl. I've lived in midtown Manhattan for years—I've sat next to actors (famous ones), so I've probably sat next to girls who were open to a variety of sexual activities. Not that I've never bought a hooker a drink at a bar—if I did, I was just unaware that I was doing it. I probably just felt super-lucky to have been sitting next to a pretty girl who didn't mind that I insisted on telling her the story of my life. And she listened, with a smile and an occasional question. Then she suggested trying a different bar, not far from where we were. I might have eventually found myself backing away, maybe even telling stories about my kids and how I had been married for a lot of years. I never sat next to a girl whom I wanted to pick up, the way guys pick up girls in bars. I was never not a married man. I don't know how to say that any stronger. I married my wife in 1973 and I promised to love her, to take care of her. I never outlived that promise until she died, and even then I considered myself married, had five children and two grandchildren. That means that although I was a widower, I was still, and am still, a married man, with zero intention to cheat on my wife.

Did I ever find myself attracted to another woman? Yes, several times. Did I ever try to seduce a woman I was attracted to as a result of a chance meeting? No. Not once. Not ever. I stayed married all the time I was married. My promises are real, and they will always be, as long as I draw breath.

The probable truth is most high-class hookers would act like high-class girls who were just interested in meeting guys to date—probably not super-different in her mind from going to a movie and dinner afterward. They tend to be very attractive, and they dress well—expensively anyway—a penchant for low-cut dresses, short hems, and understated jewelry. They also don't ask for money just because you say hi to them. I remember finding a brown-skinned girl walking next to me on 6th Avenue, near the hotel I was staying at. She looked at me and asked in an accent that said she probably didn't speak English, "You speak Spanish?" I shook my head, and she walked faster to get ahead of me, then turned at the next corner—and disappeared. I always wondered what her question was meant to convey. Was it a dirty question? Or was it a simple query to know if I spoke Spanish? I don't think it was that straightforward. I think it was code of some kind. Did she mean to offer me some kind of intimate experience? I found myself wondering, and being happy that I didn't know the answer she was looking for. I was also glad to find a nook of innocence in my head or heart.

At the time, I felt like calling my wife and telling her what happened. Not that she would have had much of an idea what the streetwalker was saying, but I wanted to share what I had heard with someone I trusted—and it wasn't like I had a trusted friend in the Peninsula Hotel on 5th Avenue and 55th Street. I trusted my wife, even though we had arrived at a point in life when we quibbled and argued a lot. I never stopped loving her. There was almost never a day when we didn't have a long talk on the telephone. I kept no secrets from her. I was in the delivery room for the birth of all of our kids. There's nothing more intimate than that. The first girl, who was named after one of my grandmothers, was over nine pounds when she was born, and my first son was ten pounds three ounces. The doctor said when he delivered the boy, "Put him on the floor and let him walk out." He was the biggest baby in the Cedars-Sinai nursery for two full days, and when we took him home, the next-biggest baby got the big-baby title by default. My wife kept a lot of secrets from me, or so I found out after she died, but by then it was too late to pursue the truth wherever it was. I did find out that she had two babies before I met her, and one of them, a boy, contacted one of my daughters through a match on her Ancestry account. They had a good telephone talk, but only one. The two babies had different fathers, but both of them were boys. I was a lucky shit that our first baby was a big healthy girl. I was disappointed at first, because my mother and grandmother wanted a boy who could keep the name alive. But I learned fast, and loved that little girl with a love that was unlike anything else I had ever felt in my whole life.

So wouldn't it just happen that Chuy's mother, Maggie Landover, was shoved onto the sidewalk! She tripped and fell, and the assailant, who was brown, most likely a strapping Latino boy, was taller than Maggie by several inches. His leverage over her left her prone on the sidewalk, where he kicked her a couple of times, and took her handbag, which had her credit cards in it, and her photo IDs and driver's license.

I was disappointed that Chuy was not only not upset when I told him what had happened, but I came to realize from his off-handed comments that he thought most girls flirted constantly, so she might have been "asking for it" (that's an actual quote). Fortunately, she wasn't really hurt, just some scrapes and bruises, and a young uniformed cop retrieved her handbag with all its contents. But it worried me that Chuy had so little sympathy with his mother, who so clearly loved him without any holds barred.

Whenever my cellphone vibrates, it's a call from Mike di Saronno. I've never programmed any other numbers to vibrate. I wanted to feel the vibration on my butt whenever the "boss" wanted to talk to me. So the day after Maggie was mugged, Mike unsurprisingly called and wiggled my left buttock. No sound, because I didn't want to have the noise where other people could hear it. I just wanted to sign on and say, "Hi, Boss," because I felt so good about working for Mike and the NYPD. I ran my own company for nearly forty years, and I would have been all smiles if my employees ever called me "boss," because I wanted to feel that my own management style made everybody in my company feel good—safe and sound. Being called "boss"—which happened sometimes—was a huge compliment to me. I wasn't just paying somebody to do a job that reported to me. I was the top of a pyramid of management that had helped all the worker-bees create a sports PR company that had a client lineup that was the envy of every sports PR company in North America. We even had World Cup heroes on our roster, which made us an international name, a PR power that could make connections for our clients—some of them became film stars, some did TV commercials, some did color fill-in with broadcast teams. I particularly liked working with the golf teams. But whenever my butt vibrated, I was happy to talk to my bossman, Mike di Saronno.

So when my butt cheek wiggled that day, I answered as soon as I could get my phone out of my back pocket.

"Maggie Landover doesn't want to press charges against the guy who tackled her on the street," he said. "I get the impression that Chuy Gonzalez might have something to do with that. Like maybe he wants his mother to be as tough as the tough guys—even with the skin scraped off her shoulder where she landed."

"What do you want me to do?" I asked. "I was surprised when Chuy told me that maybe she'd been flirting with the teenager who attacked her," I said, adding, "I've never seen her flirt with anyone of any age or sex—but it didn't surprise me when Chuy didn't seem to have any sympathy for her having been pushed down and kicked in the gut."

"What do you think I ought to do?" he asked.

"Pull it into your office instead of leaving it to the Long Island City precinct. Tell her she should think about future victims, instead of trying to be such a stiff upper lip."

I gathered he did as I suggested, because he called me again later that same day.

"Hey, boss," I answered. "How'd it go with Maggie?"

"More complicated than I expected," he answered. "Turned out she knew the guy from the neighborhood, and didn't want to get him in trouble."

"Would I know him?" I asked. "She lives less than a block around the corner from my place."

"No idea," he said. "She told me he hangs out near the Mister Softee truck right near the front of your building."

"So I might recognize him," I mused.

"Good-looking kid, looks like a gym rat. Also comes across as self-confident, well-spoken. I wouldn't be surprised if you knew him. I'm sending you a mug shot. If he looks familiar, we can do a lineup if you're willing."

The pic came through. "Yup, I recognize him. No idea what his name might be, but I did know him from hanging out at the ice cream truck. Looking for spare change, maybe so he could buy some food," I told Mike. "But I had the impression that he also carried groceries from the local supermarket, so he probably has some cashflow in addition to whatever he begs at the ice cream truck. Wouldn't want to ask him about whether he reports his income for taxes, though."

"Don't know how careful he is about reporting his income, but he told me his income from last year, and it could be spot on, from all I could tell," Mike said.

"Name?"

"Tyrone Green."

"Muscle guy? Body builder?"

"Yeah," Mike said. "And he just graduated from high school with a three point eight Grade Point Average. Planning to go to Hunter College in the fall. Says he wants to study communications media," Mike mused. "Well spoken. Wouldn't be surprised if you wanted to write him a recommendation letter."

"In that case, I'd love to meet him. My business could use any number of smart, resourceful Black guys," I said. "I wonder if he might be intern material. If he is, we might pick up some of his school fees, too."

"Happy to be Mister In-between for you and Mr. Green," he said. "That rhymes. I'm a poet and I didn't even know it."

I've never been attracted to a guy, but there was something about Tyrone Green's description that made me want to buy him a drink, or maybe just pour him a drink at my apartment—in spite of his being probably under-age.

"I wonder if he'd thought of being a cop, maybe applying to John Jay College over by Lincoln Center, to study Criminology," I said openly to Mike.

I had briefly been editor of a scholarly journal on criminology when I was just out of school at UCLA. That's where I learned for sure that I was not a candidate to be either a lawyer or a cop.

"If he hasn't, I'll make sure the idea gets into his head," Mike said enthusiastically. "Like you said, maybe an intern candidate. Could end up being a politician. Could actually end up being my boss if he's as smart as I think he might be. Like that black ex-cop who was the borough president of Brooklyn. Looks like he might be on the road to being the mayor at the election in the fall. It's a crying shame that David Dinkins is still the only Black mayor ever elected in this super-progressive city."

Mike asked me if I could do a lineup at his office that afternoon.

"Of course," I answered. "I was just thinking about having some lunch. I skipped breakfast to keep my waist from bulging—that happens at my age, as you'll find out one of these days as years pass by."

We agreed on two o'clock, and I told him I'd probably stop at Thalia for a bite on the way over.

Bryan, the longtime Thalia bartender, welcomed me by waving a bottle of Tito's Vodka. I nodded, and he poured me a dirty vodka, with some olive juice in it—and a couple of big fat olives for good measure. I asked for a plate of spaghetti with tomato sauce. Perfect lunch. Icy dirty vodka and pasta—no meat.

I kinda half expected Mike might show up, but he didn't. But he was waiting in his office when I got to the precinct building. I picked out Tyrone Green easily from the six Black guys in the lineup. Good looking enough to be a TV star, for all that matters.

Mike decided to interview Green, and to invite me to watch from behind the mirror in the interrogation room.

Green had a bulging chest and highly developed upper arms. He also had fine facial features with a distinctly small-bridged nose and thin lips, not to mention a complexion that looked halfway between black-black and white. His appearance spoke volumes about his genetic background. He would always be Black to people on the street. That could be softened by a uniform, but it wouldn't ever go away. If he had children with a White girl, his offspring could be as White as Megan Markle's and Prince Harry's son, Archie. It wouldn't matter as much as it did with the then-royal Duke and Duchess of Suffolk, but it could make a big difference for the child itself and its place in society.

Shortly after the interview was over and the interrogation room was cleared, my phone vibrated. It was Mike, as it always is when the phone vibrates.

"I think Tyrone is going to consider going to John Jay if he can get in," Mike told me. "I might write him a letter of recommendation, and I kinda hope you might do the same. As a civilian criminalist, your letter might have more weight than mine as a plain-clothes detective," he said. "I was clear that the Department was looking for diversity. If he could get through John Jay, he would have a road paved ahead of him. He wouldn't be a uniformed cop for long before he started being considered for promotions. Sergeant first, then lieutenant, maybe an office job with the media group—a way to affect diversity in a real way by attracting additional candidates to enlarge the population of people of color in the NYPD. Gone are the days of Irish beat cops swinging their batons and singing Irish songs on the sidewalks. A Black cop with a real smile is a much more *au courant* character than the old-fashioned pasty-white northern European with a slightly protruding gut that typified Officer Krupke in "West Side Story.""

Chapter Eleven

The closer it got to Labor Day, the more helpful and attentive Tyrone Green became. First of all, he stepped forward to apologize to Maggie Landover for what had happened. He didn't have to do that, and he knew it. It also turned out that he knew Chuy from sight, and quickly understood that they were mother and son. After all, they looked like twins in lots of ways, although they were far from the same age.

"Asian Hate is stupid," he told her. "I knew that, and I did what I did anyway. I'm really sorry, and I want you to understand that I owe you. I'm not going to follow you, but the next time somebody decides to pester you or whatever, I'm going to be there on your side," he said. "I can't ever undo what I did, but I can help the same kind of crap from happening again in the future."

Tyrone told her that he wanted to be a cop, and he was a hard-working student with a good GPA. "If I can be your friend, or your son's friend, I'll do whatever it takes to get there. I admire you for not being afraid of me, and for letting me talk to you like this. I can't tell you how sorry I am, and it wouldn't matter if I could. I want you to know that I owe you, and I intend to make sure you get a fair shake in the future. Same for your son, if he'll let me be his friend."

The big step happened toward the end of August. Tyrone Green was admitted to the Police Academy. He would be able to attend the Academy and then to matriculate into John Jay after the first eight weeks of the Academy. It was clearly a fast track, and a sort of internship came with it. After completing the eight weeks of Academy basic training, he would be made an intern civilian criminalist, reporting to me, and through me to Mike di Saronno. Unlike me, though, he would be on hourly pay. He would have to clock in and out, and he would get a blue uniform and a badge. No daily weapon at the outset, but he would be taking instruction on the police firing range, and could be armed in certain circumstances, like civil disturbances.

"What you need to learn is how to NOT use your weapon. We don't want cops shooting anybody. There's nothing good about a Black cop shooting a White or Asian perpetrator, just like there's nothing good about a White or Asian cop shooting a Black perpetrator," Mike said. "You'll be using all your ingenuity to figure out how to work your way through a crisis without using your weapon. We'll decide when you can be a fully uniformed police officer—trusted with a loaded weapon that is never to be used if your life is not in danger. Ask any cop about Internal Affairs. You don't want them on your back; there's no way to lose your career like a tangle with Internal Affairs. Internal Affairs will absolutely investigate everything about a police shooting. If you fire your weapon, it's going to be surrendered immediately—on the site—and the investigation will be total and without any corners cut.

"If you're not cleared by Internal Affairs quickly, you'll be walking a beat without a weapon. No kidding, no excuses, no easy way out." Mike put on his sternest face. "There'll be no easy way out, like I said. The best cop is a cop who never takes his weapon out of the holster. The worst thing that can happen to a cop is that he or she fires a weapon and hits someone. It's like a nightmare that has no end."

He paused and continued. "I've never fired my weapon except at the firing range. There I can hit the best parts of the targets with every shot. I don't even want to fire a gun at a human being. It would have to be close to the end of the world for me to do it, I believe."

By the time Mike finished his sermon, Tyrone was sweating bullets. Good reaction. I could tell he was listening and understanding what Mike was telling him.

When I got home, Tyrone was waiting in the downstairs lobby of my building. I invited him up. He was still sweating profusely. One thing you can count on in New York is summertime humidity, although in

Tyrone's case, the tongue-lashing he had endured from Mike probably predisposed him to sweat.

It was the beginning of a long-lasting friendship I was privileged to have with Tyrone. He wanted me to call him "Ty," which I tried to do, but I found myself calling him Tyrone, in honor of the family in "Long Day's Journey into Night," one of my favorite plays, and a memorable movie with Jason Robards and Katherine Hepburn in 1962, the year I graduated from high school and started my first semester at UCLA—the school I had always wanted to go to—possibly one of the most beautiful college campuses in the entire country, and certainly in the most beautiful part of Los Angeles County.

I had been a forensic debater in my Franciscan high school, and our biggest, fanciest, most difficult debate competition was held every year at UCLA, which made me feel more grown-up than I could ever have imagined. At least I was tall, so I probably blended in with some of the lower-classmen—freshmen and sophomores—but almost no facial hair, even when I totally neglected to shave. It was the northern European genes in me—Irish, English, Dutch, German and probably a bit of Viking from the eastern part of England and the Anglicized parts of Normandy. I felt fully adult because we held most of our debates in Royce Hall, which was the biggest, most elaborate classroom building on the entire campus, and the location of the biggest auditorium and stage on campus.

Some years later, I was privileged to act in a fancy-dress production of "Les Indes Galantes," an eighteenth century opera-ballet by Jean Phillipe Rameau that left a long-lasting impression on me. Glorious music, lots of original choreography in the baroque style (no dancing on pointe, even for the girls). Big choruses, and the whole thing was staged to celebrate the inauguration of a new governor of California, which gave us a generous budget that enabled us to have an active volcano on stage, and real silk costumes for all four *entrees* (acts). It was years before I could recover completely from that production, and I never gave up my love for Rameau, in particular his harpsichord suites, which seemed to be written for four hands, but had to be played by two hands.

I had earned my place as a tenor/baritone in the Rameau piece, and was able to get cast in several other productions of the Music Department, including a traveling production of Bizet's "Carmen," which for sure made me a baritone, because the high notes in the tenor chorus were far too high for me. I met my wife in one of those chorus assignments: "Les Huguenots" by Giacomo Meyerbeer, one of the biggest of all grand operas, which premiered in Paris in 1836. We married in the Episcopal Church of St Alban's across the street from the UCLA Administration Building.

My best man was my best friend at the time, a Polish citizen from Warsaw and a fine painter who was two weeks older than me, and my wife's maid of honor was one of my oldest friends, a Jewish/Presbyterian native of West Los Angeles, daughter of a deceased but famous German Jewish violinist and a noteworthy Scottish ballerina. My debate partner from high school walked my wife down the aisle in place of her father, who left when Mary (my wife) was five.

About twenty years after we were married, we were contacted by Mary's half-brother in Ohio; turns out her father remarried and had another child. His name was Stuart or Stewart, and he felt fairly certain that because the father walked out on his mother and himself just as he had Mary and her mother, there were probably more half-siblings somewhere, maybe up the Mississippi or Ohio Rivers. No way to track them down. My daughter, Annie, was in touch with Ancestry.com, and ran across a half-brother with a name other than Stuart or Stewart, but only heard from him once before Mary died. No clues about who he was, as far as I know.

Some families are screwed up more than others. My parents had problems with their parents, probably to do with the mis-matched backgrounds of the two of them. My dad graduated from Notre Dame and almost immediately enlisted in the Army because World War II had begun. The Army sent him to Fort Sam Houston for basic training, and he eventually met my mother, who was president of her sorority at the University of Texas in Austin. They fell in love quickly, as happens in wartimes I am told, but the families were less than satisfied. Dad's family were Irish Catholics, New York Republicans, urban big-city, big-company whisky-drinking people. Mom's family were Texas Democrats (keep in mind that Republicans and Democrats were strong in geographies that were almost exactly opposite to where they are strong now), Methodists, ranchers and small-town tee-totaling ruralists. Basically, the families were super mis-matched. My mother took me to New York right after the war to meet the family. While we were there, my father also arrived, having been held over in Europe because he spoke several languages, so I met my father and my grandparents at the same time. My father and I never bonded, and my mom almost immediately got pregnant with my brother, and then with my sister. Dad did bond with them. I was always the darling of my Texas grandparents, whose house I was born into.

Sorry for all that family history, but it's hard to understand my family without it. We eventually moved to southern California, where my dad had found a good job. We never lived near either set of grandparents until after I was in college, when Dad was transferred to NYC to the home office of the company he worked for. They moved to Westchester County just in time for my NY grandmother to die. Her husband outlived her for nearly twenty-five years. When Dad was old enough to retire, they moved back to Texas, but well over one hundred and fifty miles from my Texas relatives.

One of the fixed rules of my family was that we lived as far as possible from relatives. When I was married, I lived in Los Angeles. My brother and his new wife lived in Vermont, and later in northern Minnesota. My sister lived in Oregon and moved to rural Maryland. We couldn't have been farther apart if we tried. I had been raised with tens of cousins, especially at holidays. Thanksgiving was the biggest day of the year, and was always held out at the family ranch. All the women in the family cooked all day. The men went hunting for deer and various kinds of birds, especially ducks. I was the eldest of all the young cousins, and took care of them all day, chasing armadillos and various kinds of animals. My deal with my grandfather was that when it was time to have Thanksgiving dinner, I was allowed to take my dinner to the top of the windmill in the backyard (it pumped the water for the house), and adults would take over watching the younger cousins. We ate partly on china, partly on paper plates, and partly on plastic picnic plates like Melmac. Flatware was catch as catch can. Drinks were mostly lemonade and a very limited selection of chilled carbonated drinks, like Dr. Pepper, Coca Cola, Orange Crush and grape-flavored drinks. I suspect my dad drank something alcoholic from a container he brought with him (he never admitted to drinking alcohol in front of my Texas grandparents, at least not that I knew of).

The first time my Texas grandmother set foot in a Catholic church was when I graduated from high school, which was a Catholic school run by Franciscan priests. I suspect she expected to burst into flames, but she didn't. I was the valedictorian and she liked my speech. My mom (my grandmother's daughter) went to the University of Texas (a public school), so I followed suit by going to UCLA (also a public school). My dad wanted me to go to Notre Dame, but I had no interest in living in Indiana.

Dad insisted that I go to a Catholic school, but I wanted UCLA, so he promised that he wouldn't pay for any part of my college career. He later paid my sister's full freight at one of the most expensive "Little Ivy League" colleges in Ohio, but he got a free ride from me. My brother started at Niagara University, a Catholic school, but he dropped out and never finished, so that one was a stalemate. He never went back to school that I knew of, although he became a talented writer, owning and running two local newspapers, one in Minnesota and one in southern California. I always hoped he would write something in book form, but he never did, as far as I know.

Chapter Twelve

Tyrone Green looked like the soul of a man's man. It was easy to imagine him easing up to a girl at a bar and offering to buy her a drink. But like a lot of bisexual men, his eyes picked up Gabriele Cortese as soon as he appeared at my front door. I offered Gabriele a dirty vodka, which I happened to know he liked, after having spent time with him for well over twenty years.

I saw Ty massaging his crotch with his right hand. I thought immediately that if the CDC recommended a booster shot to augment his two Pfizer vaccinations, he'd be out looking for the shot, and a guy to hold his hand while the needle went in.

So that was why he was after Maggie, I thought. All of a sudden I could see him with his arm around Gabriele, waiting for Gabriele's hand to explore the area between his legs. I know Gabriele is familiar with that territory, and with having a nice guy rubbing where rubbing could do the most good.

Sure enough, Ty wanted a dirty vodka to match Gabriele's. They sat down together and toasted each other. Gabriele slid his hand inside Ty's largely open button-front shirt. It was easy to see a patch of shiny straight black hair on Gabriele's chest. I knew what Gabriele looked like naked. He looked like he did with his clothes on—a study in male perfection. If he found a girl with nice tits, his hands would know where to go until his erection was as large as it would get. In this case, Ty was in all the right places to get Gabriele excited.

Gabriele knew I was not stirred by his sexual arousal, and I knew he knew that. He also knew that it made no difference to me what he and

Ty did. They didn't have twin bodies, but almost. Small waists, round hard buttocks, a throbbing crotch, and a shirt front that fell open on its own.

Both of them also knew that I didn't want to watch them go much further than they had already gone. I sipped on my own dirty vodka, and savored the salty taste of the olive jar juice. The effect of a modest amount of alcohol is familiar to me. It doesn't make me horny or sexually voracious. In fact, nothing seems to do that anymore. I'm enough older than Gabriele that I don't want him rubbing against me. I like looking at him naked, like when he gets out of the shower and drops his towel on the floor. I could imagine how Ty would look nude. He was probably uncircumcised like Gabriele. I figured he was Puerto Rican, and most Puerto Rican men are uncircumcised ("uncut" in the normal gay parlance, just like I am "cut" in the same slang).

I was circumcised in the hospital in Houston where I was born, probably the same day. My father was circumcised as an infant, but I'm not sure it was a nearly automatic procedure as it was when I was born or when my brother was born in the smaller town of Texas City, an energy port on the south side of Galveston Bay (the side with no alligators, which are plentiful on the north side). The historical connection between Louisiana and Galveston was common knowledge in several ways. Most obviously, it was common knowledge that Jean Lafitte's pirate treasure was buried in the tidal sands of Galveston Island. When I was a kid, I never tired of digging in the sand looking for treasure: gold coins, fabulous jewels—none of which did I ever find, of course. The treasure was legendary, but not based on any kind of historical reality.

As to circumcision, gone were the days when Jews were not allowed in country clubs ("pants down clubs" in the slang). Sometime in the 1930s, circumcision became a normal procedure on a male baby. Over the years, there was an increasing belief that circumcision was healthier; that being "uncut" tended to increase the likelihood of contracting a venereal disease like syphilis. The commonplace circumcision could easily have been fostered by the medical staffs of the US Armed Services—Army, Navy, Marines. Sometime after World War II was over, we got the Air Force, which had been the Army Air Corps during the war. If being "uncut" was unhealthy, it was possible that the foreskin held the bacteria or viruses close to the opening of the penis, I suppose. Whatever the reason, by the time I was in high school, I'd say almost all of the boys were circumcised, and there was no religious tradition or law behind it. Virtually every guy in my high school was "cut." I never saw an "uncut" guy until I was in college, trying to work out and shower in the Men's Gym at the foot of the Janss Steps leading down from the central quadrangle of the UCLA campus. Probably every "uncut" guy at UCLA was from overseas someplace. American guys were uniformly "cut."

Royce Hall is the trademark, so to speak, of the UCLA campus. It's a huge Lombard Romanesque ecclesiastical-looking landmark building, and faces across the quadrangle directly across from the original College Library, which was outmoded in the late 1960s or early 1970s, when the new University Library was opened on the northern part of the campus. An extraordinarily picturesque place, people constantly snapping pictures.

Enough of UCLA. Tyrone was an outstanding specimen of a muscle jock, probably a real athlete. Taller than normal, so maybe he played basketball. I could never take elbows in the face, so I had always steered clear of basketball. I watched Gabriele's eyes survey him from top to bottom. They both clearly passed muster with each other.

I turned on CNN on the television, and we caught up on the latest hurricane to hit Florida. Hurricane Johnny, with winds of about ninety mph, gusts over one hundred mph. South Florida could expect seven inches or more of rain. Kind of a middling hurricane—not a killer like Hurricane Harvey, and not a messy tropical storm that never quite made it to hurricane winds.

After we drank our dirty vodkas, the two guys stood up and walked over to the balcony and opened the glass sliding doors. A gust of humid wind filled the apartment, but brought with it a fresh smell that seemed like something you'd smell on a sailboat in a good wind. Gabriele patted Ty on the back, and the two of them backed away from the balcony and closed the doors. I knew they'd be leaving, probably going to

Gabriele's place in Brooklyn Heights. What a couple they made! Light-colored Ty and swarthy, perfectly muscular Gabriele, looking like an Italian runway model, even in his mid-forties—bushy, shiny black hair, a little wavy, but mostly straight. Ty with enormous shoulder muscles, clearly lots of weight-lifting in his everyday workouts. Big deltoids, and big veins running down his biceps to the inner elbow, with branching veins in his forearms. Big hands, café au lait skin on his arms with traces of curly black hair here and there. They'd make a good pornographic couple, but I doubted it would get to that; I'd known Gabriele too long to think he'd get down with Ty in a big way. Something easy leading to satisfaction fairly quickly. No real sex without friendship first.

I found myself envying both of them—for their youth and health more than anything else. I was feeling the fingers of old age wrinkling my upper arms, which had always been muscular since I was a teenager years back. I wasn't interested in forming any kind of relationship—male or female. I was mentally married and not really capable of cheating on my wife, despite her having passed. My matrimonial promises were there with me every day in every way. But Ty and Gabriele were younger and probably a lot hornier. They could give each other a "happy ending" just as easily as the Korean and Chinese girls could do at the day spas on Vernon Boulevard. A man's orgasm is a fairly simple affair that's a product of friction (hand, other body parts), and sexual excitement which, for a man, is frequently a byproduct of visual excitement, sometimes nudity, almost always skin touching skin. It doesn't take long, and usually is marked by semen emerging from the penis, accompanied by moans and sometimes vocalizations that sound like expressions of what can sound like pain (even though it's not painful). As I watched the two guys leave my apartment, I realized I didn't actually envy them. I was relieved that they were gone, and looked forward to seeing them again, after their time together in Brooklyn Heights.

Just about the time I would have expected the two of them to get to Brooklyn Heights, my phone rang. It was Gabriele.

"Ty is on his way home. So am I. I need to tell you that I still only love you, will never change. I still have sexual thoughts and urges, but I doubt I will ever find myself feeling love for anyone the way I do for you. Just so you know, my dear. No sex with Tyrone Green, not today, not any time I can foresee in the future. Besides, he tells me he's going to be a civilian criminalist with the NYPD reporting to you and Mike di Saronno. Wouldn't work, would it? Ethics are ethics, after all. Take care, and let's have another vodka later today. I don't want to finish the day at home alone. I want to be with you at your apartment with your beautiful paintings and a bowl of potato chips to crunch on while we enjoy our vodkas together. Please don't invite Tyrone back when I'm there. I want to be with you, and you alone. Got it—no sex, no lovy dovy. I'm on your side, totally and forever." He said goodbye and hung up, and I noted that he was speaking proper English, no part-Italian, which meant that he was really serious.

I sent him a text inviting him for a drink around seven.

I went for a walk along the riverfront, and spotted Ty Green by the Mister Softee truck. We shook hands and I asked him how he was doing.

"Doing okay," he said. "Thought I was heading to Gabriele's place in Brooklyn, but everything changed, and we headed in different directions. He was right. I can't work for you and Mike and date Gabriele at the same time. It's like I can't push Maggie and knock her down and still be a law-abiding citizen and maybe a future cop. Red isn't green. Green isn't blue. I can't see myself naked with Gabriele, and then see him with you, my friend, knowing how he feels about you. He's honest, and I'll always try to be honest with you, too."

He ordered an ice cream dipped in chocolate, and walked away licking it, biting into the hardening chocolate skin. The last I saw of him was his back as he walked north on the sidewalk.

Gabriele showed up at seven. We had another dirty vodka, and had a short conversation about Ty Green and his ambition to be a cop. We knew we understood each other.

"Ruth ought to be here, too," Gabriele said. "Seems wrong that she's not here." He smiled. "We're a trio, you know."

Chapter Thirteen

I felt the phone vibrating on my butt while I was sitting on the couch watching CNN, picking at a half-pint container of blackberries. No fruit is more nutritious than blackberries or blueberries—packed with antioxidants in ways that even tomatoes and apples aren't.

But more important than antioxidants was the fact that Mike was calling me.

"So, big change when it comes to Tyrone Green," he said. "Turns out that the internship was being charged to the precinct house near the Vernon-Jackson subway station. So I've transferred him to my office in Manhattan, where he can be on my budget—and yours."

"So he's commuting to Manhattan from Queens now?" I asked.

"Not at all. For the moment, he's bunking with me on 49th Street. I'm looking around to find him a decent studio where he can walk to work and also walk to John Jay College where he'll be going to school."

"There's no better place in the world," I said. "I lived on 48th Street for nearly ten years—never lived anyplace so wonderful in my life. I only left because it got so expensive. Nothing wrong with Long Island City, but I'd move back to the Theater District in a hot minute if I could afford it." I paused, and then asked Mike if Tyrone was going to be free at all that day. "Any chance the three of us could have a lunch from the Halal truck outside the precinct?"

"Well, Hugo, the truth is that Tyrone grew up in Queens, and he's taking some time off right now to visit his mother and some relatives, maybe some buddies from growing up. He'll be back this afternoon; maybe we could have a drink and a snack if you're still planning to be in town. Maybe Thalia? Maybe the little Afghan place on 9th Avenue?"

"Ariana. I haven't been there in a month of Sundays. That would be great, and it'd be empty later in the afternoon, with lunch over and dinner not yet starting up."

Mike agreed, and we decided to talk later to firm things up.

I called Gabriele and asked him if he felt like a quick drink at lunchtime. "Mike and I are going to meet up with Tyrone later this afternoon, and I've got some time to waste between now and then."

We agreed to meet at the saloon part of the Oyster Bar on the lower level of Grand Central Station at around one o'clock. I was thinking of slurping down some oysters with a glass of good Italian red wine. Meanwhile, I decided to have a look at the Johnston & Murphy store on Madison Avenue. The last time I had walked by it, there was a big "Sale" sign in the window, and I can always get behind saving some money on a discount.

As it turned out, no sooner had I hung up with Gabriele than the phone chimed with a call from Ruth, who happily agreed to join Gabriele and me at the Oyster Bar. In spite of it being totally non-Kosher, Ruth never turned down fresh raw oysters with grated fresh horseradish, although she usually wanted a glass of dry white wine with hers, where I wanted a strong-tasting, southern Italian red.

Oddly enough, we all walked into the front door of the Oyster Bar at about the same time. Hug-hug, kiss-kiss. Ruth was wearing a classic linen Chanel jacket in a candy-pink color, and a pair of well-washed jeans. Gabriele was wearing jeans, too, with a tight black t-shirt that hugged every muscle on both of his shapely arms. We had a great time, and talked about the Asian Hate assignment that we were off-and-on helping Mike di Saronno with.

Prejudice based on race or appearance is common in the United States. There is a tradition of using colors to characterize people. Asians are referred to as "yellow." Native Americans are sometimes called "red," which is considered very insulting by Native Americans, just as Native Americans are very insulted by being called "Indians," which dates back to Columbus seeking the "Indies" with the idea that the Earth was round, and the islands near the east of Asia were called the "Indies." Of course, African Americans and many people from the subcontinent of India and Sri Lanka of all skin colors are commonly referred to as "Black," and Latinos and certain mixed-race people, Middle Easterners/Arabs and southeast Asians are called "brown," due to skin colors.

To be considered "White," a person should look like a European, with the potential of having colored eyes (blue, hazel, green, even purple) and hair (blond, strawberry blond, red, brown, dark brown/brunette), whereas all the other "colors" of people are typically black-haired, or occasionally with deep mahogany-colored hair. All three of us—myself, Ruth and Gabriele are "White." Gabriele can pass for "brown," because his complexion is swarthy, but his overall impression is "White" (he's Italian). Tyrone Green would be "Black" to most people, although he has few, if any, African facial features, and his skin is far lighter than most "Black" people. As far as I can tell, his hair is dirty brown and straight/European and his eyes are dark brown, so he's a combination of colors in some ways. He acts, dresses and talks like a "Black" man. I'd guess that the little prince Archie might one day look like a whiter version of Tyrone; fine European features, creamy English skin, maybe with some telltale palms and soles of feet

The reason I went through all that about races and colors is that, as it turned out, Tyrone Green had been shot and killed on the street near the subway station at Vernon-Jackson. He had been visiting his mother and sisters, and was on his way back to Manhattan. The perpetrator was a teenage Black man, who used a handgun to shoot Tyrone. He was arrested by a policeman who saw what happened. The gun was stolen and had been used in other crimes, including robberies of local businesses.

We didn't actually find that out until we went to Mike's office on 54th Street between 8th and 9th Avenues. When Mike told us what happened, it hit me like a rock thrown at my head. Gabriele burst into tears, and Ruth sobbed as though she had lost a relative.

Thus was lost a police officer in the making. Mike made a point of telling us that there was a silver lining to what happened to Tyrone. The post of intern had been created, and still existed, so Mike intended to find a youngster—maybe a girl—to fill the cop-to-be slot that would basically act like a scholarship to either John Jay College or one of the City University of New York (CUNY) colleges like Hunter College in the East 60s, or the beautiful old CUNY campus in Northern Manhattan, Brooklyn College, Lehman College in the Bronx, or any of the other twenty-five campuses scattered around the five boroughs of New York, including the Borough of Manhattan Community College, which is right near the old location of the World Trade Center that was destroyed on September 11, 2001.

My parents' wedding anniversary was September 11, 1943. I was always thankful that my parents were both already dead when 9/11 happened. It would never have been possible to celebrate a happy marriage in an appropriate fashion when 9/11 always meant a day when more than three thousand Americans were murdered by high-jacked commercial planes being crashed into the World Trade Center, part of the Pentagon, and a field in Pennsylvania where one of the high-jacked planes crashed into the ground, killing all the people aboard. We were told that some of the men on board broke into the flight cabin and crashed the plane on purpose, to keep it from aiming for the White House or another target.

I knew a woman who had a new baby that she was nursing, who took her new daughter to work that morning in the North Tower, and was incinerated with her baby when an American Airlines plane was flown directly into the side of the World Trade Center Twin Towers where Jennifer's office was. Nothing ever recovered, as far as I was able to find out. The mom was Greek and quite beautiful. Never met the husband, but he must have been Greek too, since Jennifer and her daughter had a Greek last name. I saw the mother's name in a list of "missing" people in the New York Times one day a few months later. No mention of the baby.

And of course, eventually Osama bin Laden and his crew were wiped off the map from the sky above Abbottabad, Pakistan for their part in killing all those people—for all the good that did.

Nothing glorious about the date of 9/11, just a lot of death. Every year the names are read out loud, and bells rung to commemorate the deceased. A lot of good it does to erase the massive death count of that day, something like six hundred more people than died in the December 7, 1941, attack on Pearl Harbor, Hawaii.

Chapter Fourteen

I had a brief talk with Mike di Saronno about what to do regarding a potential replacement for Tyrone Green. It seemed a shame not to continue the potential that we saw in Ty when we invited him on board. Mike's first suggestion was to turn over the replacement task to the Dean's office at John Jay College. Mike said, "We've made several scholarship endowments to CUNY schools, so no reason not to convert what we wanted for Tyrone to something for a young man or woman with the same kind of promise."

Ty was a scholar throughout high school—very high GPA—way higher than anything I ever accomplished as a student—and a more than modest amount of charm and grace to his way of talking, in spite of his having a streak of bad judgment in street antics. I would have been surprised if he hadn't been the valedictorian of his graduating class. So maybe whoever actually was appointed valedictorian should have a whack at the opportunity if he or she is interested. We need diversity in the NYPD, so there would be no disqualifying things to worry about. If a woman is interested, she could be an athlete—which helps in the Police Academy under any circumstance.

"I say let's open it up completely," I suggested to Mike. "The goal is diversity—gender diversity, racial diversity, age diversity, educational diversity. Every kind of diversity. We need more language diversity. Queens is one of the most diverse boroughs, and it's very upward mobile in its best moments. I'd say we should talk to the principals of all the Queens high schools—including charter schools—and try to get as many bids as possible for the scholarship and internship we were earmarking for Tyrone." I meant what I said. "If we could have gotten Ty Green on board, he would have been the best cop on the force in lots of ways. We would have wanted him front and center at every racial diversity demonstration—Black Lives Matter, or something as local as an anniversary of the death of Eric Garner. Both are pointed at equality for Blacks, but both are also opportunities for newspapers to feature a Ty Green type of young man or woman."

"I agree that seeing a cop in the media," Mike said, "one that looks like the people in the neighborhood—that's a good thing—especially if he or she is young and a hoodie—a local—a guy or girl with family—generations of family—in the area. We don't need Sidney Poitier or Samuel L Jackson in uniform on Page Six. We need a damned good-looking, smart young cop who can say something smart when a reporter asks him or her a question about an arrest, or a question about whether a demonstration was peaceful or not." He stared at the ceiling. "Yeah, I'd be in favor of training Ty Green Junior with a media or PR type of spokesperson—somebody the mayor likes and trusts."

"I think if every cop can say something that we'd like being quoted in the newspapers or on the TV stations, we'd be doing ourselves a big favor."

This was Mike's game to play, his basket to shoot. The last thing I wanted was to try to pick out the prettiest girl, the most movie-star-looking guy, and try to train them to think out loud. Better to find a smart kid with a good smile, and a willingness to talk to reporters about what just happened without being afraid of saying the wrong thing.

"Yeah, somebody threw a rock through that plate glass window," our guy might say. "I wish I could have seen who it was, but I didn't. What happened next was that a bunch of good guys formed a cordon protecting the bodega over there, and it didn't get wrecked or ransacked. That guy who owns that place is still in business, still making coffee for people in the mornings, still running a tab for the locals, and being a part of the family."

"Best thing that could happen," Mike said. "No machetes, no kids getting beat up, no running off with bags of stolen groceries."

"Neighbors acting like neighbors is what you're talking about," I said. "Obviously it's not always going to go the right way, but it'll go the right way more of the time with smiling, helpful cops who know how to calm a crowd down—and how to keep his foot off a man's neck while he continually says he can't breathe. The guy who runs the deli doesn't want to get his place trashed—he wants to open up tomorrow the way he always opens up. No broken glass, no mess to clean up. Just coffee to make like a regular day."

Mike was clearly doing some day-dreaming while we were talking; his eyes were wandering around the room.

"Most kids are good," I said. "They want to do good. If you scare the crap out of them, they're likely to go the wrong way. If you buy them a can of soda or a Snickers bar, you're more likely to get their good side than their bad side."

"We need a group of cops in every precinct that's looking at how to make people smile." He was staring at the ceiling again. "We need some One Police Plaza smarts at each precinct. We need to hand out cups of coffee to guys who are angry or getting ready to punch somebody. A coffee with cream and sugar goes a long way toward making youngsters feel like real people, like they want to help, not punch somebody. Sometimes it's as simple as a cup of coffee, a smile and a pat on the back."

He had a sudden grin on his face. "We don't need a replacement for Ty Green at John Jay," he said. "We need to start a Community Relations Group in every precinct. And those people need to be uniformed like cops. They just don't need weapons or night-sticks."

I had an idea. "You know what you need? You need a budget, and you need a corner of each precinct that looks like a place to have a free cup of coffee—maybe a store-bought cookie or a donut. How much could it cost? Fifty dollars a day? No better way to introduce a new Ty Green— a friendly person from the giddyup. No chance for him or her to look like a hostile cop. Not if he or she is always in the process of offering a cuppa Joe.

"Sounds like you want to teach young cops the skills they used to teach in finishing schools. The joke when I was a kid was that rich girls went to school to play the piano with their right hands, and pour tea with the left hands," I said. "When I was in college, my parents lived a couple of blocks from Briarcliff College, which was a two-year girls' school that taught manners, and maybe how to make fancy canapes. I dated one of the girls there briefly one summer—met her on the train coming back from Manhattan after going to the theater or maybe the opera.

Her name was Kayla, and she was from a Forest Hills Jewish family. Pretty girl, maybe a few pounds overweight, but well-dressed, and perfectly behaved. I remember taking her to a discotech called Arthur. I think it was run by Richard Burton's ex-wife (he had divorced her when he married Elizabeth Taylor during the filming of "Cleopatra"). I remember seeing her come to meet him after a performance of "Hamlet"—a role he was really too old for, but Shakespeare characters are frequently miscast for one reason or another. When I was a student at UCLA, I saw "Hamlet" starring Dame Judith Anderson as the male lead. Go figure. Totally lost track of Kayla. I remember being invited to her parents' house. Never went, no memories of anything like that. I think she had a boyfriend in Queens. The last thing I needed was a girlfriend in New York when I was in school in California. Of course I eventually married—twice—girls from UCLA. Maybe Kayla did exactly the same thing. It could happen.

I felt like I needed Ruth's thoughts, just to keep my mind on the straight and narrow. She answered on the first ring.

"Hey, kiddo," she said. "What can I do for you?"

I asked her what she thought we should do about filling the empty space left when Tyrone Green was shot and killed.

"Easy," she said. "Talk to the pretty Asian girl at the first one of those day spas. She's Chinese or Korean, I think. I doubt she wants to be a hooker—at least I'd guess she has something more interesting in mind than being on the bottom of a two-person sex act.

"My guess is she's brighter than you might initially think," she said. "Somebody decided she should be there, probably because she's smart, maybe resourceful. I'd be willing to bet good money on her abilities—and maybe on her breeding, too." I could see Ruth staring across the room while she held the phone to her ear. "She may be as smart as Tyrone was. Give her a chance. I bet if you give her a chance to go straight, she'd take you up on it faster than you could say Jack Robinson. Just because she's pretty and looking at you from the front room of a brothel doesn't mean she can't make sense in a normal conversation."

"Interesting idea," I said. "We originally wanted to convert Tyrone to be a good guy because of who he was in the ranks of the bad guys. If we turn that around and apply it to the girl at the day spa, it could work out just as well. She speaks good English, and probably good Korean or Mandarin—maybe other languages as well. French, for instance."

I told her I would call her back, and hung up. I laid out the conversation with Mike, who started to stroke his neck and nod his chin almost immediately. "Of course, she could be a total loser, but I'd like to try talking to her before I try to come up with reasons to say no to Ruth's idea. Women are cleverer than men think they are. If whoever put up the money for the day spas put his bet on her, I'm ready to give her a chance at bat."

"Why don't you come over to my place and we can walk up to the day spa and see what we think of her?"

He agreed, and suggested that Gabriele and Ruth come over, too. "They're as smart as a whip, each one of them. And don't forget that Gabriele was in the same line of work that she's in, for a while. Never got in trouble as far as I've even been able to find out. And seems to have gone totally straight—that is, straight and narrow, not straight instead of gay."

Within the hour, the four of us were convened at my apartment, and I had poured a couple of fingers of scotch into my grandfather's Irish whiskey glasses over a couple of pieces of ice. Enough to taste good, but not enough to blur the mind or the outlook.

We walked up to Vernon Boulevard and knocked on the front door of May Ling Day Spa. There were several men hanging out near the door, but none of them looking like they were looking for trouble. To tell the truth, most of them looked wealthy, or at least well-off. Well-dressed, clean shaven, well-tailored linen or cotton sport jackets with colorful shirts open at the collar.

We walked into the small front room and Mike asked the pretty Asian girl if she was May Ling.

"No, I'm Grace Kim, and I'm here in the United States legally. Used to work at a beauty salon in Manhattan, doing fingernails and pedicures. Been here most of my life, which is why my English sounds natural." She directed her conversation to Ruth, who introduced Mike as Detective di Saronno.

"Detective di Saronno's office is in Manhattan, and we'd like to talk to you about the situation we all face here. We lost a young police intern, who was shot and killed here in Long Island City, and we'd like to ask you some questions."

"I want a lawyer," Grace Kim said.

"You don't need a lawyer," Mike said. "We're not going to accuse you of doing anything illegal. We'd like to talk to you about how you want your career to take shape. No reason for you to go from working in a mani-pedi salon to working in a small day spa covered with smoked glass. We may have an alternative path that you would find worth considering. It could pay more, could have better benefits, and almost surely could offer a better future career path."

Mike held his hand out to her. "I'd like to shake your hand, and invite you to come to Manhattan to my office to have a conversation. I think what we have to tell you, to offer you, may be very attractive to you. Do you have a Green Card?"

Grace pulled a Green Card out of her handbag and flashed it at Mike.

"Great," he said. "We can't give you a Green Card tomorrow if you don't already have one, although there are a lot of ways we can make your life easier and more comfortable."

She smiled at him, but with a puzzled look.

"We might be able to offer you a job," Mike said. "We need to talk. I need to learn more about you, your education, your past, and your vision of your future. You're not going to get in any trouble from what we want to talk about. All that can happen if you like what we tell you, is that your life will get better. Your income is likely to go up, although I don't know what you're getting paid now—and I won't ask you about that—I promise.

She took his hand and shook it.

"I'm game," she said. "I don't like where I am right now. I want to be on the right side of things, not the wrong side of things. I want to be respectable, and I want to have a family—children, a real husband. I have the same dreams as other girls my age. I'm twenty-four, and I want to still be a young person when I have my children—and I want my husband to be in the delivery room when my babies are born. If that's where you're going, I may be your girl."

Chapter Fifteen

Grace was Korean, of course, not Chinese. That's one reason why her name wasn't May Ling. Her family name, Kim, was quintessential Korean, the same as the ruling family of North Korea, in fact. But she had the bloom of beautiful young girl, no matter what ethnicity. There was no doubt in Mike's mind that his message had gotten through to her, and that she was ready to move to the side of the angels if he offered her the chance to do that.

As usual, Ruth and Gabriele and I were in the room behind the mirror, so we could see and hear everything that was said.

"Where did you go to school?" Mike asked her.

"Marymount 5th Avenue, right across from the Metropolitan Museum of Art," she said, and added, "Then I went to Hunter College for two years, put together enough credits for an associate's degree, but never applied for it. I want a bachelor's degree, a four-year degree."

"A four-year degree in what?"

"Computer science. I know girls aren't supposed to study computers, but that's what I want to do. I want to be able to hack other people's computers, like working for the cops."

"Working for the cops? How's that gonna happen?" Mike asked.

"You're gonna help me," she said. "I can tell. That's why I'm here, right?"

Mike nodded slightly, but said nothing.

"So what's the indication of the name May Ling?"

She explained that May Ling was one of three sisters who were famous in China. May Ling was the youngest, but she married an important man. "Every Chinese in the United States would know that name," she said. "Especially girls. May Ling married Chiang Kai-shek, and became the first lady of China until the Communists took over in 1948."

"The guys wouldn't know who she was? Why the name on the door then?"

"She was like the Marilyn Monroe of China. Great beauty, very sexy woman. And very rich. For Chinese man, best woman is beautiful and rich. That answer your question?"

She looked at the mirror as though she could see us behind it, which we knew she couldn't.

"You got friends back there listening to what we're saying?"

"Your English is very American. Did you work on it?"

"I have been here since I was a baby. I speak some Mandarin, but mostly I speak English. My parents speak English, too. That's why Gonzalez boys hired me, because I am more American than the American men who I talk to."

"And why do you want to be a hacker?"

"So I can work with the police. I want to help the police keep an eye on the bad guys."

"And what is your ultimate goal working for the police?"

"Police Commissioner. First Asian woman to run the NYPD. I will show them how smart a woman can be. I wanna be your boss, Mr. Mike."

Mike gave her the short version of what happened to Tyrone Green—high GPA, smart, presentable, well-spoken. The NYPD was going to sponsor him through John Jay College to study Criminology as a police intern. He'd have a blue uniform, and by the time he was ready to be on his own, he'd be a police officer on his way to being a sergeant. He'd also be working for the Commissioner part-time, in the Media Department. So he'd be talking to reporters and news people, helping improve the image of the police across the city.

"I can do that," she said. "And I know more about computers than anyone else in the NYPD. Promise you that. If somebody hacks a big bank, I'll find out who did it. Promise. I can trace anything. Give me a blue uniform and a desk, and I'll prove to you what I can do. I'll also lighten my hair color and change my look. Nobody will know who I used to be. No May Ling here. Only Grace Kim, who grew up in Jackson Heights and went to school in Manhattan. Might as well be an American. Pay for it and I'll even have eye surgery, make me look European."

"Not gonna do that, no surgery here," Mike said. "I like you the way you are."

She smiled.

"What was your high school GPA?" he asked.

"4.2."

"How does that happen? I thought 4.0 was the highest possible GPA."

"I had extra-credit courses in Marymount College. Two courses in Computer Programming. Let me at 'em. I'll find the hackers before they even get in the system."

Mike smiled. "You'd start off as a civilian criminalist—uniform but no weapon. No badge."

"No badge?" she asked plaintively.

"No badge until you complete the full program in the Police Academy and take the pledge. Then you'll have a special title of something like 'Computer Specialist'—and all the computer power you can dream up."

"When do I start?"

"As soon as you leave the day spa business. No more happy endings."

"I don't do happy endings," she said.

"Maybe as a cop you'll do some happy endings, but of a different kind. We like to solve mysteries, you know. One of the other civilian criminalists you'll be working with is as sharp as a tack, and has close to forty years in PR and business. He may be able to give you some pointers. And just in case you were going to ask, yes, he's behind the mirror with a couple of his colleagues."

She smiled.

Mike held his hand out and Grace shook it.

"Deal," she said. "I just took a step I was afraid I might never get to. I joined the NYPD. I'm gonna make you one happy cop, Detective di Saronno. I may even learn to speak some Italian, just so we can tell secrets when we want to. I've always wanted to wear pants, instead of flimsy little dresses. I want to be able to toss a full-grown man across the room, too."

Chapter Sixteen

The next time I saw Grace Kim, she was wearing a blue uniform with an NYPD patch on the left shoulder and a patrol cap with a shiny brim. She was wearing zero make-up, and had lightened her hair a couple of shades, so that it was a pale brown with some blondish highlights. She had also gained a crease in her eyelids that may have been encouraged by tape while sleeping. It made her look like British actress Emma Watson, a born Caucasian.

She didn't even vaguely resemble the girl we had thought of as May Ling. She was sitting at a large wooden desk wearing black-rimmed glasses, just outside Mike di Saronno's office in the precinct building on 54th Street near the corner of 8th Avenue on the west side of Manhattan. If you looked carefully, there were criminology textbooks on the same desk, which was just a few blocks from John Jay College, where Grace was matriculated as a baccalaureate candidate in legal affairs having to do with criminal behavior. A casual observer would have thought she was European; her masculine outfit made her look taller and more muscular than she would ever have looked in the silk, floral-print, short dress she'd been wearing when she left the day spa on Vernon Boulevard the day before. She looked like a gym rat, which she could have been, I suppose. I would have taken her for a yoga enthusiast, but she could easily have been a Nautilus user that might have made her arms more muscular. The overall impression was that even someone from the "Gonzalez" group that theoretically had a hand in opening the three day spas would not have recognized her.

The name "Gonzalez" being half of Chuy's hyphenated name was a telltale clue. The name was associated with several drug groups in Guadalajara, not to mention Manuel Acosta-Gonzalez, who had been killed by Maggie Landover. He was the same guy who had stuffed his wife's vagina with condoms filled with cocaine years back. Also the same guy who was the sperm donor who was Chuy's birth father. Also the very same fellow whose neck was slit that night when Gabriele and I heard screams from the open balcony doors that night several months back.

Lots had happened, and it looked like the permanent change would be Grace Kim rapping and tapping on her computers, finding previously unknown information on the guys who signed the leases and hired the employees of the three day spas that were looking like fronts for prostitution in the heart of Long Island City, which had become an extension of Manhattan in Queens, and where I lived.

"I bet she could grab a guy and flip him over her back," Ruth said when she saw Grace stand up from her seat at her computer spread, which had three screens, two of which were fairly constantly searching for data that scrolled down the screen at a fast pace.

Mike di Saronno crept up behind Grace with a Styrofoam™ food container. He put it down on her desk, somewhat startling her. She opened it; it was falafel, which is made from ground garbanzo beans (or other types of beans like fava beans, but more commonly garbanzo beans or chick peas, which are the same beans that are used to make hummus, a food staple in the Middle East and in Halal eateries). It was hot and fresh, on a bed of yellow rice, soaked with a white sauce that looked like it was made with mayonnaise and yoghurt, and had a sprinkling of pickles and crispy French fries on it, and diced tomatoes mixed up in the rice.

Grace lighted up like a child at Christmas. Little did she know that there was a Halal truck that was semi-permanently parked in front of the precinct house. Nowhere in New York can you find a more delicious and nutritious lunch than Halal falafel and rice—usually for no more than seven dollars for a couple of pounds of totally delicious food. Totally vegan except for the eggs in the mayonnaise and the dairy in the yoghurt, falafel is reputed to have been developed in Egypt before it was taken over by Muslims. The ancient Copts (Egyptian Christians whose language still is descended from ancient Egyptian hieroglyphics) are said to have invented falafel to substitute for meat on days when early Christians were supposed to abstain from eating meat—such as during Lent and Advent.

Most Muslims, Jews and Christians are unaware that monotheism probably originated in Egypt during the reign of Pharaoh Akhenaten. He was possibly the originator of the Judeo-Christian version of monotheism, although he died young, and was succeeded by his sickly son, Tutankhamun ("King Tut"), who returned to the polytheistic religion of earlier Egyptians. Of course it was King Tut's tomb that yielded the richest treasures of any tomb opened during the modern period (in 1922, accompanied by what was reputed to be a curse that killed all the people involved in opening the tomb). The solid gold funerary mask of King Tut is probably the most well-known artifact of the ancient Egyptian state. It has traveled all over the globe, including a memorable series of museum exhibitions in the United States in 1972 (originally opened by Queen Elizabeth II in London), and seen by hundreds of thousands in the United States with exhibitions from state to state across the country.

I invited Grace to join Gabriele and Ruth and me for dinner in Manhattan. Gabriele is a half-owner of a wonderful Italian restaurant called Ora di Pranzo ("Dinnertime") in the SoHo area of Manhattan. It's impossible to get a table, but because of my friendship with Gabriele, I can get a table at the last minute. In addition, Gabriele almost never charges me for anything; his cousin Dante is the chef and owns the other half of the restaurant. One of my favorite meals is a roasted branzino (fish), filleted at the table and then bathed in olive oil and herbs. Also, Gabriele is a wine expert, and always keeps a bottle or two of *aglianico del vulture*, an ancient Greek wine preserved through the centuries by the people of Basilicata (the instep of the Italian "boot"). Perfection. Great way to celebrate Grace's first day on the new job.

Chapter Seventeen

It was easy to tell from her facial expressions that Grace had never been in a restaurant as fancy as Ora di Pranzo. The gaudy red, gold and green heavy satin and silk curtains, the gold ropes holding up the curtains to keep the windows clear. Even Gabriele in his tuxedo looked like he was at a palace ball, with Gabriele playing the Prince. Ruth and I arrived moments after Grace, who was dressed in navy blue—the same color as her uniform during the day, but her evening outfit was dark, un-pre-washed Levi's denim, made like a pants suit, with a plain jacket, slim lapel, a red rosebud pinned on the right side of the lapel with a hatpin. No jewelry. But looking beautiful with perfect skin, shining eyes, and slightly curled brownish hair that was shorter than shoulder length. Gabriele sat the three of us (Ruth, Grace and me) at a table for four in the rear of the restaurant. He clearly planned to sit with us, because his place was set just as Grace's and Ruth's places were set—and mine as well. The puzzle was that there was a fifth place at the table. I had no idea who that might be for.

What I didn't know was that Mike di Saronno was going to join us, too. He'd be sitting between Grace and Ruth, but we didn't realize it would be him until he walked into the restaurant, and Gabriele met him with a big hug at the front door. This was going to be a huge welcoming dinner for Grace. I wondered if Grace was potentially the only up-and-coming Asian female detective on the NYPD team. Mike greeted Ruth with a cheek kiss and a hug. As it turned out, we had a choice of two entrees—each of which was a specialty of the house. One was a roasted whole branzino—a small sea bass farmed in the Mediterranean and filleted at the table, usually by Gabriele himself, who could have fileted a fish facing the wrong way with his eyes closed. Of course, the entire skeleton of the fish was lifted out intact, with no little fish bones left in the flaky white flesh. The other choice was chicken parmigiana with a side of penne with red sauce.

For the most part, the only "parm" dish that is served in Italy is eggplant, but the Italian population of the United States was undoubtedly the second largest such in the world, and for whatever reason, in the US, chefs made chicken parm, shrimp parm, even veal parm. All of them were breaded and fried before being casseroled with red sauce and lots of cheeses, in particular mozzarella and parmesan cheese, with torn basil leaves between all the layers. More of a home-made treat than a restaurant invention—a sort of one-dish meal that Mom made at home, and that restaurant made fancier and prettier. It was still odd that what was in Italy a largely vegetarian dish, was represented in the USA by almost any kind of meat a cook could find in the restaurant fridge. Even so, the most flavorsome "parm" remains eggplant or *melanzane*, probably because a vegetable hosts the many tastes of "parm" better than any meat. Oddly enough, the eggplant parm in the US is most often relegated to the appetizer part of a meal, which makes no sense at all, it being the "mother" of the dish without a doubt. Frequently, the eggplant is rolled around melted cheese under the name *rollatini*, which means exactly what the Italian name indicates.

Anyway, Grace elected for the fish, which I did as well. There is nothing like roasted branzino (which is called *spigola* or sometimes *barramundi* in much of southern Italy, *loup de mer* in France and sometimes Italian sea bass in England and the United States). The mildest of roasted Mediterranean fish, it's usually served with the olive oil the fish was roasted in, and some fresh lemon, sometimes along with a house mix of green herbs like oregano, basil, and flat-leaf parsley. Heaven.

Gabriele brought over two bottles of *aglianico del vulture*, my total favorite Italian red wine; always the best when it comes from Basilicata, an area of the Italian "boot" that usually represents the insole, and that—as one might guess, is an Italianization of a Greek original name ("basil" is a word "root" for "king" in classical Greek). Italy was settled largely by Etruscans, who may have been native to the area, and colonizing Greeks, many of whom were Corinthian, like the founders of the amazing towns of Taormina and Siracusa on the south coast of Sicily. Sicily has been invaded and conquered by more foreigners than any other piece of land within the boundaries of Europe. Sicilians always say the Greeks gave Sicily grapes and olives; Arabs gave Sicily citrus fruit and date palms. The Spanish gave Sicily tomatoes, peppers and prickly pear cactus. The Romans didn't give Sicily anything in particular; they just collected taxes.

Gabriele didn't ask who wanted wine, just poured a glass for each person at the table, and then raised his own glass in a toast to the table. No question that everyone tasted the wine. The *aglianico* grape is not only ancient and Greek, it is a super-flavorful and dark-colored fruit that has survived thousands of years because of its excellence, particularly in making wine.

Ruth stood up with her wine glass in her hand. "I want to toast Grace and welcome her to our family. She's a super-smart person, and will be a knowledgeable and well-informed team member," Ruth said. "We needed—and continue to need—somebody who's worked with the bad guys, but who has a mind that favors the good guys. I trust her, and look forward to working with her, and with her sterling boss, Mike di Saronno, New York's foremost detective, and a lieutenant with well over twenty years on the force. We all look forward to Mike eventually taking the captaincy exam, and becoming a superior officer in the NYPD detective force."

She turned to Grace, and said, "We all expect Grace to move up the ranks faster than most girls. No glass ceilings for her. We want to go to her graduation from earning her four-year degree from the John Jay College Criminology Department—might as well establish your reputation in the Lincoln Center area—it's only about three blocks from the Metropolitan Opera. Maybe that'll be about the same time she passes her sergeant's exam. You never know, especially when Grace is smarter and has more experience than most of the guys wearing blue office uniforms."

"I have an announcement," Gabriele said, standing up. "I've applied to the Police Academy, and I look forward to becoming a full-fledged New York cop. My wonderful cousin Dante can run Ora di Pranzo, and the wait staff is way more than just good. The best in all the Big Apple. So maybe there'll be more than one graduation sometime soon. I'm thinking I can make it through in six months or so. I want to be part of the blue line of cops in out wonderful city. I live in Brooklyn, and would be very happy to serve in Brooklyn or Manhattan, where I've built a reputation as a restaurant guy and a friend of restaurateurs all over New York. Maybe a competitor to Danny Meyer—who knows? But if I can make it through the Academy, I'll have some stripes that Danny Meyer doesn't have, although he's way richer than I will ever be—and more famous than I would ever dream of being."

The waiters brought Caesar salads around the table. Perfect, with the distinct taste of brown anchovies proclaiming them accurately made. Then the famous northern Italian soup, *pasta e fagioli* or *pasta fazool* in the more familiar Neapolitan (Naples) dialect. "I used to know a girl in Brooklyn who called herself Lena Fazool," I said. "That name made everybody laugh when I was younger, especially me. I've totally forgotten her real name, but I remember her as Lena Fazool even all these years later."

Well, Grace was no Lena Fazool—Lena was Italian with an hour-glass figure, where Grace is a slim, almost boyish woman, with a modest bosom, and long legs, with a perfect complexion, and almost no hair on her arms or forearms. Lena was married, with two small children. Grace doesn't seem to be attracted to men much—not that she's LGBT+, but she doesn't seem to cozy up to guys—which may well have been a strong point of hers while she was at the May Ling Day Spa. Nobody wants a forward Madame trying to pair up guys with her girls. She was pretty as pretty can be, even dressed in navy blue pants and a Levi's jacket with a navy blue shirt beneath the jacket. She didn't look like a cop, unless you were looking for someone who looked as little like a cop as possible. She didn't look like she could wrestle a grown man to the floor; she didn't look like she'd been lifting weights for years. More like than not, she looked like a slim young girl who would rather flee than fight. Well, maybe that's a little too exaggerated.

I know for sure that she liked the roasted branzino, and she watched really closely while Gabriele filleted her fish. Could she do it herself if she needed to? I doubt it—having tried it myself from time to time. What I got usually when I tried to do that was a mushy plate of flaky small bits of fish, with little white fish bones easily visible all over the plate.

Chapter Eighteen

While we were finishing up our entrees and talking about desserts, Mike took a call on his cellphone and stood up, motioning to me that he wanted to talk to me privately.

"I just had a call," he said, "to tell me that Maggie's son, Jesus Emmanuele Acosta-Gonzalez, apparently hot-footed it out of town about two hours ago."

"Any idea where he went?" I asked in a soft voice that I tried to duplicate from the way he talked to me.

"Apparently back to California," Mike said. "He flew on American from LaGuardia to Dallas-Fort Worth, then to Palm Springs. One way fare. He rented a car at Palm Springs and drove someplace. My guess would be he went home to his father's place—which would be his now, since he inherited his father's estate when his dad died. I've asked my colleague at One Police Plaza to see if he can locate the young man so that we'll have an idea where he is."

"I wonder why he headed back to California," I mused to Mike. "I would have thought he'd be interested in Grace Kim's defection from the day spas to be a student at John Jay College studying criminology."

Mike frowned slightly, and said, "I doubt he knows she's also enrolled in the Police Academy, but somebody in California obviously found out about something. It could put her in a difficult position if some of his buddies find out she's working with the NYPD—to put it bluntly. It could also make trouble for him if they thought he was not paying attention to the new business in Long Island City."

"You mean the day spas?"

He nodded. "Look, I'm going to have to tell Grace what's up, and maybe put her in a safe house someplace in case Chuy's friends want to get rough with her."

"Hopefully her name isn't really Grace Kim, so NYPD can protect her in case she needs protection."

He walked over to where Grace was sitting, and motioned her away from the table. They walked outside and talked for a few minutes.

I was wondering if Maggie was in Dutch with the bad guys. After all, Chuy kept saying she had killed his father, so somebody in California—Guadalajara toughs would be difficult to avoid if they wanted to find her in New York.

Mike said, "Her name isn't really Grace Kim. She's really Korean, but her real name is Margaret Susan Park, and her father was a Baptist preacher in Seoul when she was a kid. Probably hard to track her down from what they might know about her. They probably call her Grace like everybody else does." He looked worried with his forehead wrinkled. "Might be safer if we all went to California together. I doubt they'd be looking for her out on the west coast." He looked up at the ceiling and said, "It might not be a bad idea to get her some eyelid surgery, turn her into a White girl, instead of a pretty Asian who might be more what they're looking for."

Just then there was a gunshot outside. No holes in the windows, but it was a warning shot across the bow, and worth paying attention to, even in Manhattan, one of the most dangerous gunfight places in North America. Mike trundled Grace out of the restaurant and whispered to me that he would take her to his apartment. He could sleep on the couch if they got sleepy. She could sleep on his bed, which had a good mattress, he said. I knew Mike would be the perfect gentleman.

"I get freaking tired of guns and bullets," I said, feeling some sweat dripping down my forehead. "My grandfather hated hand guns— he always said that rifles were for hunting, and hand guns were for killing people. And just watching the TV news in the evening—it seems like a shoot-em-up most evenings."

Gabriele stood up, apparently realizing from the change of mood that had disrupted the table that the shit had just hit the fan. Ruth did the same and marched off with Mike and Grace, and I watched them put Ruth in a taxi that would get her back to her apartment on Park Avenue and 60th Street. Unless somebody was keeping a close eye on Grace, where they could have spotted Ruth sitting across the table from her, I figured she was safe, at least for the time being.

Mike was on his phone checking to see what he could find out about Chuy's home address. His smile told me he found out what he needed. He talked to the travel department and got some flights set up— all on his cellphone, while standing on the sidewalk outside Ora di Pranzo.

"Did you find out Chuy's home address? I think it's in Rancho Mirage," I said. "Maybe Palm Desert."

Mike nodded vigorously "Rancho Mirage, but almost in Palm Desert, near a big Marriott hotel called Desert Springs—big tennis and golf resort. I bet Chuy's a member of the golf club there. His hand-eye skills are excellent. You can tell from watching him throw a baseball that he'd be good at golf. Same skills, especially swinging a bat at a ball pitched by the pitcher to the catcher."

"Did you have a look at Google maps to see what the house looks like?" I asked Mike.

"It's huge," he said. "On a big piece of land, too, as far as I can tell from the picture on Google Maps."

"It's always been cheap to build out in the desert. It's expensive to AC houses, but not particularly expensive to frame them, build them out. And the land isn't expensive like it is near the ocean," I said. "I have a friend who has two homes—one in Big Bear up in the mountains, and one in Palm Springs itself. One works for the winter, and the other one works for the summer. It's like the Native Americans taking cover in the mountains in the hot weather, and fleeing to the desert when it's snowing in the ski country."

"It doesn't look like they built two houses, and there's no record of a second address either," Mike said. "They probably have a backup generator that allows them to keep it cool indoors, even if there's a failure in the electric grid."

"For some reason, I think Chuy is very well-off," I said, using a hand gesture to indicate an exclamation point on the "well-off" part. I paused and then emphasized, "No money problems anyway. I suspect he owns the house outright, for instance. Probably inherited it from his father," I told Mike. "I'd guess he would tell you that he's been visiting his mother for the last few weeks. You know her as Maggie Landover, but her married name would have been Acosta-Gonzalez, like Chuy's last name. She was married to Chuy's father. Probably a church wedding, because Chuy was brought up as a Catholic, which was probably a legacy from his father. There's an underworld potential in the family, father was from Guadalajara, probably drug cartel, as you might guess. I think he was a naturalized US citizen when he died, so I'm guessing that Chuy is a US citizen today, too. Like father like son."

Mike was all in favor of hot-footing it to Palm Springs to pay a call on Chuy Acosta-Gonzalez, who might be trying to expand the family businesses to Queens, and maybe other NYC locations as well as just Long Island City. I volunteered to go along, but Mike was ready to go it alone, maybe taking a fellow detective along with him. He particularly had little if any interest in taking me alone—someone Chuy knew fairly well, and would certainly suspect if I knocked on his door. No question after all the time we spent together on the trip to Cooperstown (and remembering that we shared a room as well) that he would know who I was, and likewise he would know who Mike di Saronno was.

Then it turned out that Mike had discovered that Maggie Landover was apparently not at home in Long Island City. He was positing that maybe she had followed her son to Rancho Mirage, even though she had probably never been there before, since she was way divorced from Manuel before he built or bought the Rancho Mirage house. Maybe not the best idea, but she may have been feeling more secure visiting Chuy than might have been warranted. If anything was true about Chuy, it was that he might be acting on the spur of the moment. He might well have been flying to California to meet with some of his Mexican cartel buddies, which might not be the right kind of party to walk into uninvited.

I believe Mike ended up taking one of the Manhattan detectives with him, and the two of them met up with a Los Angeles detective with experience in drugs and vice, in case there was a parent organization in California that was in charge of the "day spa" business that had suddenly appeared in Long Island City, under the possible aegis of a Mexican cartel group. They stayed in the Marriott Desert Springs, which came with the beneficial side effect of having a very fancy spa and exercise facility, including a massage and salt-scrub group that could make you feel younger with softer skin if you were willing to go through the experience—and were willing to pay for it. I think the massage was around seventy dollars, and the salt scrub was in the same range. Clearly the price was based on the time the masseur or skin technician spent with the client.

Based on the physical appearance of the masseurs, many of whom were mildly overweight, the likelihood of a "happy ending" was low to nil at Desert Springs, unlike the upside-down economics of the day spas in Long Island City.

Anyway, I stayed in Queens, and invited Gabriele over to cook dinner for Ruth and me while Mike was cavorting around in Rancho Mirage. I know it sounds odd that I would invite my close friend, the restaurateur Gabriele Cortese, to cook dinner, but chalk it up to a long friendship, and a close relationship between Gabriele and Ruth to boot. He made my favorite dish—pasta with sausage, garlic, oil and chopped rapini, topped off with handfuls of parmesan cheese. Perfectly healthy to start off with, and it would pass muster with any diet, too. Nothing fattening, nothing to annoy your stomach or your bowel. And I knew Ruth liked the dish anyway.

I scratched up two bottles of Barbaresco to complement Gabriele's cooking. Barbaresco is considered an everyday wine in northern Italy where Barolo is almost always a Sunday bottle. Barbaresco is fruitier than Barolo, which is more aged, with more tannins. At the risk of being offensive to Northern Italians, Barbaresco is a lighter wine than Barolo, maybe a bit like California Zinfandels compared to a complex wine that has been aged for years at least, and decades potentially.

At any rate, the wine matched Gabriele's cooking very well. And

Gabriele understood the place of Barbaresco in the hierarchy of fine Italian wines, too. Maybe the Italian equivalent of what might be called a "hamburger wine" in New York. It was almost worth missing a trip to the California desert, and I was able to top it off with strong coffee and a chilled limoncello, which is basically vodka that has had bottles of lemon rinds soaked in it for months at least (and years in lots of cases). In my case, I get several bottles of limoncello made with lemons from Capri every Christmas from Gabriele, who gets a couple of cases from his mother, who still lives in Capri, with her very own lemon trees in the back yard.

To make it all perfect, Mike and his detective buddy who had been in California with Mike, got back without incident, and they never saw Chuy during their whole time in Rancho Mirage. From all they could tell, Chuy had been in Guadalajara for well over a week, while Mike and his detective buddy were only in Rancho Mirage for three days or so. The fact that Chuy was totally absent made it more suspicious that something illegal was being hatched in Queens, or that at least, a larger version of the day spa business was being contemplated. I managed to take a bottle of limoncello to Mike's office, so maybe both he and his detective colleague managed to have a sip with their morning coffee at the precinct in Manhattan. Wouldn't Gabriele's mother like that? Her lemons and her limoncello sweetening the morning coffee? No mother would be capable of overlooking that.

Chapter Nineteen

The longer the drug cartel was involved, the more their operations resembled the old-fashioned mob businesses of what used to be called the Mafia in New York. Prostitution was a well-known activity, but the most lucrative parts of the business were gambling (numbers) and drugs. That meant that the day spas in Long Island City had to be tilted to drugs in order for the cash return to justify the risks that the cartel was incurring.

It occurred to me that Maggie Landover would have been a real asset in setting up and running the operation. After all, she had been a drug mule when she was a flight attendant on the routes between Venezuela, Mexico and the huge markets for cocaine, opioids like heroin, hydrocodone, fentanyl, morphine, codeine and the rest of the street drugs, not to mention the brand names like OxyContin®, which was sold in patches that didn't require needles and syringes.

OxyContin also had the advantage that it was a privately owned family business, so skyrocketing profits were perfection—especially since a huge majority of the users were on prescriptions and could buy the drugs legally—or apparently legally—as a result of many years of pain relief medications that simply led the user from one drug to another. Fentanyl was similar to morphine, but up to one hundred times more potent. Best of all, almost all fentanyl was made in China for years, and trans-shipped without leaving a track or a footprint through countries like Mexico, in order to be distributed more or less legally by major drug distributors like McKesson, Cardinal Health and AmerisourceBergen.

That didn't stop the Guadalajara cartel from taking its cut during the transfers of products from a plane that landed in Mexico City to a plane that flew from Mexico City to the Promised Land—originally in the urban hubs of the USA think Chicago, New York, Los Angeles, San Francisco, and most of the college towns across the country—and later to the exurbanites in the far suburbs of the Midwest in states like Ohio, which became a significant user of fentanyl and even oxycodone—a "legitimate" prescription drug that was just part of a long conga line that started with marijuana and heroin from street vendors, and ended up flowing through pharmacies in small towns that filled millions of prescriptions for areas where there were not nearly enough patients to legally consume them.

Not that the huge drug business represented by substances like fentanyl had anything to do with the day spas in Queens. Those were start-ups, most likely hugely profitable, but mostly small fish; not someone that would come under the eye of the DEA or any other federal agency.

It's hard to believe that's where Chuy Acosta-Gonzalez fitted into the puzzle. He wasn't smart enough, for one thing. He was well-placed to introduce useful people who could make the business more and more profitable every time more young girls and boys took over selling drugs or sex. He was most likely not ever going to be connected with the three day spas in Long Island City. He also didn't get a fair cut of anything. He just got a payment every month—enough to pay some of his bills. He was already rich, having inherited his father's estate when the Old Man was killed by his ex-wife across the street from where I live.

Chuy was just not the brightest bulb in the room. He was a baseball fan like his dad, but he never had a thought that would change things for the better. He didn't need to be bright—he was rich, had a big house and probably lots of financial resources, which was all he needed. He had a general idea of what was going on, so that he could be part of the operation. He could run some of the girls, and maybe could get a cut of referrals to bookies who worked for every gambling vendor in New York City. Chuy was somebody to blame if things went wrong. In fact, when Manuel had his throat cut, the Guadalajara big hombres thought he'd been eliminated by somebody who was getting his feet stepped on.

Maybe a smart guy who had some boys who sold opioids on street corners—and who Manuel got in the way of. Manuel was not the smartest person in the cartel either. No surprise he got sliced up. It was almost inevitable that he'd get eliminated sooner or later, because he wasn't bright and wasn't careful in who he talked to. His wife was never suspected of going after him for personal reasons, probably because she kept claiming that she had no idea who he was because of the damned surgical mask he was wearing. She'd never seen Chuy in person since he was an infant, and had not seen Manuel in well over twenty years—so why would she know who he was? Stupid female. She just managed to get caught with his blood all over her. Might as well let her take the rap for whatever the addle-pated cops felt like pinning on her. Murder? Probably not, but some kind of mayhem, maybe accidental manslaughter, which still could run anywhere between three and a half years and fifteen years, depending on the judge's take on the sentencing guidelines. When police officer Derek Chauvin was convicted of murdering George Floyd, he got more than twenty-two years in the slammer, although his lawyer appealed the sentence.

Thing about a woman accused of manslaughter is that if she starts to cry, the jury is likely to vote more in her favor. In Maggie Landover's case, crying could mean that she really didn't intend to hurt the man she killed—who turned out to be her former husband. Or it could be simply self-pity as she starts to think about being penned up in Sing Sing for a bunch of years.

From what I knew about Maggie, she could be a Niagara Falls of tears if she thought her son was in trouble with the law—which would be nothing short of what anyone who knew his father would have predicted. Like father like son, as they say. Manuel—Chuy's dad—was a born drug dealer, and probably at least an accomplice in some fairly gory murders on the drug trail. The group of drug pushers he was with had killed tens—maybe more than tens—of people who had crossed the cartel's plans or trails. The differences between Mexican justice and American justice is that American justice is pointed at putting criminals behind bars, where Mexican justice is more inclined to give a bad guy another chance to avoid punishment. Think about Joaquin "El Chapo" Guzman, who not only escaped from Mexican prisons on several occasions (including using a nearly mile-long tunnel that seemed directly designed for Guzman's escape). The same man has avoided Mexican courts and penalties over and over again. Since being handed over to the US for trial, it's been a different story. Could easily be the same with the Guadalajara cartel group.

I doubt Chuy could be nailed on a felony that would put him away for a long time, and of course his father—who may well have been more deeply involved in illegal matters during his fairly short lifespan—is no longer answerable for crimes he may or may not have committed while he was alive. Manuel was never convicted of a punishable crime in Mexico.

He was surely not a total innocent, but he was able to avoid any serious clashes with the Mexican *Policìa* Federal (also known as *Federalis* in the common slang). Possibly the wealthy folks in the cartel were part of a family tradition—maybe even partly dependent on relatives. It has never been uncommon for Mexican patricians or rich people (*gent erica*) to play both sides of the law, so it could easily be believed that Manuel's father, whose name was Santiago ("Saint James" in English, just as Iago is a Spanish version of James used by Shakespeare in "Othello"), could have been a more than respectable land-owning ranchero, someone who was part of a business cartel in Guadalajara—and willed that relationship to Manuel.

Manuel could easily then have been a high-class playboy who spent most of his life having a good time. That life-style seems to have been handed down to Chuy, so it makes sense that Santiago handed it down to Manuel, who eventually died as a result of attempting to rape his ex-wife, who didn't have a clue who he was due to his wearing a surgical mask to comply with pandemic rules in New York. She killed him by grabbing a kitchen knife while she was pinned to the refrigerator, and then accidentally slicing open his carotid artery when he moved his head.

It was seen as self-defense at the arraignment.

Chapter Twenty

Might she have given in to Manuel's rough sex if she'd known who he was? Maybe, if he had spoken to her to let her know who he was. It could have happened. Maybe Maggie was interested—hard to tell from talking to her today, after the fact. She's certainly no puritan. She had gone along with his drug habit when they were married, and he stuffed condoms full of cocaine into her vagina so that she could smuggle them into the United States, as she was flying back from Venezuela. Her husband's family had a vacation home in the super-high-class resort-style Los Roques islands (think about Malibu on the Caribbean when you think about Los Roques). She had been an ideal drug mule, partly because she had a Hispanic married name even though she had native US citizenship and pale skin. In addition, she was an American Airlines flight attendant with all that appropriate education, training and union memberships—American Airlines had taken over the Eastern Airlines air routes and airport gates between Caracas and JFK Airport in New York City. Not only that, she was pretty, and obviously part Asian—so she had that international look that made Manuel feel like a celebrity.

When they were in a group of people, he treated her like the celebrity he thought she looked like. In some ways he was a gentleman like own his father and probably his grandfather had trained him to be. He was a hand-kisser, for instance, in the French style, keeping his eyes focused on her eyes as he held her hand and kissed the back of it lightly, like Maurice Chevalier in a pre-war movie. In some ways, knowing Maggie as she was when I met her, I could see her thinking Manuel was a prince among men. Wealthy, handsome, polite (at least when people were watching), and very frank with everybody that he thought Maggie was the cat's meow, as they used to say.

I could see her looking at Chuy admiringly. He looked like his father, acted like his father, dressed like his father. Everything Maggie had liked about Manuel, she liked about Chuy, too. Chuy was her son, and she didn't flirt with him the way she more or less did with other men.

The two of them grew up in the Eisenhower years, when the last thing governments wanted was a war. Even Dwight Eisenhower watched the creation of jobs and the strength of the American infrastructure more than he paid attention to international affairs or military movements like the newly independent Israel in 1948, and the split of India into India and Pakistan in 1947, as the British Empire began to crumble faster and faster. President Eisenhower's biggest project was the creation of the Interstate Highway System—which needs a lot of repairs all these years later. It was fashioned after scenic routes like Route 66 and California's Highway 1 through the central seafront in areas like Big Sur. Eisenhower was a futurist of his time, understanding that the family automobile would take the place of trains and public transportation—this at a time when commercial airlines were growing bigger and faster than any other transportation segment, and airports sprang up like corn plants in the early days of summer.

LAX was doubled in size more than once, and so was San Francisco International Airport, and Idlewild Airport in Nassau County New York morphed into JFK Airport after John Kennedy was assassinated. Then Dulles sprang out of the ground in Virginia near the District of Columbia, and all of a sudden there was international air traffic over the skies of the nation's capital. Ike also understood that service and gasoline stations were the keys to making cars work as the backbone of transportation—especially commercial transportation that depended on 16-wheelers to move all kinds of products from one side of the continent to the other. Every mom and pop could find a gas station for fuel under Eisenhower's plan, and most of those gas stations had service bays where at least basic repairs could be made on the spot—in those days, you didn't need a computer to read out what was wrong with a car. Today, even a grease monkey has to be a rocket scientist on the side. That's a perfect change that makes the infrastructure of our highways old-fashioned and virtually useless.

What Eisenhower didn't know was that automobile exhaust would pump what's now called "greenhouse gases" into the atmosphere of our planet, and that the gathering of carbon dioxide and other carbon compounds/greenhouse gases would cause the average atmospheric temperature to go up, up, up, year after year—melting polar icecaps, glaciers that cover places like Greenland, and stunting the snowfalls that are the mother's milk of rivers and streams all over the world. As the Colorado River is increasingly fed by lower snowfalls, Lake Mead has progressively started to dry up, for instance. The same is true of the Great Salt Lake in Utah, where the drying up of the lakebed frees dust that contains arsenic and other super-unhealthy minerals and compounds.

Until we get the annual snowfall back to where it was in the 1950s, we may not have the amount of water we got used to using in the Kennedy, Johnson, Nixon, Ford and Carter years. That's when the central flatlands and deserts of California and Arizona became "the breadbasket of North America." That same disappearing water supported the hugely important California wine industry, concentrated in places like Napa County, Sonoma County and the agricultural areas in central California near Paso Robles. The same is true of Oregon and the State of Washington, where some of the most costly white wines in North America are produced—less and less, unfortunately. The same will be true in the Mendoza area of Argentina, which has become a boom-land for red wines such as malbec and even cabernet sauvignon in the Chilean Andes. Just trying to remedy the climate change in the USA will do no good for South America, or the codfish industry, the sailfish fisheries, and the salmon runs in the western part of the United States and Canada.

The final thing that Eisenhower didn't know was that livestock were generating greenhouse gases of their own—particularly cattle, which burp and fart methane, which accelerates the warming of the atmosphere even more than the carbon dioxide that blows out of the exhaust pipes of cars, trucks, factories, energy producers—and even the kings of transportation—the small propeller and gigantic jet planes that make cars and trucks look like toys that created jet fuel exhaust streams that dwarfed the use of gasoline for cars.in climate change problems. As travel increased, the bigger the planes got, the more exhaust they generated, and as the globe became totally circled with plane routes for business people and tourists, the biggest polluters of the air and atmosphere turned out to be some of the most exotic and fastest-growing places in the world. Places like Australia became huge tourist destinations. So did Java, Bali, Tahiti and other areas of the south Pacific. Hawaii, which had been a cruise destination since it was a kingdom of its own, bloomed aircraft and airlines—and Honolulu became a way-station between California and Sydney, with gigantic Boeing 747s taking off and landing every few minutes, followed by 777s and 787s, both wide-bodies that carried more and more passengers.

As of a few years ago, China has become the largest polluter in the world—primarily because the amount of carbon dioxide generated from gasoline, jet fuel and coal being burned to create electricity was larger than other countries with slower-growing economies and slower-growing populations as well. The more people, the more cars, trucks, buses, trains and planes.

Today, China is still the biggest polluter, just recently surpassing the United States at a fast pace, and growing at a much faster rate than the USA. In other words, China is likely to be the world's largest economy pretty soon—and it's highly unlikely that climate change can be effective without China leading the world in controlling greenhouse gas emissions. Until then we'll have uncontrollable wildfires that burn millions of acres every year, major lakes drying up, water shortages in a bigger way every year, that cuts into farms, orchards, truck farms that fill up our produce aisles all across the USA.

Chapter Twenty-one

Meanwhile, the Asian Hate movement, the Black Lives Matter movement and the Me Too movement picked up speed, and hit the TV news virtually every evening. For some reason, New York City has one of the largest Asian populations in the United States. It was also one of the most segregated cities in the country with names to underscore that segregation. Thus, Koreatown and six (or up to nine, depending on how you count them) Chinatowns in five NYC boroughs, to complement the largest ethnic Chinese population in the western hemisphere, That's not to mention two free-standing Chinatown areas in Nassau County (Long Island) and in several New Jersey cities such as Edison and Newark.

When we think of Chinatown, for some reason the city of San Francisco comes to mind—but San Francisco is a smallish city, and it has a smallish ethnic Chinese population, compared to the gigantic Asian populations in greater New York City. All told, lots of Asian people to blame for whatever needed blame—like the COVID-19 virus, which is rumored to have originated in Wuhan, China. So if it's a Chinese disease, why not slug Chinese people in the nose to punish them for it? After all, a former US President was very forward about calling COVID-19 the "Flu Manchu." If he can do it, why not angry homeless people? Guys who hate Asians? People who equate Chinese with Communists?

Lots of sucker punches had been delivered in all five boroughs—most commonly in or near subway stations. Two or three Asian seniors (all women) had been pushed onto subway tracks, where they could be killed by trains or by being electrocuted by touching the "third rail," which provided electrical juice for the subway trains (and elevated trains in many places outside of Manhattan). Fortunately, nearly all of such victims had been rescued by Good Samaritans (for the most part also seniors, many times related to the victims and even out walking with them).

However large the Asian population in New York might be, the Black or Afro-American population is larger—and the Black Lives Matter movement took to the streets more and more in marches and demonstrations with banners and signs that concentrated principally on police clashes with Black citizens. Black Lives Matter marches and all kinds of demonstrations portrayed the danger of losing Black lives as more likely to be caused by police wielding guns at Blacks.

The Me Too movement was interested in women who had been the victims of sexual harassment or abuse—especially by men who were privileged or powerful, or in positions of power in companies that employed women. The poster child was a Hollywood movie producer, Harvey Weinstein, who was accused of sexual mistreatment by well over eighty women—a number that was exceeded by Bill Cosby, a television comedian whose sexual habits seemed to include drugs such as Quaaludes. He was convicted of sexually assaulting one woman due largely to expired statutes of limitations, but on the testimony of five or more other women with similar stories. His conviction was eventually overturned, and the superannuated Cosby was released from prison, apparently at little if any danger of being re-tried due to double jeopardy.

Nonetheless, Manhattan seemed to have more demonstrations than any other major American City. Portland, Oregon, was plagued by Black Lives Matter marches and demonstrations, as well as riots and even invasions of a federal court building, which brought in the National Guard to protect the federal property that had been invaded.

Minneapolis was the locus of a notorious Black Lives Matter incident, when a potentially high Black man named George Floyd was strangled by a group of police officers led by a police veteran named Derek Chauvin, who was later convicted of murder in the case. The George Floyd murder probably caused more marches and demonstrations than any other single case of police-caused Black death, other than the

Staten Island death of Eric Garner, who was also strangled for the crime of selling single cigarettes on the sidewalk. The banners of both Floyd and Garner demonstrations carried the quote "I can't breathe" prominently, because both men were strangled.

But the most pointless group of assaults were the Asian Hate incidents, very few of which ended in deaths, but many of which were inflicted on aged or feeble people of apparently Asian looks, and for no obvious reason other than pure ethnic hate. It ramped up in Long Island City after the Chinese-named day spas opened on Vernon Boulevard near the Vernon-Jackson subway station. Mostly caused by homeless or drug-high toughs, these incidents usually consisted of punching or knocking down elderly Asian women and men on the streets of Queens—frequently with Hate Speech accompanying the violence. "Go Back to China!" was a common yell, although the victims were usually obviously not recent immigrants, due to their advanced ages. Most of the victims were helpless, or were attacked without warning. Most of the injuries were from kicking, punches to the face, knocking down to the sidewalk—and theft of handbags and wallets.

Asian Hate is a long-term American form of prejudice, harking back to the California Gold Rush, when waves of Chinese immigrants provided manual labor for gold miners. There was the Chinese Exclusion Act of 1882, which prevented Chinese people from entering the United States legally—and there were scabrous posters of Uncle Sam kicking and otherwise mistreating Chinese people, many of whom had long queues of hair, which was a historic artifact of the takeover of the Chinese government by the Manchu people, also known as the Qing Dynasty of Emperors (1644-1912, and succeeded by the Republic of China under Sun Yat-Sen).

Asian Hate is an ethnic form of prejudice that is based on Asian facial and physical characteristics, particularly almond-shaped eyes and pallid skin tones, together with smaller stature than Caucasians. It is also colored historically by the mid-nineteenth century history of opium use in China, due largely to the various Opium Wars between China and Britain. If Chinese were opium addicts, what kinds of other evil traits might they have? If Chinese emperors had hundreds of concubines, what was the likelihood that Chinese women would take to prostitution? What kinds of diseases did they carry? And why was Chinese food so much in fashion if Chinese people were unhealthy and possibly diseased? It never made sense, and still doesn't.

As it turned out, most Asian Hate attacks in New York City were charged to young minority toughs, primarily Black and Brown males— not so different from arrests on charges of robbery, assault, use of lightweight drugs like marijuana. Even in New York City, federal hate charges were seldom pinned on perpetrators unless the media had video of the crimes being committed—which happened more often than one might think a camera might be catching sidewalk or streetside activities.

It was also unusual that the day spas on Vernon Boulevard didn't attract other crimes, and seldom were accused of soliciting prostitution. Apparently most of the activity was thought to be a standard massage followed by a standard "happy ending"—something that happened on teen-age dates every weekend in every town and city in the United States. Ha! Not something indigenous to Chinese or Asians at all. Just hate, just intolerance of people who look different from people of European ancestry. Pointless. Stupid. Simple prejudice, not much different from all other kinds of racial prejudice. If you're not White, you're not acceptable in polite society. Screw you.

Chapter Twenty-two

So, what was the danger—if any—to Maggie Landover? She was clearly Eurasian, and even she would admit easily that her father was a Catholic priest who was a missionary in China. That made her illegitimate, because her father wasn't married to her mother when she was born. In fact, her mother wasn't, strictly speaking, her mother at all. Her birth mother was a Chinese maid or servant girl. Because her father was a priest, he actually had to adopt her jointly after he left the priesthood and married the woman Maggie called "Mom." They were not related by blood, except that his semen had caused the Chinese servant girl Lily's pregnancy that turned out to be baby Maggie (she was named after her adoptive father's grandmother, whose name was Margaret Mary, after a French female saint who started an order of nuns that adopted the name of Religious of the Sacred Heart of Mary—and established schools under the name of Marymount around the world). She wanted to be called Maggie, and she grew up preferring to use the name Maggie Orangeman, which was her birth mother's family name, although her birth certificate read Maggie Gaston. Her real grandparents would have been Mexican on one side, and Chinese on the other side. As her father told her, she was a mutt, not a pure-bred pooch.

For some reason, although he had done everything wrong regarding his daughter, she loved her father, and she loved sitting on his lap. When he stopped being a clergyman, he became a teacher/tutor, and hired himself out to prepare foreign—largely Chinese—teenagers to be graduated with high honors from American high schools. It was a more lucrative way of earning a living than one might have thought, because the American parents of small children who spoke both English and Mandarin tended to have deep pockets when it came to their children's educational upbringing.

Her father had left the priesthood when she was not yet a teenager, and subsequently he married her adoptive mother, whom he called "Snookie" all the time, although Maggie knew her real first name was Winnie Helena. He sent Maggie's birth mother, Lily Orangeman, home to her family, worried that he might lose the child he wanted to keep. Maggie never saw her again, that she knew of. She only knew one mother, and that woman was a former nun who died relatively early, probably from a virus that she might have caught in the missionary operation where she lived with her mate, the former priest. Lots of children around, and of course they were from a variety of homes and could have been exposed to almost any kind of contagion. The mortality rate among Chinese commoners was very high, and her father (the former priest) seemed to accept illness and death as parts of life that sometimes could be avoided— and sometimes not.

Maggie kept the attitudes of her childhood throughout her adulthood. She never trusted that men would treat her fairly. She was attracted to men—a lot—but she couldn't bring herself to trust them. It was a thousand wonders that she was only pregnant once. Some types of men seemed to get her trust. One of those is Mike di Saronno, and I think I may be one of the type of guys she can make an important bet on, although I doubt she would have trusted me if we agreed to bet on a baseball game.

She doesn't seem to trust handsome, sexy men like Gabriele, although her trust in Ruth Jensen seems to rub off on Gabriele when they're both in the room at the same time. She also seems to admire Gabriele's hard work at his restaurant—and the quality of the food he serves. She seems to respect hard work, whether male or female. She doesn't look down on people who are less than respectable. She would have been friendly with the prostitutes in the day spas, but she would never have been able to manage the business, or handle the money in a way that would make a profit regularly and dependably. She would also have leaned toward trusting the girls, which might not have been the best pathway. She might have been better off trusting the male clients, who would at least have paid the agreed-upon price for services rendered. Most men would understand that some types of services deserve a tip—and that most likely includes a "happy ending" to a massage. Of course the Madame gets a cut of everything. Usually well over fifty percent of the cash, as long as the manager or boss isn't standing there while the cash is counted. If the boss is there, then his cut is the biggest—always the biggest.

My phone vibrated, indicating Mike wanted to talk to me. I was at home, watching CNN on TV, and sipping on a dirty vodka. No reason not to pick up the call.

"Hey, Mike," I said jocularly, "how's it going where you are?"

"Well, more or less the way you might have expected. Chuy showed up again in Queens, just in time to decide to plug his mom into Grace Kim's job at the May Ling Day Spa." He paused. "What do you think?"

"I doubt Maggie has a managerial bone in her body, and I also doubt she has any sympathetic feelings about the girls that work the spas. If she doesn't take care of the merchandise, she's not going to get much in the way of repeat customers."

"Well, in fact, two of the girls disappeared after Maggie took over," he said. "I doubt you know them, because I doubt you've been there since Grace left to join our Red Rover team. Now that Maggie is their team captain, she's set up for trouble. I hope somebody tells her what the rules of the road are, given that she's head of all three spas because of being the head of the May Ling operation, which seems to be the home base for the whole kit and caboodle."

"What do you think we ought to do?" I asked.

"I think it might be a good idea if you—and maybe I—could have a talk with Maggie. A down and dirty talk, so she'll know she's not a princess in this operation, but a schlemiel—the kind that might jump out a window for no particular reason, except that she doesn't want to get shot or otherwise done in." He paused, and added, "She has to know she's at the bottom of the ladder in this operation. Anything that happens, she's likely to get blamed. And Chuy is likely to be the Lord High Executioner if something goes wrong. If she sees her son pointing a gun at her, she needs to run and duck as fast as she can move."

"What about we invite her to lunch at the Oyster Bar?" I asked. "We should be able to talk about anything there without being overheard or watched. I think she's more naive than she looks, or than her history might indicate. She needs to take care of herself, and not assume anyone else is going to have her best interest in their heart or mind. That includes Chuy."

"If Chuy is his father's son," Mike said quietly and thoughtfully, "he knows that cash is king. Nothing is as important as cash. Cash is the only financial device that can't be controlled or traced. No credit cards, no checks. Cash. Small notes, no hundreds. If she understands that, she can probably even start to skim some off the surface without getting caught and losing at least one finger on each hand."

"Up to you," I said. "If I call Maggie, it'd be like hearing a siren in her world. I need to not be a surprise. I don't mind being part of the conversation, and I'm not afraid of whoever she's in cahoots with. But I don't want to walk into a room full of drawn guns cocked and ready to fire."

"Okay," Mike said. "I'll set it up. Just plan to be at the Oyster Bar tomorrow at one PM. I'll arrange to have a table in the back, not near any other table. If I'm not mistaken, cops are probably cock of the walk at the Oyster Bar. The last thing he'll want to do is fuck me over—or you, for that matter. The days of free donuts are still here for a cop in a uniform, or with a shield shining on his beltline."

"I think all that works better if your name is O'Reilly or di Saronno." The cops that restaurants love are all Irish or Italian—the Pope's troops. Black hair and a blue and orange striped tie. Nothing says New York like blue and orange. Like the Mets, or the New York City flag. The flag of New York City is a vertical tricolor (designed like the French tricolor), orange on the left, then white, then blue on the right, with the seal of the City printed in navy on the white bar—in the style of the

Dutch Republic from 1625 (long time passing, but not a lot has changed over the years—note the Dutchman and the Native American if you see a flag that fits the description—like at New York City Hall).

I went back to watching CNN, and saw two new videos that showed two elderly Asian women getting knocked to the ground and then kicked and robbed of their handbags. No sooner had I seen these stories on Asian Hate than Mike called back.

"I'm not sure she can keep a secret," Mike said, "but Maggie will meet me and a friend—that's you—at the Oyster Bar at one PM tomorrow." He paused and then added, "I'd recommend that you show up five or ten minutes late. If we see a group of Mexicans watching Maggie, we'll cut the program to nothing, just lunch, some laughs, a glass of beer or wine and a talk about her plans for the day spas on Vernon Boulevard. Nothing racy or that would look suspicious to our friends from south of the border down Mexico way. Maybe I'll hint that the guys at the Long Island City precinct might like to see their palms greased a little.

"Last time there was a cop that didn't want a few bucks on the side was a long time ago. If we decide to fall back on that crap, let me do it," he said. "Don't try to drop that bomb yourself. Leave it to me. I'll take care of you. Trust me."

"I completely understand that this whole sideshow is about Maggie, not about Chuy or his business colleagues," I said. "If we want anything out of this, we want to have an ongoing relationship with Maggie, so we can have eyes inside the operation on Vernon Boulevard."

As it happened, Maggie wandered into the Oyster Bar alone, and there was no gaggle of Mexicans following her or keeping an eye on her. Neither did her son show up. But Maggie herself made sure that the meeting was memorable.

"I want to work as closely as possible with you, Mike, and with my neighbor Hugo," she said. "I want to do as little damage to the neighborhood as possible, but I have to say that the girls I work with are going to be a high priority for all of us. I want to get these ladies to be American citizens—tax-paying citizens. I came by my citizenship because I was born American—my father was American and I've had a passport since I was a little tyke.

Then she changed the subject very abruptly, and made me feel like I knew her better than I actually knew her.

"I love fish and chips," she said. "So I knew this would be a good lunch when Mike told me to meet him here. I had lunch here one day a couple of years ago, and I asked the same question that a bunch of people ask here every day. I wanted to know what kind of fish was made into fish and chips here. Cod was the answer. Not pollack; not any other kind of cheap fish. Cod has been a principal food for people for thousands of years. In the Middle Ages, the Christian Church created 'fish on Fridays' to support the cod fishing people of North Europe. I love fried cod, and I love tartar sauce, and put them together and I love them twice as much." She smiled broadly, and continued.

"Anybody who's a fan of fish and chips is good people. I think these two guys—Mike and Hugo—are good people," she said, pointing first at Mike and then at me. "I want to work with you both, and I want to make sure that everything we do helps people who need help and friendship. Immigrants, people without documents to say they are here legally. People who don't have any place to live, no address to give to the government to make them legitimate. You can't vote without a home address, you know."

She was just getting up a head of steam, and it was clear that she didn't much care that she was on one side of the law, and Mike was on what most people would see as the opposite side.

"I want all the people who work in the day spas where I work to be able to vote. They came here because they want to be Americans like the rest of us. My son, Chuy, is an American. I'm an American, and I want all the people I work with to have a way to be Americans if they want to live good lives, raise happy families, and want to pay taxes to help raise the millions of Americans who don't have a sense of what they need to do to help other people."

She stopped talking, and Mike picked up the conversation. "Nobody has to be a saint to do good things for people," he said. "Happy to work with you in whatever ways we can help."

I jumped in. "I've been retired for several years. And I agree that fried cod and tartar sauce are an ideal combo. I could eat that combo every day of every week of every month of the year. Consider me a friend, and I'll make pan-fried breaded codfish any time you feel like stopping by my place."

I decided to backtrack a bit. "I want to make sure I understand you. And that you understand me." I stared at her directly and she clearly calmed down. "I want to help all the people you work with. Mostly I want to make sure they don't get into trouble. I don't want anyone to get raided, arrested for any reason at all. I don't want undocumented foreigners to get shipped back to wherever the last stamp on their passport is readable. No smuggling of foreigners just to put them in danger of deportation. Smuggling undocumented people can land people in jail for up to ten years—even when that smuggling is perfectly well-intentioned—when all you're trying to do is help people lead productive lives, raise their children, live like American's are supposed to live. No point being in prison when what you want is to help people. If you're not a lawyer, you'll have a hard time helping people if you're in prison."

Maggie looked around to see if anyone was listening or watching. The place was almost empty, at least in the corner of the dining room where we were sitting. She was safe, and as far as I could tell, so were we.

"Listen to me, Maggie," Mike said. "If you want to help somebody who's not doing something bad, call me." He handed Maggie a business card. "There's almost always a legal way to help people—almost always a way to help without getting in trouble."

She looked troubled and her lips began to tremble.

"And what if I want to help somebody who's in trouble?"

"Call me anyway. We can sit down and talk, and figure out a way to help the person you want to help without getting both of you in trouble. There's almost always a way to get good things done. Believe me. I'm not a cop because I want to put people in the slammer. I'm a cop because I want to help people do what they need to do without getting in trouble. I know the ways to cut corners, the ways to help people who are in trouble with the law, the ways to help people who have been arrested. If a girl in one of your day spas is arrested for offering a hand job to some fat guy who wants to be treated like a guy who looks sexy and more handsome than the evil-smelling unshaven porker he looks like to the rest of the world, call me."

"Sometimes you can't really tell much about what kind of person a guy is just by looking at him," she said.

"Totally true," Mike said. "But something I can tell you for absolute truth. There's almost always a legal way to get something done. There may be faster ways to get the same job done. There may be easier ways to get the same job done. But it's the legal way that you need to know, and to follow, to not only get it done, but to make sure it STAYS done, and doesn't end up putting somebody behind bars. Your biggest weapon in getting things done is a smart cop. In my case, I'm not only a smart cop with a good record, I'm also a smart lawyer. Never been in private practice, never ran for district attorney, but I'm one heck of a lawyer at the defense table, too."

"It sounds to me," Maggie said, "like you're telling me you know how to go around the law, how to cut corners so that you can avoid the difficult parts of the law." She rolled her eyes and then made eye contact with Mike again.

"There are some things that you can't go around," Mike said. "You can't shoot somebody and get away with it, for instance. Once the forensic scientists match your bullet to the bullet that killed somebody, you're in a pickle that you can't get out of." He took a breath and ran his right hand through his hair. "But there are almost always ways to avoid getting in trouble. Nothing magic can make you innocent when you are guilty. The trick is not being guilty in the first place. And the best help you can get is a smart cop who knows how to work the loopholes to keep you out of trouble."

"Gotcha," she said. "Sounds like I ought to have you on retainer so I can call you when I'm in a pickle."

"You don't need me on retainer. All you need is my phone number. I don't charge for being smart and knowing how to handle the edges of the law. I can't help you get off a murder charge, because murder is a crime no matter what. You murder somebody and you will end up in jail for a long time. But if you call me when you think a crime is your only choice—that's when I can help you. No magic, but there are almost always ways around situations that are just difficult."

Chapter Twenty-three

As New York summers get hotter and more humid, storms become more and more common. When I was a kid visiting my grandparents in Fleetwood, I found the lightning and thunder exciting at best and frightening at worst. My grandmother would count between a bolt of lightning in a dark sky and the thunder that almost inevitably followed. At the time, it was beyond my understanding that the lightning traveled at the speed of light, and the thunder traveled at the speed of sound. The two speeds are dramatically different, so you see the lightning way-way-way earlier than you hear the thunder.

So the reason my grandmother counted was to compare the time between seeing the lightning bolt and hearing the thunder. The theory was that if she counted slowly, you could tell how many miles away the lightning was when it struck from the cloud to the ground. If she counted to five, it meant the lightning was about five miles away. If she couldn't count even to one, it meant that the lightning was virtually on top of us. That meant getting away from the windows immediately, although outrunning lightning was like trying to fly off a cliff—a totally useless endeavor. If lightning struck the tree outside the second-story window, there was no point in trying to avoid it.

When I was a teenager, the family went on a vacation in Mount Lassen National Park. It was at a time when recreational vehicles were just becoming interesting for family groups. So we rented a small trailer that slept four people, had a tiny toilet, and had a rudimentary kitchen, including a fridge and a stove top that hooked up to outside pipes and wires that powered not only the kitchen accessories, but also provided electricity to a loud and windy air conditioner that theoretically made it easier to sleep at night when it was hot, and insects were everywhere.

It made little difference to me, because, being the eldest of three children, I slept outdoors every night anyway. There wasn't room for all of us to sleep in the trailer, so I slept in a sleeping bag outdoors— sometimes on a lunch table, sometimes in a hammock that could be hooked up to a tree on one end and the trailer on the other end. It was far easier for me to fall asleep, and it seldom rained at night in the Sierra Nevada, which was the mountain range where Mount Lassen was located.

But one day while we were there, my father decided we would hike up Mount Lassen, an active volcano but not a frequent erupter. The scars on the northern flank of the mountain still remind the locals of the 1914-1917 eruptions. The fact that Lassen was a volcano didn't deter my dad from wanting to hike up the nearly ten thousand five hundred-foot-high peak, though the top part of the hike was across a glacier. When we got to the top, my mom broke out a picnic hamper and dad decided it was time to eat.

I looked west, which was the direction easiest to look—and the direction the weather blew in from California. Storms came from the Pacific; sometimes from the north and sometimes from the west. This particular day, the lightning in the distance was due west (I had a compass), and I decided that it was unsafe to sit on the edge of the glacier and eat lunch as the sky was darkening quickly, and there was visible lightning all over the grey clouds that seemed to grow larger and larger.

Dad poo-pooed the idea of hiking back down the mountain to the parking lot the car was in. I was scared of the storm, and headed back down to the car in spite of my father's snide remarks about my masculinity. It was faster going down than it had been hiking up, and I slid down much of the glacier and found myself in a small grove of evergreen trees, probably some kind of redwood trees. I could see the car, and made my way to it, and got there just as the rain began to pelt down, spiced with quarter-sized hail, so I slid under the chassis to avoid getting soaking wet. Shortly after I got under the car, I heard a crack of thunder that sounded really close. I stayed where I was, under the car.

Not very long afterward, a group of park rangers appeared in the grove of trees above the parking lot. They were carrying several stretchers, which, as it turned out, were filled with my mother, father, brother and sister, who had been close to a lightning strike and had been knocked out. By the time the rangers found their way to our car, I had wriggled out and recognized my family. They were all awake, but all had major-league headaches. The rangers called for a couple of ambulances, which took my relatives to a small hospital not far away. I had keys to the car, and followed the ambulances. My parents were feeling better, although Dad still had a headache. We all got back to the campground, and Mom made some dinner, hamburgers as I remember it. I don't know if there were any concussions, but my dad never made a comment about my running down the mountain because of the coming storm.

I never ignored a lightning storm, even when I visited my grandparents in Westchester County. I found myself hanging back from windows during thunderstorms until I was well into late adulthood.

Back to the evening after the lunch with Maggie at the Oyster Bar. There was a humongous lightning storm that started up around five o'clock, which was not uncommon. It was not unlike a tropical climate where there were storms on a daily basis as humidity increased in the air. I remember going to see an opera at the Santa Fe Opera House during the month of August, which is squarely in the middle of the late summer monsoon—not dissimilar to the summer storms in India, Sri Lanka and the areas around the Indian subcontinent. Fierce daily storms, lots of flooding from rivers that overflow their banks—but creating a greening that is more or less the opposite of the New England autumn colors. In New Mexico, it rains almost every day around four or five o'clock. Since the Santa Fe Opera is an outdoor amphitheater, the storms can really be frightening. The Opera is roofed but open on the sides, so it could get wet in the orchestra seats. One particular night I remember seeing a production of Richard Strauss's "Elektra," where much of the second half of the opera was nearly overwhelmed by lightning and thunder as it sailed across the valley below Santa Fe. I found it frightening, just as I had found lightning scary since my experience in Mount Lassen when I was about sixteen.

At any rate, Maggie knocked on my door that evening. I was surprised when I opened the door, because I had no idea she was going to show up. At any rate, we had seen enough of each other that I wasn't startled, although I fleetingly thought I should call Mike to see if he wanted to join us. I didn't call him, although I sent a text telling him that Maggie was at the door. He texted me back that he was on his way over to my place from his apartment in Hell's Kitchen. Normally it would take half an hour at most.

Meanwhile, the sky came crashing down, rain lashing sideways in buckets full of water. My balcony was awash with rainwater as Maggie and I sat and drank scotch on the rocks from my grandfather's Waterford whiskey glasses in the Lismore pattern.

"These are beautiful," Maggie said sweetly.

"They were my grandfather's, and should be about a hundred years old." I told her that my grandmother thought they were juice glasses, but Waterford never made juice glasses. "They're whiskey glasses. I looked them up in the Waterford catalog online."

My family name is English, but over the centuries, a lot of Irish blood was added to the family gene pool. I found out some years back that the word "whisky," refers only to Scotch whisky. All other types of whisky are spelled with an "e" between the "k" and the "y." That includes Irish whiskey—and Irish whiskey glasses, even when they're being used to drink Scotch whisky. It's supposed to hold bourbon, too, but spelling in the United States is hit-and-miss, meaning sometimes it's one spelling, sometimes another. Probably some distillers were Irish and others weren't. But the Irish ones would have used the "e" spelling most likely. The Irish Gaelic word for whiskey is "*uisce beatha*" (pronounced like "ish-ka ba-ha"). When it's translated it comes out as "water of life," like *aqua vitae* in Latin, which has the same meaning: a liquid with a lot of alcohol in it, like *Poire William*, which is a very alcoholic after-dinner drink that's made with a whole pear inside a bottle that is essentially filled with the equivalent of vodka.

My phone vibrated in my back pocket, and there was a text saying that Mike was downstairs, and on his way up. The doorbell rang, and of course it was him.

"Hey, Maggie," he said to her across the living room. "Good to see you. Have any chance to think about what we were talking about at lunch yesterday?" He looked like he might be out of breath, like maybe he ran all the way from the subway station, and then up the stairs.

She gave a sort of sour smile, like she was trying to laugh but felt like crying. "I think if I had a best bud who was a cop and a lawyer, I might get into more trouble with my boys than I would if I shot somebody on the sidewalk."

"Sorry to hear that," Mike said. "Like I said, what I want to do is keep you out of trouble, not get you into it. Even if your bosses think of your business as being on the wrong side of the law, they have to be happy if it makes money—especially if it makes more money than they expect it to. What's business about if it's not about making money?"

"How am I going to make money for my bosses if I'm not running the business the way they want it run? They want pretty girls earning dirty money from guys with cash in their pockets."

"And everybody will be better off if nobody gets in trouble with the cops."

"How does that happen? You get on the take?"

"Nope. I don't want any of the money you earn. Don't want any of the money in the cash register. I want the cash tray to be full to the top when the bosses come by to pick up the day's take."

"So how does Cutie-Pie make money from Fatso the Plumber if she doesn't grab him between the legs and help him get rid of his load?"

"If it goes just a little different than you just described it, it can be almost completely legal. If Fatso the Plumber hands you a couple of twenties before he gets off, then when he gets off, nothing illegal happened. Cutie-Pie did what she wanted to do, and Fatso got what he wanted. You got the two twenties, and some of that went to the bosses. If you wait until Fatso gets off to get the money, then Fatso is paying for something illegal. It's that simple."

"Are you saying that if a girl gets a couple of bills in the restaurant—to tip the lady in the restroom—then what happens in the bedroom later on is okay?"

"What I'm saying is that it doesn't matter if it's okay or not, as long as Fatso isn't paying for something illicit. No harm, no foul. How many times have you been out with a man who paid for everything—the drinks, the food, the dessert, the limo to take you home? I bet you're really familiar with that, even getting some folding cash in your handbag. And no cop would be ready to accuse you of doing anything improper or illegal. I told you yesterday that there are ways to handle things where everybody's okay after it's over with. If Fatso shoots his load, and Cutie-Pie doesn't hold her hand out for payment, then you probably didn't do anything wrong. If Cutie-Pie wants a tip, and takes a couple of twenties from Fatso, then there's reason to say something illegal happened. Better a date than a trick, right?

I decided to put my two cents worth in with Mike. "Maggie, I went to a Catholic high school in California. Boys had classes separate from girls, although we had both sexes in the same school buildings. I took the Homecoming Queen to my Junior Prom as my date. I worked like a slave at a fried-chicken restaurant for months to pay for everything. I paid nearly one hundred dollars for a limo, another hundred dollars for an orchid corsage, and another hundred dollars for the tickets to the Prom. For me, at that time of my life, three hundred dollars was a fortune. When the limo dropped my date off at her house, I walked her to the front door. I kissed her in a way that I had to confess to a priest, and I felt her tits with my hands. Maybe it was a mortal sin, but there was nothing illegal about it, in spite of the three hundred dollars I spent on the evening."

"I don't know if you ever got felt up by a guy you were on a date with, but it wouldn't surprise me if you said you had. Guys do what guys do, and girls do what girls do. Is it always okay?" Mike asked Maggie. "Maybe yes, maybe no, but you learned a lot along the way. Some of it you learned helped you deal with guys while you were still young. Maybe some of what you did was a mortal sin. Maybe even when you killed your ex-husband without ever realizing who he was—maybe even that was a mortal sin, although it was clearly an accident, no matter how you look at it. But if it was an accident, it wasn't a crime, wasn't illegal. It was self-defense.

"There are almost always ways of doing things that stay on the right side of the law," Mike said. "I can help you with things like that. I'm not a priest and I can't forgive your sins, but I can help make sure you stay on the clean side of the law. That's important, just like your sins may have been important. But maybe staying legal is even more important than staying innocent of sin."

Maggie gave a shrug and hugged Mike. "You got me, for whatever that's worth," she said to him.

Chapter Twenty-four

The storm picked up the longer it went on. I kept thinking it would blow off to the east, which is the direction weather usually disappears to. Comes in from the west, goes away to the east. For some reason, there was no slowdown to the lightning and thunder, and no slacking of the rain, which continued to "fall" sideways due to the wind. The streets were awash with rainwater, and people walking outside were trying to protect themselves with inverted umbrellas.

There was a knock on the door (not a doorbell ring), and I opened the door. It was Maggie, soaking wet. I invited her in and handed her a beach towel to dry off with, and almost simultaneously sent Mike a text message saying that Maggie was back at my place.

"Wet outside, eh?" I asked.

"Very wet indeed," she said with a series of explanation points in her voice. "The clouds have opened up and it's like Noah's flood outside. If we're at all short on rainfall, we won't be by tomorrow," she said. "Reservoirs should be full to the top after this is over with. Wish we could send some of it to the western part of the country. It would be great if we could direct some of this water to Lake Mead," she said as she toweled off her hair. "I've been reading that it's at the lowest level since the Hoover Dam was finished in 1936. If this keeps up, agricultural water allotments are going to be cut back more than farmers will be able to cope with. We're gonna lose a lot of citrus from the Southwest—oranges and grapefruits. They're thirsty plants, so I hope they survive."

I offered her a heavy cotton bathrobe so she could sit down in the living room.

"Mind if I put on the news? I wonder if there's going to be an update on the weather. Maybe there's some clear weather that might push some of this storm over toward Nantucket—or even Bermuda, even though that's pretty far south of where we are geographically."

I told her not to worry about the upholstery, but to make herself comfortable. "Want a scotch on the rocks?" I asked her. "Maybe it'd keep your blood warm. I offered her one of my grandfather's whiskey glasses and waved a magnum of Dewar's blended scotch, thinking she might nod or just say yes. I was very aware that Mike wasn't there. Last thing I wanted was to have her toss down a couple of scotches and get high. She was a small person, probably not capable of handling any real amount of whiskey. She probably knew her limits, and I offered her a glass of red wine if she didn't want the scotch—*montepulciano d'abruzzo*—a tasty and easy to like red wine from the flat-lands to the east of Rome.

I took a chance, without Mike being there to referee. "Mike is an honest guy," I said. "If he tells you he can keep you safe, he means it. He has a Columbia University law degree, and he's been a gold shield NYPD detective for more than twenty years. He lives a stone's throw from the precinct office, and walks to work. I used to live about two blocks from where he lives in Hell's Kitchen, and I consider him a real and valuable friend. I'd trust him with anything I have."

No sooner had I finished my endorsement of Mike than there was another clap of thunder and the doorbell rang. It was Mike.

"A little wet out there?" I asked him, and handed him a fresh towel. "I was just about to have a finger or two of scotch. Seems like the right kind of weather for whisky."

"I'll join you in that," he said.

He reached over and patted Maggie on the shoulder. I poured him a couple of fingers of Dewar's blended scotch over a couple of ice cubes.

"That's a cute little glass," he said.

"My grandfather's whiskey glasses," I answered. "Probably a hundred years old. My grandmother thought they were juice glasses, but Waterford never made any juice glasses. They're whiskey glasses. I looked them up on the computer. Waterford is one of the most collected labels in the world. Maybe it's just a characteristic of the Irish diaspora after the Potato Famine that raged in Ireland from 1845 to 1852, and starved literally millions of Irish residents, and caused a huge emigration of Irish citizens from Ireland to the United States."

"I had no idea you were Irish," Mike said.

"I'm not," I said. "The family tradition is part German and part English. "The whiskey glasses are Irish—as all Waterford crystal is." I added, "Ancestry says I am a mish-mosh of Northern European genes, but Irish slipped in when millions of starving Irish fled to New York and New England just before the Civil War. My great-grandmother and great-great-grandmother were both full-blooded Irish. I have photos of both of them: Mary Haney was my grandfather's mom, and Mary Ann Clare was my grandfather's grandmother, who married Alphonso, the scion of the family in the mid-nineteenth century.

"Mary Ann's husband, Alphonso, was decades older than she was—he was a long-time bachelor with no romantic history that we've ever been able to find; no ex-wives and no children. He met Mary Ann on the road as he was driving a mule team from Grand Isle, Vermont, to Niagara Falls, New York. Alphonso was a nephew of Ethan Allen, who was a well-known name from the American Revolution—he surprised and captured the formerly British Fort Ticonderoga (at the south end of Lake Champlain on the border of Vermont and New York not far from the Hudson River and Albany) with the aid of the Green Mountain Boys (a small group of Vermonters; Vermont means Green Mountain). The Allen home is still in Deerfield, Massachusetts, on the border of Vermont. It is a museum, and can be toured by visitors. Deerfield is primarily known for the Deerfield Academy, founded in 1797 and still one of the oldest secondary schools in the United States.

"Ethan's daughter, Frances Margaret 'Fanny' Allen, was the founder of the first order of Catholic nuns in the United States, after she was sent to Montreal for safety during the Revolution. Ethan Allen himself was Protestant, but his daughter was the first New Englander to become a Roman Catholic, a legacy from the formerly French areas called Nouvelle France (today called Nova Scotia), following the ethnic cleansing of the Acadians ('Cajuns' when they found their way to Louisiana) when the British took over Canada after France lost the Seven Years War with Britain, known as the 'French and Indian War' in America, because many of the Native American ethnic nations like the Iroquois were allies of the French."

"Sorry to circle back around just because we're having a thunderstorm," Mike said to Maggie. "Hugo is a civilian criminalist with the NYPD—he's not a cop, not a detective, doesn't carry a shield or a weapon. He can't arrest anyone, and seldom gets involved with criminal cases, unless he has independent knowledge that helps the detectives figure out what happened to whom, and when it happened. Hugo and I were neighbors for years, and now we've become good friends. His colleagues, Ruth and Gabriele—whom you've met—have skills that come in handy from time to time. And keep in mind that virtually everything that Hugo does for the NYPD is what they call *pro bono*. In other words, he doesn't get paid for the work he does. He doesn't get a salary or benefits, and usually be doesn't get reimbursed for expenses he incurs. The same is true of Gabriele and Ruth. Gabriele doesn't get paid when one or more of us has dinner at his restaurant—even though it's one of the most in-demand eateries in the entirety of Manhattan. Gabriele's restaurant pays for everything—drinks, wine, desserts, aperitifs, pasta, fresh fish—you name it. The NYPD doesn't foot any of the bills.

"I grew up in a lower middle-class family," Mike said to Maggie. "I worked my way through school, and I have climbed up from being a beat officer to being a lieutenant Detective. I don't want to brag, but I'm one of only three lieutenant Detectives in the entire NYPD—and the only one officed in a Manhattan precinct. The other two lieutenant Detectives are officed at One Police Plaza, and report directly to the Police Commissioner. They seldom get involved in day-to-day police business. One of them is primarily assigned to the Media and Public Relations Department on the same floor as the Police Commissioner. You may have seen them on television from time to time."

Chapter Twenty-five

The rain kept up, and the thunder didn't fade away either. The three of us—Mike, Maggie and me—stuck together for most of the evening. Mike gave Maggie some background on what Mike's career had been.

"Time was," he said, "when vice was most common in what we now call the Theater District." He paused and added, "Eighth Avenue was called the Minnesota Strip for years. Why? Because every day, buses pulled up at the Port Authority and discharged young girls—and sometimes good-looking young boys—who were swallowed up in the flesh trade almost immediately. The girls became streetwalkers right away, and picked up pimps who helped them out sometimes, and sometimes beat them to a pulp."

He stared into the ceiling of my apartment. "The boys had the same future as the girls, but they had to get used to same-sex relationships. Some of them took dance lessons, and a few even got chorus-boy jobs in musical comedies. It wasn't like any of these kids found themselves in a brothel or whorehouse. Nobody wanted to provide a total amateur hooker—boy or girl—with a free place to work. Some pimps let apartments where some of the cuter kids hung out. And some of those kids found their clients based on what they used to call 'agencies,' which acted like other kinds of agencies. Some were representing young actors or singers, but most of them were just sending kids out for sex based on phone calls that came in because of flyers that were left at bars and low-class restaurants all over the west side.

"Those were the bad old days," he said. "It's not like things are a lot better now. Kids and young people are still treated like slaves, for instance." He looked up and rolled his eyes. "Healthcare is virtually non-existent. If a hooker gets syphilis, he or she is going to get an antibiotic to get rid of the infection, but if that same kid gets pneumonia or bronchitis, the pimp's idea of healthcare is the Emergency Room at the closest hospital. That, unfortunately, may mean an overnight stay in the waiting room with a roaring fever, and by the time morning has come, there may have been no headway made at all. The kid may be as sick as he or she was the night before. That may mean another night in the same ER with the same result—no result at all.

"The truth of the matter is that when you take a kid or a youngster to a hospital without any insurance, they aren't going to get any help beyond the kinds of medicine that the state will pay for. If a young girl is pregnant and getting ready to deliver a baby, the ER will respond with real help. Nobody wants a dead baby or a dead mom, and no ER is going to let that happen without trying damned hard to make the outcome better."

Mike looked really troubled. "Health insurance is a real thing. Kids with no insurance need to qualify for Medicaid as soon as possible. But you can't just walk into the ER with no insurance at all and expect to get modern medical treatment." He looked down at the floor. "And if the ER thinks you have more than one infection, they may admit you and take a pint of blood for tests. You may end up taking all kinds of antibiotics and antivirals, with almost zero follow-up."

He started to wring his hands. "Remember that healthcare people—including ER people—want to help, but they can't help without a budget most of the time. They can't admit you to a hospital without some means of paying for the treatments. Hospitals don't get paid for delivering healthcare when there's no insurance. If you're a bleeder or have a fever, you may stand the chance of a snowball in Hell of getting some help. But if you give up and leave, forget it. You're more likely to be picked up from the sidewalk or the subway, and you may or may not be salvageable at that point.

"So look back at the pimp, who doesn't make a lot of money to start off with. If he wants to help his prettiest girl—the one with the biggest tits—he may be able to strike a deal with the ER. That may mean he writes a check or hands them a credit card that will pay some start-up costs. It doesn't take a lot of time to use up a lot of money if you're doing lung x-rays, MRIs of the gut, or major blood work-ups that might lead to contagious diseases."

Maggie was starting to cry.

"Look, Maggie, I'm not trying to upset you," he said. "If you take on a bunch of seventeen-year-old hookers, you may end up with major healthcare issues faster than you ever thought possible. And if you think the bosses are going to help out, you're wrong. Those girls are more likely to be shot than to be healed in a hospital. Once they're shot, they have a better chance at healthcare, because they'd be victims of a crime—and that means their bills can be covered with normal budgetary avenues. Every state makes ways for real emergencies to get paid for. If you're in a car crash, you're going to get help. If you're in a fire, same thing."

All of a sudden, the sky began to clear and the rain stopped fairly abruptly. I turned on the TV to one of the major networks. There was a weather report that was up to date, and said that things were clearing up, and that tomorrow was likely to be warmer and less rainy, with a good chance of some fair weather during the afternoon the next day.

"I know we need to lighten up," Mike said. "I still think I can help you stay on the side of the angels if that's what you want. I can pull some strings sometimes. Maybe I can even help with an ER that's overcrowded and has no beds available. I know some doctors who might be able to help here and there. Try not to worry a lot. If you want to help people, then that's what you want to do. I can help you do that. I can't solve all the world's problems, but I can do a lot to help when other people don't know how. I know some charities that can help. Believe me, a cop with a good reputation can work some wonders with people who want to help people who need help in a big way.

"Go home while the rain has stopped. Have a drink of something and put yourself to bed. Think about what we've talked about, and remember that I really want to help. I'm not Jesus Christ, but I'm trying to make the world a better place. And I still know how to keep you on the right side of the law. That's important. Remember that."

Maggie stood up and held out her hand to me. We shook and she waved at Mike as she left. I didn't know what, if anything, had been accomplished. But Mike looked like he had just had an ice cream sundae.

"You think things are going to work out?" I asked him.

He nodded. "We've got a better chance than we did at the Oyster Bar yesterday."

As if Mother Nature was making a comment, there was a streak of lightning and a speedy clap of thunder.

"You never know what's going to happen next in weather like this," Mike said. "But I'm going to head home anyway. This time I may be able to make it without getting soaked to the skin."

I poured a dirty vodka and turned the television back on to CNN. Once a news junkie, always a news junkie. As I watched the screen, I found myself going back over the morbid talk about young hookers trying to get healthcare help hanging out in some big, dirty, loud Emergency Room someplace. Depressing, but if Mike can help out, there's nobody I'd trust more. Mike taking care of scared little hookers—still people, still needy, still worth helping, no matter what the situation—whether they're burning up with fever or bleeding from having been assaulted in some grotesque way.

Chapter Twenty-six

Meanwhile, Grace Kim had already started the early stages of basic training for her time in the Police Academy. She'd started, I later learned, with daily yoga lessons, and added on weight lifting at the local gym (which gave her a huge discount as a potential police officer registered in the Academy). Instead of the slim, pretty Korean girl we'd seen at the May Ling Day Spa, Kim was increasingly a woman with strong upper arms—big biceps, big triceps, very well developed deltoids. When she went for her COVID-19 vaccinations, the nurse commented on her arms.

"Hey, you have real deltoids, sister. That makes it easy to get the needle in your arm. And I bet you can hardly feel it when the needle goes into the skin," she said. "Most of the deltoids I see are on guys. Nice to see a young woman who's working out these days."

When I saw Grace, I almost didn't recognize her. She looked two or three inches taller than she had been the last time I saw her, right after she jumped on board Mike's train to make her a promising young cop instead of a combination hooker and gangstah gal. Not only did she look taller, she looked prettier, and had almost no Asian features that I could discern. I wondered whether she had been wearing make-up when I first met her—something accentuating the almond shape of her eyes. Hard to tell looking backward in my memory that wasn't the clearest in the first place. A lot of Asians don't have "Asian" eyes, after all—particularly if what you're looking for in Asians is what's called the "monolid."

A lot of Asians have a crease that divides the upper eyelid into two parts—rather like a Caucasian eyelid. Eastern Asians tend to have these monolids, and are frequently difficult to differentiate from Europeans—especially eastern Europeans who may have genes from the Mongols who owned all of Asia and eastern Europe for centuries after Genghis Khan's invasions of the mid-thirteenth century. It's not uncommon to see eyes in Russia, Poland, or the Ukraine that have a distinct Asian shape. These people are sometimes called Tatars, and take pride in their Asian blood. Historically Tatars are a Turkic ethnicity that was part of Genghis Khan's confederation nearly eight hundred years ago. Many Tatars maintained their Asian appearance; Russians frequently thought of them as a different race—fierce and reminiscent of the Mongol Hordes. The name Tatar was also used for food, but usually spelled and pronounced Tartare or Tartar; "steak tartare" or "tartar sauce" are examples.

Mostly Grace was wearing police blue top to bottom. She wasn't graduated from the Academy, so she didn't have a shield, but she had the patches on her chest and shoulder. She had the shiny brim on her hat, and a metallic NYPD insignia above the brim that gave her the look of a street cop. No weapon, but a lot of cops don't have a weapon that's worn where it can be seen. Nobody would be able to tell that Mike di Saronno was carrying a revolver, because it is always holstered under his arm inside his suit jacket.

On the whole, I was super-impressed when I saw Grace. She looked like a film star—far too attractive to just be a cop. Far more attractive than she had ever been when she was on the wrong side of the law. I found myself going back over Mike's conversations with Maggie Landover when I just looked at Grace, but I never mentioned that to her.

I waved to her, and she waved back to me—she was standing outside one of the interrogation rooms on the second floor of Mike's office building. I noticed that she was drinking a paper cup of coffee, and walked over to her. She was standing feet from the coffee machine, and I had a quarter in my pocket, so I got a cup of black coffee myself.

For some reason, if there had been an accent in her speech when I met her, I didn't recall it, but I was impressed with how "American" she sounded when she talked to me. I told her some of the details of Mike's and my discussion with Maggie Landover, emphasizing how Mike wanted to work with Maggie to keep her out of trouble.

Grace didn't take very seriously Mike's idea that it was possible to operate a whorehouse legally.

"You mean if a guy pays before he meets the girl, it's legal?"

I nodded. "Paying after sex makes it criminal." I paused and then added, "At least that's what I took from what Mike was telling Maggie. And the way he put it, it sounded like it made sense. He kept saying the problem Maggie should worry about was keeping the girls healthy. If they got pregnant, the hospitals would take care of them. If they had syphilis or gonorrhea, the Emergency Rooms would help them. But if they got something common, like pneumonia, trying to get healthcare without insurance was nearly impossible. If a girl was a victim of a crime—like she got beaten up by a John—then the ER would treat her as the victim of a crime. If you're seriously hurt in the commission of a crime, you're covered by the state or the federal government."

"And you believe that?" Grace asked me, implying that if I believed it, I was crazy.

"I had a friend in my twenties—long time ago—who tried to kill himself," I said. "He took a bunch of pills that he thought would kill him. When somebody called 911 and the EMTs came, there was no question. He was totally unconscious and his pulse was almost not there at all. Basically dead." I waited and then continued, "He was the victim of a crime."

She rolled her eyes.

"Suicide is a crime," I said, "even if it's something you do to yourself. You're covered if you try to kill yourself. I visited my friend in that hospital for a couple of weeks, and they had a psychiatrist on his case. I don't remember how long they kept him in the hospital, but it was a long time. When they let him out, he went back to his work in a publishing house as an editor. No bills, no legal problems. Never served a day in jail. That may not make everything Mike said true, but I know what happened to my friend, and how he got the best Beverly Hills medical attention, in spite of not having much insurance."

"I gotta go to law school to make sense of that," she said. "If Mike tells me what you just told me, I have to say I'd probably believe him." She looked askance at me. "But I think if he told me what you told me, he'd be telling me something more, not just what you said."

Grace wanted another coffee. Mike showed up and bought her one.

"You wouldn't believe what Hugo just told me that you told Maggie," she said.

"He told you I could keep the girls at the spas out of trouble. Not permanently, not all the time, but most of the time, and in most situations. I spent nearly five years in Columbia Law School, and I've been a cop since your mother was a teenager." Grace stared at him. "I know my goddamn way around. You listen to me and you're gonna get by most problems without getting in trouble."

"And what happens if I go to the PC and tell him one of his detectives is protecting my girls?"

"Well, he should applaud, because the more we keep people out of trouble, the better we're doing our jobs." I stared at her. "Okay, maybe he'd want to dive deeper into what I was doing to help you. But once I explained to him what I was advising you to do, he'd shake my hand— and want to arrest whoever the bosses are—maybe Chuy and his guys. The bosses had no intention to keep the girls out of trouble, and they're the ones who ought to be in the slammer."

Grace waved at a young cop who had just walked up the stairs. He came over, and it was obvious that he had a detective's shield on his uniform.

"Hey, Dave," Mike said to the young man. "How's tricks? Did Grace here tell you that I've been trying to keep some hookers out of trouble?"

Dave smiled broadly and looked at Grace. "You didn't think that Mike's spiel was new, did you?"

"I thought it was bullshit," she said. "And I still think that."

"I'll grant you that a cop who works to keep people from violating the law seems a little off the wall. Cops are supposed to arrest the bad guys, put them in the slammer. Right?" He turned silent. "Except when it comes to Mike di Saronno," he said. "Mike was born to keep people out of trouble. That includes people on the wrong side of the law, but not the bad guys themselves.

"Mike's not after the kid that steals a bag of chips." Dave leaned back against the wall. "He doesn't want to trap people in those interrogation rooms. He wants to save their skins—as often as possible." Pause. "He for sure doesn't want to sweep up all the hookers. Hell, if he did that, they'd just be worse off than they were when they were working girls."

"So it's just about saving the whores?" Grace asked.

"Not at all. It's about saving the people who aren't causing any real harm. No shoplifters. No guys drinking from a hip flask to get high. No kids rolling marijuana cigarettes. Nobody jumping subway turnstiles."

"What does that leave?" Grace asked.

"It means he wants to get the guys with guns, the ones who stick a knife under your neck and grab your handbag. He wants to lock up the drunks who drive cars or ride motorcycles the wrong way on the parkways. He wants to grab the guys who snatch little kids from the back seats of cars, and then hold them for ransom."

"Í don't get you," she said.

"If Mike was the king, he'd go after everybody that hurts other people, everybody that steals what you need to make dinner for the kids, everybody that uses your debit card to empty out your checking account."

"So basically he's gonna be in favor of giving a free pass to people who sleep on the street, people who litter by throwing away burger wrappers on the street. He's gonna chase after every young scallywag who tries to sell his girlfriend's sex, or who hooks kids on cocaine or crystal meth. He hates people who peddle machetes and guns, but he doesn't give a shit about guys who swipe a pack of smokes because they're hungry and don't have any money." Dave stroked his chin.

"Watch Mike sometime," he said. "Watch him buy dinner for somebody that obviously didn't have anything for lunch. He's single and has no kids. All the kids on the street are his kids. He puts out stacks of books on his stoop for kids to take home and read." Pause. "Mike's no saint, but he's no sinner either. He wants to help people. That's why the heck he became a cop. Cops help people. If you keep that in mind, you'll be the kind of cop that everybody in New York loves."

Grace smiled. "I promise to listen when Mike tells me something," she said. "Every goddamn time he tells me something. He straightened me out. I'm gonna pay that forward, and save someone else every time I get a chance to. I hope Maggie does the same—she's smarter and nicer than me anyway. I wanna be more like Maggie when I grow up. Wait and see!"

Chapter Twenty-seven

I found myself more and more puzzled by what seemed like Mike di Saronno's split personality. I knew he wasn't schizophrenic; didn't add two plus two and get five. But I found it difficult to listen to his palaver about keeping people out of legal trouble when he clearly was a law enforcement officer. I knew better than to doubt Mike's intentions. His intentions were similar to my own. I had no wish to put people in jail, although I had no particular feeling that jail would help them go "straight" if they were guilty. Jail is punishment or penitence—not intended in the USA to be rehabilitation. After all, most prisoners are eventually released back into society, and then a large percentage of those released end up back in prison again.

But when I saw him cozying up to Maggie Landover after she took over the day spa business that her son was clearly involved in, I found myself wondering whether I knew the man as well as I thought I did after all the years and cases we had worked on together. I always thought of him as a guy with a stiff upper lip and a strong backbone. Yes, I knew he had a law degree—from Columbia Law no less—but I had never heard him defend the little people—the kids who swiped bags of chips from the bodegas, the girls who shared their bodies with their boyfriends—and frequently ended up single moms as a result.

From what I gathered, he had been telling Maggie that he could help the girls at the day spas stay out of the way of legal problems. One of the key ideas was to get paid in advance. If a girl gave a man a hand-job (often called a "happy ending") and then got a "tip," it could look illegal, like sex for money. But if the same girl picked up a couple of

Jacksons (twenty-dollar bills) before the massage started, with no negotiating afterward for tips or bonuses, the sex was hard to prove as a money ploy. How was it different from a little nookie after a high school date? The boy pays for a nice dinner and a movie, and the girl balances it out by dropping her panties and/or loosening her bra (if she's wearing one). How is it different from a grocery shopper eating some of the produce while they shop? You gotta try the apples before you buy them, right?

I trust Mike di Saronno completely. There's not a phony bone in his body. If he tells you he's going to do something, he means it. He's been doing what he's doing for more than two decades, and he seldom promises things he can't deliver. If he told Maggie that he could keep her whores from getting in trouble, I tend to believe him. He's not going to break the law while he's doing it either. I'm theoretically an employee of the NYPD myself—put there by Mike after I worked with him on a few homicide cases. I don't claim to know what he knows. I think I have some good instincts about how to figure out who did what to whom—and I think I've been more than a little helpful to Mike and the NYPD on a bunch of cases.

Ruth's father was a rabbi at a wealthy synagogue when she was growing up—she is the only girl with four brothers, so she's up-to-date on sports and business. There are no two people in New York City with better instincts than Gabriele and Ruth—a gay Italian guy and a widowed Jewish woman with one of the broadest groups of rich-people acquaintances I've ever come across. Every time I've tried to get in touch with somebody famous or otherwise difficult to meet, Ruth has come through by calling on people she knows—she has a memory like an elephant, and never seems to forget a face or a name.

It also happens more often than you would think that Gabriele and Ruth know many of the same people. Ruth, for instance, has been a member of the Opera League at the Metropolitan Opera for decades—a real opera fan, and hugely knowledgeable about individual operas. She knows the names of the arias in the language they were written in. She knows the music of well-known and little-known operas. If you want to know the name of something, just ask her. Same goes for the hundreds of other Opera League members whom she considers close friends. Opera League members show up on Monday evenings every week during the opera season—always in black tie attire. Ruth has a seemingly endless panoply of evening gowns—enough that she never seems to wear the same gown twice—and they don't all go to floor, by the way. They're just all fancy and expensive-looking. I used to go with her to some Monday nights (always black tie) at the Opera League, and took a lot of flak from her for not wearing patent leather shoes to match the satin lapels and pants stripes of the outfit. You don't get invited to the Metropolitan Museum Costume Gala every year easily. Ruth has been an invited member on the red carpet for the last two decades at least—longer than Anna Wintour and her famous sunglasses, as far as I can tell.

By the same token, the number of overlap people who go to Ora di Pranzo and also belong to the Opera League is astonishing. First of all, Ora di Pranzo is not only Italian, it's run by cousins who are both Neapolitan (from Naples). Are they opera fans? Is the Pope Catholic? The Metropolitan Opera is basically an Italian Opera house. These days they do Wagner in German, but it hasn't been all that long since *Tristan und Isolde* was sung in Italian—and so was "Boris Godunov," which for years was sung in more than one language during the same performance at the Met. When Feodor Chaliapin sang Boris in Russian at the Met, all the other characters sang in Italian. There are famous recordings of Maria Callas singing Isolde's death scene in Italian—the piece known as "Liebestod" around the world ("Love Death"). That recording was made in Venice at a production when Callas took over the role at the last minute—and she learned it in Italian because she spoke Italian fluently (although she was Greek ethnically, she grew up in Brooklyn, which was dominantly Italian for years upon years).

There are lots of puzzles in the world. Gabriele Cortese is a puzzle inside a puzzle. I first met him when he was a "person of interest" in what might have been a homicide. The victim was a musician who lived in a very posh apartment above Carnegie Hall. He was also gay, and Gabriele had developed a personality that was a sex worker. He later told me that he came to the United States via Florida, where he landed as a waiter on a huge ocean liner. He had grown up on the island of Capri, but moved to Barcelona as a teenager, and almost immediately married a teenage girl, who promptly got pregnant.

The boy was born with Gabriele's good looks, and his dad had him working out bigtime as soon as he was able to walk around the apartment they lived in. Gabriele was straying away from waiting tables, not staying with the ocean liners he signed onto—one of which was Norwegian, and the rest of which were Italian—one Genoese and one Venetian. All three of them were flagged in Liberia, which is a major international home port for ocean liners. Hard to trace.

Anyway, Maria, Gabriele's wife and the mother of Giuseppe, (or Beppe, which is a normal nickname for Giuseppe, the Italian version of what in English is Joseph) sailed away on a Dutch ocean liner, and was never heard from again. She was headed for Bali and French Polynesia, and apparently got there, but never reported back. A few short months later, Beppe fell off the roof of the school he had been enrolled in. It had to do with a soccer ball that went over the edge of the building. Anyway, he went through the roof of the building next door and was killed on the spot. Gabriele's passport said his name was Rafaele (Raphael, also an archangel like Gabriel)—had the same feast day on the Catholic calendar of October 29 and known widely as the Feast of Saint Michael and All Angels, Michael being the most famous archangel, and of course the one who threw Lucifer out of Heaven and into Hell. Whether his "real" name was Rafaele or Gabriele, or even Michele, which, like the other archangels, has an extra syllable on the end of his name, but it's usually not pronounced, just to be clear, though his actual or assumed name has no part in the rest of Gabriele's story.

When I met him, he was known as Rafe Aker, not particularly Italian-sounding, but it matched his passport, because the "Italian" version of his name was Rafaele Avernetto, as I saw his outdated passport years later. The fact that he was a "person of interest" in a homicide persuaded him to change his name to Gabriele (another archangel, which kept his feast day on the same day, which probably consoled his mother, who still lived on Capri). Where the name of Cortese came from, I have no idea; maybe a family name from someone else related to him. Cortese is a common Italian name, and has an etymological relationship to "courtesy" or "courtly."

He dropped the sex worker position totally, and went into the restaurant business with his cousin Dante di Benedetto), and almost immediately had a homerun. From the first day it opened, Ora di Pranzo was sold out. Want a reservation? Plan ahead three or four months or give up.

My friendship with him dated from the homicide, which I was working on with Mike di Saronno. I liked him. He's easy to like, which is probably half the reason for his restaurant success (the other half is probably his extraordinary good looks and freakishly friendly smile. I've watched rooms full of people—men and women—follow Gabriele with their eyes when he walks into a room. He's always been an eye-catcher. Even Ruth agrees on that. "He's sexy no matter who you are looking at him," she said to me in London one time.

He told me at one point that he had married a lesbian who was American, and that's how he got his US Green Card and eventual citizenship. She was an Ohio native, and they divorced after Betsy (that was her name) had a baby boy, Michael or Mike, with the last name of Cortese. He did well with Ora di Pranzo, and upgraded his living style to a nice apartment on the Brooklyn Heights Promenade, one of the most expensive and gorgeous places in all five boroughs. He seemed to have no interest in a family, a wife, or a guy to live with. He has always been super-attached to his cousin, Dante. Their first restaurant was destroyed in an explosion that was related to a natural gas pipe that had been improperly (and illegally) installed—and blew up the whole building. That place was near Madison Square Park, and the new Ora di Pranzo is in SoHo. No matter where they were, there were lines waiting around the block to get in, even if just to elbow their way up to the bar.

Chapter Twenty-eight

Just as I've always thought of Gabriele as my son, I've always thought of Ruth as my sister. I actually have two sons and two sisters, so I didn't need another one of either. My sons were from my second marriage, and I never had a close relationship with either one of them. I sent birthday cards and gifts, and Christmas gifts every year, but I haven't seen them, other than in the kinds of photos that arrive in Christmas cards, in years and years.

My sisters both live in the South, which is where my mother was from originally. We always kidded my mom when we were kids because of her Southern accent (actually her accent was Texan, although it just sounded drawly Southern to most Americans—especially people from the Northeast and the Far West). When my kids were young, they used to kid me when I would call my mom on the phone. I would pick up her accent almost immediately, and it made my kids laugh at me when I talked.

Ruth and I have been close friends forever. We were matched up by a former client of mine—a stock brokerage financial research analyst. When he found out that I was divorced, and Ruth was dating a married man who apparently had no plan to divorce—he decided that she and I would be an ideal couple.

Not.

I had been married twice, divorced twice. Like I say to most people, "three strikes and you're out." Ruth had four brothers and didn't need men in her life. I tended to be a "best friend" type of guy for her, and when she and her somewhat elderly and rich boyfriend broke up (he went back to his wife, whom he never planned to leave anyway), we both briefly considered what might happen if we had started dating. Didn't happen, but we did become business partners. I hired her from time to time to help with my Sports PR company, and then I convinced her to volunteer with the NYPD like I had done to become a civilian criminalist—which put me on the same level approximately as the people who put together sketches of people of interest, people described by crime victims, etc. Not police, no badge, no weapon, but the ability to put X and Y together to find the person whodunnit, as they used to say.

Over time, and over numerous shared cases, Mike di Saronno put a real value on the trio of Hugo, Gabriele and Ruth. We were able to put together logic that tended to point to the person or people the police were after. Fortunately for me, I get the lion's share of the praise. On two occasions, I've been promoted, so that now I am a civilian criminalist Level 3, which theoretically means I should be getting a monthly check from the NYPD. My original agreement specified that I would work *pro bono*—in other words, at no charge. The term implies that it is a charitable effort—that I give my efforts to the NYPD for no cost. But the two boosts up to Level 3 means I'll be getting about one thousand dollars per month, prior to withholding taxes, etc.

I'm retired, so I'm not sure how that would work out. I've been with the same CPA for several decades. He tells me that I should get the entire one thousand dollars per month, especially because I haven't been submitting expenses over the years. I should get my expenses reimbursed over the past five years at least. My CPA is ready to submit years of expenses, plus enough expenses for the current year to outdistance any deductions I might otherwise have to put up with. That includes a portion of my telephone and internet costs, not to mention my software expenses, such as the annual ninety-nine dollar fee to Microsoft to give me the use of Office 360, which includes Outlook 10, which I need to communicate with Mike di Saronno. I also have to pay annual fees to GoDaddy relative to Microsoft software, and something like two hundred and fifty per month for my cellphone and internet access. Without those, I would be useless to Mike or anyone else at the NYPD.

But whether I was being paid or not—expense-reimbursed or

not—I've never enjoyed any part of my life as much as I have enjoyed working with Mike. It's frankly not usually difficult to figure out who shot somebody. There's physical evidence lots of times—shell casings, fingerprints, eye-witness testimony, and sometimes even recollections by the victim, who frequently saw the perpetrator prior to being shot. The challenges came with homicides that could have been accidental—not just as simple as a bullet through the lung.

One of the cases I worked on—in fact the one where I met Gabriele—involved a fairly famous musician who flew out a window of his apartment and landed on the pavement of 7th Avenue.

Splat!

Could have been homicide (if he was pushed or thrown out the window, for example). Could have been suicide. Could have been an accident. Nobody heard a scream or any kind of noise from when he catapulted out the window. He'd been smoking hashish—as it turned out, mixed with some PCP, which was notorious for making people think they could fly. I could testify to that, because I had partaken of the same drug mixture (which also included some LSD just for good measure), and very nearly tried to fly off the third balcony at the Metropolitan Opera that evening—but I was eighty-sixed from the Met instead. It took me nearly three days to recover from the "high" I was suffering from. "High" is a piss-poor word for what happened to me. I was dizzy for days, felt like throwing up constantly, and had several injections of "downers" over the period of time that a friend had a medical doctor take care of me after the Met threw me out.

Nothing about that potential homicide was a slam-dunk. As it turned out, the musician had two potential male sexual partners in the apartment with him when it happened—and either of them could have been part of what happened (or both of them).

Just for good measure, it turned out to have been an accident. He apparently did think he could fly, and he jumped out the window (which is also why he never screamed—he was flying after all). But we could have tried to pin the whole thing on several different people, not least the two potential sex partners who were in the apartment that evening. They had nothing to do with it whatsoever, although it was this case where I happened to meet Gabriele Cortese, who had been there as a sex worker—he was hiding in a closet while I was there that evening for a quick smoke of hashish (no word of any other drugs being mixed in).

Imagine what could have happened if Gabriele had been nailed for the man's death. First of all, Gabriele would have been in jail for a long time, instead of becoming one of the most successful restaurant owners in Manhattan. Second, he and I would never have become friends. Third, Gabriele might have stayed in the sex business (which he didn't—the whole thing scared the shit out of him, and he quit that very same night).

That whole thing could easily have been evidence of Mike di Saronno's thesis about people being not guilty even when it appeared that they might be. For one thing, I myself had the same mixture of drugs in my system that the musician had, which could easily have proven that I was at the scene of the crime when it happened. I wasn't in fact at the scene of the crime when he flew out the window. I had left with my friend from California to go to a special performance of "*La Boheme*" at the Metropolitan Opera—and had his testimony (and the usher's outraged testimony from the Met) that I hadn't been within a mile of what happened when the man hit the street. I tried to tell the police detective who was questioning me that I wasn't even there—he was Mike di Saronno, whom I knew from the neighborhood where I lived, but had no idea he was a cop at that point. It took the usher to convince Mike that I was at the opera house when Hubert the musician had died on 7[th]t Avenue. There was no reason to think the usher wasn't telling the truth—and Mike understood that right away. The usher wasn't even a regular employee of the opera—he was ushering in exchange for a seat at "*La Boheme*," which happened to be featuring operatic superstars Luciano Pavarotti (tenor) and Mirella Freni (lead soprano) that night (it was a special night, much higher ticket prices than usual—it was also the week between Christmas and New Year's, which meant the house was totally packed each night for the entire week).

I was totally convinced that Mike knew what he was doing. It would have been impossible for him to have jumped to the right conclusion without the real detective clues he managed to scrape up. It also helped that Ruth was a Trustee of Carnegie Hall, which was where the musician jumped out the window. She was the one who got access to the apartment where it happened—and where Mike found Dante di Benedetto's keys on the floor of the bedroom closet—the keys to a not-new Lamborghini Countach that had been a gift from Hubert, who had been Dante's boyfriend for several years. It had been parked in a garage across the street from the apartment building, and managed to testify to Dante's innocence, since Dante managed to get his car out of the garage with a duplicate set of keys that were in his coat pocket at the time.

I wrote about this case in a book called *The Monteverdi Manuscript*. The title had to do with the actual perpetrator who mixed the "extra" drugs into the hashish that night. He also had created a fake manuscript of "lost" music by the early seventeenth-century composer who is reputed to have invented the format of dramatic opera, among other things.

Monteverdi was said to have written nearly sixty operas over his years, but only three have survived the centuries, with all three getting regularly performed at the great opera houses of the world. If there had been a real manuscript, it would have been worth millions—but of course, it wasn't real, so it wasn't worth the paper it was printed on. And the counterfeiter ended up with a long sentence of community service at his home in California (he had been a professor of mine at UCLA—and had also plugged a bullet into the wall of my apartment shooting upward from the street below). He pleaded guilty to mixing the drugs with the hashish, but swore he never knew what the drugs were—just that he had bought them blind from a street vendor a few doors down 57th Street from Carnegie Hall. The drug dealer had never been identified, but it was rumored that he had also been a student at UCLA at one point—and that he had been an extra in a number of Hollywood-made movies over the years.

Chapter Twenty-nine

The next evening was another Hudson Valley thunderstorm—one that lasted hours and hours, and that dumped several inches of water in addition to tens of thousands of volts of lightning and thunder. Maggie showed up at my door as though she had been paged when the thunder started. I invited her in when the doorbell rang and I found her standing in the hallway.

"How about a scotch?" I asked her. "It'll help you put up with the thunder and lightning. Just stay away from the windows as long as there's lightning."

Oddly enough, shortly after Maggie showed up, the doorbell rang again, and it was Chuy, accompanied by Mike di Saronno. Pretty soon there was scotch being consumed around the room, including by me. I'm a sucker for blended scotch, and particularly for Dewar's blended scotch, which is the brand preferred in the Business cabin of international American Airlines flights overseas.

I happened to fly to London pretty regularly, because I had opened an office there after having made the New York office profitable over the first six months of my tenure there. New York and London were media capitals of the world, so the Sports PR operation had plenty of work to do. After all, sports stars were real stars, and endorsements were worth lots of money from companies like Nike, Coca-Cola and various brands of automobiles, including a variety of sports cars. We managed to make a fair amount of money on Corvette television ads, since we were able to collect ten percent of the net on TV commercials.

Anyway, I flew well over one hundred thousand miles per year for several years, and became what American Airlines called "Executive Platinum" as a frequent flyer. It meant that I was upgraded pretty regularly and predictably to Business Class when I booked an Economy seat (Economy was an attractive term used for "Cattle Class," with skimpy food and liquor, even flying across the ocean at night). I always flew on the plane leaving at midnight from JFK to Heathrow. Given the five-hour time change and the seven-hour flight, it meant we landed at about noon the next day. By the time I spent two hours getting into London, my hotel room was always ready for check-in—and frequently had a good bottle of red wine sitting on the side table by my bed.

Nothing makes it feel more like home than a good bottle of wine. I never met a good red wine that I didn't enjoy, particularly if it came from the southwest of France or Italy. My favorite glass of red in most restaurants was *montepulciano d'abruzzo*, a delicious but affordable everyday wine from an area about an hour east of Rome itself. There are actually two wines in Italy called *montepulciano*: the one from Abruzzi (called Abruzzo in the wine name—a singular version of the name of the area, which is a plural for no particular reason that I ever knew. The other is from a town called Montepulciano in the southern part of Tuscany (one of the wine heavens in the world). The Tuscan wine is called by the fancy name of *Vino Nobile de Montepulciano*, and usually costs something like three times the price of the Abruzzi wine of the same name.

One of the great things in a businessperson's life is a real frequent-flyer program. I had been part of an ad-agency team that invented the AAdvantage program, the first frequent flyer program ever invented. It set the airline industry on its ear for months—even years. It was the first way to show business flyers that they were valued customers. Business flyers were usually charged more than economy flyers, and resented it—especially having to sit between an adult and his/her children, who clearly had paid a small fraction of the fare charged to a business flyer, who frequently had to make a reservation at the last minute, and almost always wanted an aisle or window seat (not the dreaded "middle" seat).

The AAdvantage program made it possible for business flyers to upgrade to Business or even to First Class by using accumulated mileage traveled on American Airlines and what they called the "One World" group of airlines, which included British Airlines, KLM and Qantas (in case you were traveling to Australia). I managed to fly to London almost monthly, which gave me not only high mileage, but bonus mileage and the much-admired "upgrade" coupons that moved me up from Economy to Business by simply putting a code on my reservation on my computer. It took United Airlines the better part of a year to duplicate the AAdvantage program.

Even today I get special treatment from American Airlines when they see my AAdvantage number, which is one of the original numbers given out to team members. All numerals, no alphabetical letters. You'd be amazed at what something like that can do, if you purely want something as simple and everyday as a window seat, or a seat in the last row of Business Class, so you don't have to worry about putting your head in the lap of somebody behind you when you recline your seat to flat or "nearly flat" to take a snooze. I can also get special treatment for my daughter, who is a disabled Navy veteran and a former Hospital Corpsman (nurse), just by using my AAdvantage number. Since she's tall like me, it's a special treat to be able to have her upgraded to Business Class.

One of her legs is problematic, and she needs a wheelchair to get to connecting flights in airports like Dallas-Fort Worth or Chicago O'Hare. "No problem, Mr. Miller. No problem at all. And thank your daughter from us for her service." It's amazing how many telephone reservationists are veterans, and how many of them were tended to by Hospital Corpsmen, who take care of not only Navy, but Marines, who have no medical corps of their own. My daughter spent most of her hitch at a Marine Corps camp on the East Coast. She wears a Hospital Corpsman baseball cap in the airport and on a plane, and it's uncanny how many passengers call her "Doc" in recognition of the help they were given by her colleagues over the years. And forget charging for a drink—not gonna happen.

I'll never forget Istanbul. I had been in Cairo some years before, and for some unknown reason, I was expecting Istanbul to have that same sandy, gritty texture that Cairo has. Cairo, in spite of the Nile River, isn't a gardenlike city. Istanbul is—green, green, green forest, and the Bosporus is as blue as the sky. It's easy to understand why Constantine wanted his new capital to be where it is. Hard to blame him for naming it Constantinople, too. Istanbul is also astounding architecturally. Just walking through the ancient Hagia Sofia is a revelation. It was built under Justinian, who was emperor from 527 to 565 AD. For many centuries, it was the largest building in the world, and had the biggest dome in the world. Even today it is astonishing, especially since some of the original mosaics have been restored. It's now a museum, by the way—not a church. It was a mosque for centuries, but became a museum in 1935 after Turkey became a republic. Today it still functions as a mosque, but most of the people who visit it want to see the ecclesiastical architecture, not the four tall minarets that were added after the conquest of Constantinople in 1453, the same year that Gutenberg invented movable type and the printing press—together the two great events frequently mark the beginning of the Renaissance, because of the huge number of Greek scholars who emigrated to Italy and the new availability of books due to Guttenberg's invention, admittedly based on ancient Chinese devices.

I said I'd never forget my first time going to Istanbul. One of the comic reasons I remember that flight was that it was at a time when smoking was increasingly being forbidden on airplanes. Where it was allowed, it was restricted to small sections of the planes—frequently the last few rows of each class of flight. All but on Turkish Air, which was a member of the One World group of airlines that let me fly virtually free using American Airlines air miles. On Turkish planes (remembering that tobacco was a major crop of Turkey at the time), smoking was allowed on the left side of the plane from front to back, and forbidden on the right side.

Totally useless, of course. There's no way to keep smoke from invading the air on one side of the aisle, but not the other.

I was not a smoker, although I came from a smoking family, which made me a secondary smoker, inhaling the smoke from other people's cigarettes. I'm sure the paint in our house was yellowed from smoke—

but most restaurants were similarly polluted—there was no way to avoid smoke other than to spend your life outdoors in the "fresh" air. My mother smoked like a chimney, lighting one cigarette from another. She smoked Kents, which were "filtered" to help keep pollutants out of her lungs (ha! it probably added splintered glass to her lungs instead of purifying anything). She died with clean lungs, by the way, but with colon cancer, which is blamed on a history of smoking by many—or most—oncologists. She had surgery to remove a blockage from her colon, but refused chemotherapy. The surgeon told her she had three or four months to live, but she survived well over eighteen months, although the tumor seemed to have metastasized to her brain, as she became somewhat demented the older she got. Anyway, not everybody who smoked got lung cancer—just most people, it seemed. John Wayne was the poster child for lung cancer.

My grandfather died in his early seventies from heart problems. He was a heavy smoker, too. My grandmother lived to her late eighties, and never smoked a cigarette in her life, although she lived in a house that was home to smokers. She spent a lot of time outdoors, working in her garden. Maybe that helped. Or maybe it helped that she wasn't inhaling tobacco smoke. Who knows?

Chapter Thirty

Anyway, I lost my way writing about Istanbul. Chuy had just arrived. It was amazing how much alike he and his mother looked. Chuy was a bit taller; I'd say he was five foot nine and she was five foot six or five foot five. But facially they were virtually identical.

They were anything but alike in their personalities. Chuy would never have agreed to take over the day spas on Vernon Boulevard. Maggie jumped at it without a whimper, apparently. Maggie was also willing to listen to Mike di Saronno's offers of help in preventing legal entanglements.

Mike didn't see anything wrong with sex. Maybe it was because he was Italian, or maybe it was because he was a cop and had seen it all before. He saw no reason to put pretty young girls in jail for getting paid for sex.

Prostitutes have been around since the world began, as far as I can tell. I certainly had some experience with the way whores work.

Even when I was in high school—a Catholic high school run by Franciscan priests—I knew that if I took a girl to a fancy restaurant on a Friday night, I was most likely going to have sex afterward, most often in the back seat of a car, or sometimes standing up against a wall with her dress pulled up. It was her job to take pills to prevent pregnancy, although I carried condoms with me in case the birth control fell to me. If she forgot to take her pills, I'd put on a condom. I would confess my sin to the priest in confession, but I wouldn't confess her sins—that was up to her.

I grew up on a ranch. Sex was natural. Babies were natural; calves were natural, foals were natural, rabbit kits were natural, puppies and kittens were natural. Piglets were natural—hell, they made bacon as they got fatter and fatter. It was unnatural to wear a condom, and unnatural to take birth control pills—so maybe the unnatural part was the sinful part, not just the natural need for sex, or wanting to have a baby.

Catholic girls were my dates, of course. Nobody promised the girls remission from mortal sin., just like nobody promised me that I could do what I did and not be sentenced to Hell or Purgatory when I died. I had been baptized as a Protestant because when I was born, my Catholic dad was overseas in France after the Normandy invasion.

My Protestant mother (Methodist) had me baptized as an infant, but when my dad decided I was to become a Catholic instead of going to church twice every Sunday, I was re-baptized. Baptism is not a sacrament that can be given more than once. But there was no way to guarantee that the Methodist baptism was done properly, according to the Catholic idea of baptism. So it was re-done, and I was able to make my First Communion after about six months of catechism studies. "Whiter than the whitewash on the walls," the priest said to me after my First Communion. Father LaGana was his name—Italian, my dad said. Most priests were either Italian or Irish in his experience. We lived in Texas at the time, and there were almost no Catholics compared to the number of "Christians" (a synonym for "Protestants" in normal Southern English). Catholic churches were little, and they seldom had bells to ring.

I stayed Catholic through high school, but when I started at UCLA when I was eighteen, I stopped going to church—any church. I guess I had never really become Catholic, although I had learned how to feel guilty. They used to say Catholics got their guilt from the nuns. Jews got their guilt through their mothers' milk.

Through no intention of my own, I met my second wife, who had grown up Baptist, but had settled down as Episcopalian. I found the Episcopal liturgy homey as compared to Catholic liturgy. The big difference was that it was in English, not Latin, but the timing was right, because it was right after the Second Vatican Council, and the Catholic liturgy was quickly converting to the local tongues. If you were in a Spanish parish, the Mass was in Spanish, with a guitarist. If you were an

English speaker, the Mass was in English, maybe with a piano or a small electric organ.

Chuy's dad was Catholic, at least in upbringing, so his Mass was in Spanish, since his native tongue was Mexican Spanish. I have no idea what religion, if any, Maggie was, but if she was Catholic, it would be either English or Mandarin—or maybe Spanish, since she probably spoke that when she was married to Manuel. She had never considered herself remarried after her marriage with Manuel broke up—never saw him again until the day he attacked her on the subway without her knowing who he was.

There was nothing natural about what he was doing to her, especially since she had no idea he was her husband, or ever had been. They'd never been divorced according to the Church, but it had been twenty years since they'd seen each other. Some Latin guy on the subway grabbed her ass and made it clear with his hands what he wanted. She wasn't giving him any, but when he followed her home, she grabbed that knife when he had his hands in her bra. But she didn't even swipe the knife at him.

He did it to himself. It wasn't her fault. It was self-defense.

She dropped the knife on the floor, and the blood covered her all over and his shirt was dripping with it, although it stopped bleeding a bit at some point. She was bloodied from head to foot. He still had his goddamn surgical mask on, and he still hadn't said anything. Maybe it was the knife wound—maybe he couldn't talk. Maybe he was just stubborn and didn't care.

She tried to explain it to Chuy a couple of times, but he was his father's boy all the way, and he didn't want to see it her way.

"What would you do if some guy grabbed you and tried to pull your pants off? Some homo guy maybe. Somebody you had no idea who he was. What would you do?"

"I'd slug him in the nose, break his fucking nose and whack him on the side of his head with my other fist," Chuy said.

"And what would happen if you found out he was your father?"

"I'd spit on him."

"But you wouldn't try to kill him?"

"Nope, not if he was my father."

"And what would you do if you saw him trying to rape me? Would you help me?"

"Not if I knew who he was. He was my dad, after all. He had every right to you. You were his wife. You weren't ever divorced, right?"

"Never divorced according to the Church, but he used to hit me, beat me with his belt. I had to leave or he was going to kill me."

"He wasn't going to kill you. You were his wife You're my mom, even though we didn't see each other for years and years."

"And if he did try to kill me? Then what would you do?"

"I'd yell at him. I'd make sure he realized you were my mom. What am I going to do without a mother?"

"But you wouldn't hit him?"

"Hit my father? Hard to imagine doing that. Even if I thought he was going to punch you and really hurt you. I know him. I knew him, anyway. He wasn't a killer, especially of women, and especially of you. If he had wanted to kill you, he would have gone after you a heck of a lot sooner than he did. Don't you think so? How did you feel about him? Were you in love with him?"

"I was in love with him when we got married. I was in love with him when you were born.

"But when he started to punch me and whip me with his belt, no, I wasn't in love with him anymore. I was afraid of him. Hard to be afraid of someone and still be in love with him. He was a lot stronger than me, and he made it clear. You'd don't remember seeing me with black eyes and purple bruises all over my body. You were just a kid. Kids don't see things like that. You don't remember him hitting you, do you?"

He shook his head. "I don't think he ever hit me."

"He did, yes. He used to slap you upside the head whenever you talked back to him."

"I didn't talk back to him, not ever."

"Yes, you did. When he hit you, you'd tell him not to hit you. You even made a fist like you were going to hit him sometimes."

"That's what men do. They make a fist like they're going to hit somebody."

"You gonna hit me? What if you hit me and I hit you back?"

He crossed his arms and refused to answer. "If my dad was here, I would tell him not to hit you," he said softly.

"And what if he hit you instead for talking back to him?"

"He wouldn't do that."

"I told you he used to do it when you were a little kid."

"You must have been lying."

"Me? Your mother? Lying?"

He was a little over twenty years old, and strong guy, although he was shorter than most American men, and maybe less muscular than a lot of baseball players. He made a fist and waved it at her.

"You gonna hit me? You little punk you? You gonna hit a woman? Your own mother? I nursed you when you were a baby, even though it hurt me to do it."

"It hurt you to feed me when I was a baby?"

"Having a baby is very painful, and feeding a baby can be very painful too, although my friends told me that it wasn't always painful to feed a baby. Imagine somebody chewing on your nipples. Grab one of them and twist it. See what it feels like. That's what it's like when a baby sucks hard on a mom's nipples. There's milk inside, but that doesn't stop it from getting sore and hurting."

He pulled his shirt up and twisted one of his nipples. "Ow!" he yelled. "I'm not gonna hit you, Mom. Not now, not ever. I would've hit Dad if I thought he was going to hit you, but you left us when I was still a baby. I don't think I was even walking, if I remember what Dad told me. He told me you left him before I could even stand up."

Chapter Thirty-one

Chuy stalked out after that unrewarding conversation with his mother. She was supposed to look at things the way he did—at least that's what made sense to him.

He loved her even though he never knew her. He'd forgotten about her over the years, but when he visited her, and when they went to Cooperstown and played catch, his heart melted and he knew she was his mother. He loved her. He was angry with her for arguing with him, but he understood what she was saying. If somebody hit her, she would hit him back. If somebody hurt her, she would protect herself. If somebody tried to hurt her, Chuy would do everything in his power to stop it from happening.

He started thinking about Maggie working at the day spas on Vernon Boulevard. What if some Fatso old guy wanted to have sex with her? What would he do then?

I'd kill him. I'd find Dad's gun and kill him. Kill him right there on the spot, just when he pulled his dick out to do it to her.

She's my mom, not his girlfriend. He, whoever the fuck he might have been, thought he could pay her for sex. That's fair if he paid her fair, I suppose, but I'm not going to fucking tolerate it. She's my mom, after all. Not just another female. She's my own mother. She not only gave birth to me, she nursed me until I was able to eat on my own. My dog had puppies one time, and I watched her raise those little critters until they were dogs like they were supposed to be. That's a big deal, and I don't have any intention of letting some horny guy do things to her just because she might be willing to take his money to let him do what he wanted to do.

Like I said, I'd kill him on the fucking spot. Shoot him in the crotch to make sure he knew why he was getting shot.

It was a turning point in his life. Most kids bond with their moms at birth. In Chuy's case, it was like she wasn't there when he was born. He didn't remember any of that baby stuff. She must have changed his diaper and wiped the shit off his little ass, no matter how it smelled. But he had no recollection of anything. He remembered his dad teaching him how to ride his tricycle, and teaching him how to slide into a base. All that was super-clear.

But of course Mom wasn't there, because she had stayed in New York when they moved to Rancho Mirage. They never went to visit her until nearly twenty years later, when he grabbed her on the subway. Manuel remembered the desert cities as the best places in the world when he was growing up.

Chuy was Asian looking, like the mother he hadn't known. There was a wedding photo of Maggie and Manuel at City Hall in Manhattan, so he knew what she looked like. She was wearing a white dress and had a white bouquet of flowers, some of which were white orchids. But he didn't remember ever having seen her in person until recently.

"Your dad did a lot of the dirty work for you, too," she said to him. "You shit your diaper one time when it was all over the crib and you, and all over your sheets, your hands and your face. What did he do? He took off his clothes, picked you up and took a shower with you. You thought it was the best thing that ever happened. You were laughing out loud, the way only a baby can laugh," she said. "I'll never forget it.

"As a matter of fact, when I found out that the man, I killed was Manuel, that's what I remembered. It made me cry like I had never cried before. What a great guy he was when he was at his best. I hadn't seen my son for years—almost twenty years to tell the truth. And what I remembered was Manuel totally naked, covered with baby shit, taking a shower to get the baby cleaned off completely. By the time he was finished with you, you were as clean as you were in the hospital where you were born, which was Cedars-Sinai Hospital in West Hollywood."

After she finished telling him about the Great Shit Shower, she was smiling the biggest smile he had ever seen on her face.

"It's hard to imagine what the best memories are when it comes to babies. I'll never forget that shower that Manuel took you into, and how sweet and clean you were when he finished rinsing you off." She thought for a minute, and then said, "If he had just talked to me, I would have recognized his voice, and I would have remembered that shower he took you into and cleaned you off. That was one of the happiest moments of my life."

Chapter Thirty-two

Grace Kim's temporary replacement at May Ling Day Spa was shot in the face with a shotgun, and left with a dollar bill pinned to her blouse. It meant in gang parlance she was a traitor to the cartel, and had sold out some of the cash receipts for no reason at all—in other words, just to rob the bosses of the money they thought they deserved. The implication was that she pocketed some of the profits herself, even knowing that she was being watched moment to moment.

Grace felt like a traitor when she found out that Sheila had been shot and left with no remaining facial features and a single one-dollar bill pinned to her blouse. In other words, a cheat of the worst type, and a worthless money-grubber to boot. Hard to believe, given that Sheila had been a longtime masseuse for the cartel—someone who never took anything for herself, but always did everything she could for the girls she was in charge of. Her dead body was found on the floor inside the May Ling Day Spa, with blood spattered all over the room.

Grace was safe from all kinds of retaliation, because she was basically a non-person, now that she was in the Police Academy and a danger to the cartel from any angle. She had managed to change her apartment to a Hell's Kitchen address, where she was less than a block away from Mike di Saronno. Mike had struck a deal that gave Mike nothing in terms of payment with Maggie Landover to train her girls to stay out of trouble while making profits for the bosses.

It was a big gamble on Mike's part, since he had committed to Maggie that her girls wouldn't get in trouble for selling sex to men who were willing to solicit prostitution, especially from minor girls. It was transparently obvious that several of the girls in the new day spas on Vernon Boulevard were under eighteen, and maybe under seventeen. It was back in the days of the Minnesota Strip, when young girls got off the buses every evening and went to work on the Avenues of Manhattan without further ado. Have pussy will sell was the idea of the day. Taking the young girls to Queens was a big change from the day to day. Unlike Mike was telling Maggie, if you take a flat fee for the massage and then include the "happy ending" in what you were paid for in advance, you probably weren't in any trouble with the law.

The "extras" were all the best of the illegal activities. If you get paid fifty dollars for the whole deal and the whole deal includes a handjob without further negotiation, that's what Mike was saying was avoiding the whole illegal side of the business. You get Fatso off after he gets hard, and you got your own tip included in the fifty you got to start off with.

The youngest girls were left with the simplest decisions. Get paid for the whole thing with a single fee on a single credit card debit, and you had the whole thing taken care of without any extras. No tips, no extras, nothing other than shooting a load, and you got a safe good time with Mr. Fatso. Why are they all Mr. Fatso? Because most men have a belly, and most men are not super-worried about the size of their bellies. So whether it's a handjob or a blowjob, and whether it's a handjob mess or a mouthful of load, you got what you wanted to give.

Grace Kim was safe. She was becoming a cop, and she was working with Mike di Saronno. She was an officer in the making at the Police Academy, and her brief history at the day spas was a ragged piece of the distant past. Not that there was zero danger in her life. She was still recognizable as the person she was before. True, she looked a little taller, which was largely a matter of posture—it also helped that she had been lifting weights, so she had muscular shoulders and deltoids. Maybe it would be just as easy to say she was looking a little more masculine than she did when she was concentrating on being pretty. It was difficult to learn to be a cop when you were not only not a guy, but Asian to boot. She was short, about five foot five or so, even though she looked a lot taller due to the way she held her shoulders and her backbone

That morning, she knocked on Mike di Saronno's office door. When he let her in, she was blunt with him. "I want to help the girls in the day spas. They're going to turn out to be floozies for sure if somebody doesn't teach them how to be more respectable." She paused. "Any progress with Maggie? If she gives you access to the girls, everything will change."

Mike looked at her in her navy blue uniform head to toe, and could envision her with a shiny brass shield that would mark her as a police detective one day soon, after she managed to pass the exam.

"You're on your way to where you want to be. You're a real adult now, making yourself a strong citizen, trying to help people who need help." He patted her on the back. "Yes, I've had some good chats with Maggie, and I'm going to start working with her girls to help them stay out of legal trouble. The last thing those girls need is to be arrested for soliciting prostitution. They need to train their imaginations to find something likeable about the guys who show up in their massage. They don't have to be attractive to be likeable. It doesn't matter that they have to pay for sex. They can still be real people, worth a smile and even a kiss—maybe.

"Lou Gehrig was thirty-seven years old when he died," Mike said. "For the last months of his life, he worked as New York City's parole commissioner, trying to rehabilitate guys and gals who had wandered off the straight and narrow in a variety of criminal activities. He was a hero in baseball and a hero in life.

"You're going to be a hero for the girls you used to work with," Mike said. "You're going to help them be strong and learn to take care of themselves. I'm going to be at your back, and gonna help you help your friends and family at the day spas. That's what life is about—helping people you care about, helping people you can help without getting in their way. You can teach the girls how to do what they do, stay healthy, and never get in trouble with the cops."

The truth was that Grace was afraid more of her girls would get killed—for nothing, for trying to stay alive under circumstances where it was almost impossible to stay alive. Half the girls were smuggled from Korea or Taiwan. Almost all of them had no immigration permits. If there was one girl with a Green Card, it would be a surprise to everyone. In fact, not having a Green Card gave the bosses extra leverage over the girls.

"Maggie is the key to giving the girls a chance to survive," Grace said to Mike. "Maggie is smarter than most people, and she's been around hookers and drug dealers for a lot of her life. She knows what to expect from them. It's just that Mike has to keep his distance. If the bosses think he's involved with the girls, they'll get suspicious, and if they get suspicious, some of the girls are going to get hurt—or killed.

"Not if Maggie is there, probably, because Maggie is Chuy's mom," Grace said, "and that gives her some leverage that the girls will never have. Chuy is rich. He doesn't need money, because he inherited all his dad's fortune when he died, and he probably gets a cut of everything that goes on too." Grace looked tentative, but continued. "If it turned out that Chuy is a millionaire, I wouldn't be surprised at all. For sure Manuel, his dad, lived like a rich man, and he had a huge income stream from Mexico, from his buds in Guadalajara. Chuy probably has money stuffed under his mattress—there's nothing like cash, you know—that's true of people like Chuy, who never go anyplace without a pocketful of hundreds, even though he acts like a normal guy, and pretends like he doesn't live in a mansion in Rancho Mirage."

As it turned out later, Chuy did have the kind of deep pockets that Grace suspected. He did in fact stuff his pockets with hundred-dollar bills—because who needs twenties or tens? Hookers wanted twenties, and gay escorts wanted anything that was legal tender. A boy whore is a twenty-dollar whore—whether he gets a hundred bucks for a session or just a couple of twenties or whatever he can bargain his way up to.

Chapter Thirty-three

It had been a long while since I spent any time with my best friends—Ruth and Gabriele. It had been a time of distraction and upset, of murders and fright. Ty Green was gone. So were more than one of the girls whose lives centered around the new day spas on Vernon Boulevard. The happiest thing that had happened was the crossover of Grace Kim from the cartel side to the NYPD side, but even that had been an after-effect of an out-and-out murder—when Tyrone Green was killed and Grace was able to jump in and fill the empty space that Ty left behind, and that Mike di Saronno had held open for her when he found out she was interested in what he had offered Tyrone.

I texted Ruth and Gabriele to see if they felt like coming over for dinner, or maybe meeting at one of our favorite hangouts, like Chez Napoleon, a little family café on the west side where the grandmother was still the queen of the kitchen and the food was straight out of Brittany. The best duck confit in New York City. As it happened, I had lived about two cross-town blocks from Chez Napoleon, and it was where I actually met—as in actually shaking hands with—Mike di Saronno for the first time. Mike lived a few steps from 51st Street and 9th Avenue, which was where Chez Napoleon was located. One fair night in the spring while I still lived in the Theater District, I found myself dueling with Mike for a table for one in the tiny dining room where every waiter was a family relative.

We turned out to be seated at the same table, since there were two chairs. I realized that I had seen Mike around the neighborhood, but I had no idea he was a cop until that evening. Fortunate turn of fate that night when Mike and I ended up at the same table for dinner.

But the way that night turned out was that Gabriele invited us to Ora di Pranzo to have dinner with him. Perfect for all of us. Gabriele could have dinner without missing work, and Ruth and I could eat New York's best Italian cuisine without standing in line for an hour and a half, like the common people who wanted to "walk in" to one of the most popular restaurants on Manhattan Island.

Gabriele took the additional step of inviting Maggie Landover to join us, since she had never been to his restaurant that he could recall. After all, Maggie was a neighbor of mine.

I made a secret promise to myself as I set out for Ora di Pranzo that I would, within a few days, drop in at Chez Napoleon for some of the world's most perfect duck confit and french fries. Maybe I could arrange it to meet Mike there, since I knew he was as much addicted to that little French *boite* where everybody knew my name, like the theme song from "Cheers" said for years and years. A well-known actor named George Wendt was a regular (his character was "Norm") on the program, and lived in the same building I lived in on 48th Street. I used to see him on the elevator from time to time. That elevator was a place where everybody knew his name, as you might guess.

Ninth Avenue was becoming a go-to place for Thai food, especially if you wanted take-out food. Even though I no longer lived in the neighborhood, I walked over there to pick up some Thai noodles as a surprise for Mike—I thought I would drop in unannounced.

But I was surprised when I got to one of the Thai take-out places, which were lined up like tin soldiers on the east side of the avenue. I stopped to look at the menu, which was pasted on the window so you could read it from the outside.

But there was a robbery going on. With guns pointed at the counter people, but no sound of shots. The three men who were masked and holding guns had apparently ordered some food, which they were lugging as they moved out the front door, perilously pointing the guns at their own feet, or at the legs of anyone waiting outside.

"Here," one of the guys, who looked Latino, said to me as he handed me a bag, ostensibly full of food.

I opened it, and it turned out it was full of money—probably what had been in the cash register before the stick-up happened.

There were cops on the street, and the robbers scurried across the avenue and off west on 47th Street. There was a hue and cry from the Thai place after the robbers exited, and the cops took off chasing after the three probable perpetrators of the robbery. I was surprised to see Mike di Saronno among the crowd standing outside the place that had been robbed. He waved to me, and I walked over to him with the bag of money, which I handed to him.

"Hard to believe they left this with you," Mike said. "They must have been really confused to hand you all the money, and run off with the noodles."

There were gunshots from somewhere west on 47th Street. Mike walked off in the direction of the sounds, following a group of uniformed cops who were pursuing the probable robbers, who had taken off with the bags of food (and left the money with me).

"Lack of planning," Mike said as he walked back across 9th Avenue to where I was standing.

"I was actually planning to surprise you with some Thai food for lunch," I said to him.

"Well, thanks," he said, "but next time give me some warning," he said. "This place is one of my faves these days. Cheap, good food, and they give me more food than most of the take-out places in the area. More food, better food, less money, what's not to like?"

"Did the uniforms catch the guys who ran off with the food?" I asked Mike.

He shook his head negatively. "They didn't know what they were doing, obviously," he said, grabbing the bag of money that I had tried to hand to him before he walked off toward west 47th Street. "Did you know that when I was a kid, 47th Street was a row of whorehouses? It got cleaned up as I grew up, and now it's a kind of upscale neighborhood with rents that are probably among the highest in Hell's Kitchen."

I knew where he lived, less than two blocks away. "I would have thought there would be plenty of take-out on your street," I added.

"All Italian, old-fashioned, same menu every couple of doors. This area used to be Puerto Rican, so I have no idea where the Italians came from. You know, this was where 'West Side Story' took place back in the original production in the 1950s. At that point, they still smoked real cigarettes on stages. And they sang and danced at the same time. Go figure."

"Well, that was kind of a non-event, wasn't it?" I said to Mike.

He nodded. "At least it wasn't an Asian Hate incident," Mike said. "No old Chinese ladies pushed onto the subway tracks. Could've been worse. Too many cops here to have had any real problems. Kinda surprised no guns were discharged, given how many guns there were in the area. All the cops in my precinct come here for take-out food for lunch. Imagine how many service revolvers there were here—holstered."

"You mind if I come over to your place if you're headed back to the office? Maybe the Halal truck will be there and I can get some fresh falafel and rice with white sauce all over it."

There was what sounded like a gunshot, but could have been a firecracker.

"Sounds like at least one shot was fired," Mike said. "Either that or somebody has some cherry bombs that echo around these old stone and brick buildings. Sure, come on, I don't expect things to calm down here any time soon, so the Halal truck is as good a bet as any under the circumstances."

We started to walk over to Mike's office, and of course the rains came. There were several cracks of thunder in a row, and some flashes of lightning, but too many of both to be able to guess how far away the lightning bolts had hit the ground. I was wearing a suede sport jacket, and was worried that it would get totally drenched. I took it off and folded it up, tucked it under my arm. Then the rain stopped, so it was another not-to-worry, like the robbery itself.

I ended up with falafel and some NYPD coffee. Grace Kim was there, also eating Halal food. She was much entertained by Mike's account of what had happened in the Thai-food village on 9th Avenue. She was wearing a regulation blue uniform, but had a name-plate, which I hadn't noticed before. She also had a weapon and a shield pinned onto her chest. There must have been a graduation event at the Academy over the last week.

"Congrats, Officer Kim," I said to her. She beamed a big smile at me. "The PC gave a speech—good one. I still have a lot of work to do at John Jay College, but when that's done, I'll be ready for the sergeant's exam. I think I'll do okay on it, been studying every day. I want to be the best cop in Manhattan, and I want to be Mike's side-kick."

"I don't think Mike's ever had a side-kick that I know of," I said.

"You mean you don't think you were his side-kick for years? The guys tell me you and Mike were like glued together for years. Some of the most colorful cases over the last ten years were the two of you—and Gabriele and Ruth—working together."

"Well, good luck. I don't think I was ever anybody's side-kick, except maybe Gabriele's."

Grace smiled a big smile that belied my comments. Then she waved at Mike, who motioned her to his office. He was all smiles, and waved good-bye to me.

Chapter Thirty-four

My cellphone rang. It was Ruth. I have long been attracted to her, and it has always been a treat when she calls me, or drops by to visit. We were both vaxers when the COVID-19 vaccines were first okayed by the FDA to prevent the scary new respiratory illness that seemed to have originated in southern China, and may have been transmitted by bats to other animals, and by the other animals to human beings. By the time of the writing of this book, well over six hundred thousand Americans have died from COVID-19, and the effectiveness of the Pfizer and Moderna vaccines has been extraordinarily strong. I had my first Pfizer shot in March of 2021, and the second on Easter Sunday of the same year. That Easter was also the hundreth birthday of one of my aunts, so I considered it a good luck charm.

Now it seems like the CDC and/or the FDA may be considering a booster shot to increase the strength of the protection the vaccine gives us from the novel coronavirus disease (COVID-19 is a shorthand version of Corona Virus Disease, which first appeared in 2019).

Ruth is a lot younger than I am—I was born two weeks after the day my father landed on Omaha Beach during the Normandy invasion in 1944. It's safe to say that my dad had no idea I had been born the day that my mom took me home from St Joseph's hospital in Houston, where I was born. I was brought up in a small town in Texas. My dad was born in Sault Ste Marie, Michigan, but grew up in Mt Vernon, New York—a town that borders on the Bronx. He was from the time he was a tyke a Yankee fan, and he grew up going to Yankee Stadium and getting children's tickets. He caught a foul ball that was hit by Babe Ruth, and had the ball signed to him by the Babe. He also had a relative who lived in New Rochelle, in the house next door to Lou Gehrig's parents. So he had a Lou Gehrig autographed ball, too.

I could read the Babe Ruth autograph, but I had no way of reading the Lou Gehrig autograph, and I destroyed the Lou Gehrig ball when I was a kid. We needed a ball to play with, and I knew where my dad kept a baseball in his chest of drawers. I took it and we used it in a game, where it got grass-stained and was scuffed up pretty good. I thought he was going to kill me when my mom told me what THAT baseball had been.

My grandmother was a huge Yankee fan, too. Those were the days before baseball games were on television, and she used to have long conversations with the radio in the living room—frequently telling Casey Stengel (then the Yankee manager) to take out the pitcher and bring in Whitey Ford (elected to the Baseball Hall of Fame in 1974), who was Grandmother's favorite pitcher (and everyone else's favorite, too).

The Yankees Fan Club didn't stop with my dad and my grandmother. My father's youngest sister became a nun in her late teen years, and eventually became known as Sister Yankee in her convent. I was a Dodger fan as a teenager, when the Dodgers moved to Los Angeles, where I was living. When I moved to Orange County, I became an Angels fan, because the Angel Stadium was less than fifteen minutes from where I lived. Besides, Nolan Ryan pitched for the Angels from 1972 to 1979, and Reggie Jackson played for the Angels from 1982 to 1986. Overall, I'd probably say I'm an Angels fan, but when I go to Yankee Stadium, I wear a Yankee cap.

Anyway, Ruth and I go way back. When I first met her, she was a hostess at a financial research trade show. I had several clients who were making presentations to brokers and institutional investors at that show, and ended up spending some time with Ruth. She had a boyfriend who was a bigshot in the music industry, but she and he never really clicked, and he never divorced his wife, which was part of what Ruth was looking for from him. She eventually married Manny, who worked in the ladies' clothing industry. I never divorced my wife (she died when we had been married for nearly forty-eight years), so there was never an opening for

Ruth and me. I was an opera fan and she was an opera fan. We both wanted to see all the shows that opened on Broadway, although I think she came closer to doing that than I ever did.

She has always been a clothes horse, and is the only woman I've ever known who can wear linen suits in the summer and have no wrinkles in the fabric after a day's wearing. She is a collector of classic Chanel (usually used clothing, second-hand shops). She mixes blue jeans and Chanel jackets with great panache, and generally attracts the attention of every woman in the room when she walks in. She has never been a great beauty, but she is a one-of-a-kind woman with a very distinguished way of wearing her clothes. She is a widow these days, as I am a widower. Will anything ever come of it? Probably not.

I drove Ruth to the area around Woodstock to find a suitable place to strew her husband's ashes. He ended up in a small lake near where the greatest rock and roll concert of all time took place. When my own wife died and was cremated, my daughter scattered the ashes on a mountaintop in California, which was not only appropriate, but thoughtful. My wife was a Virginian by birth, but spent most of her life in California, and our children still live there. I don't know what will happen to my ashes, but worse things could happen than having them strewn in the Pacific Ocean.

Oddly enough, I was not much of a rock and roll fan, especially when it came to outdoor concerts like Woodstock in 1969. It rained and everything turned to mud. It smelled terrible and the smell of drugs being smoked was everywhere. There was no good food and no place warm to sleep. I can say I was there, but I wouldn't be so dishonest as to say I would do it again if I had the chance. I did see Janis Joplin at Woodstock—that was with Big Brother and the Holding Company. She later became the girlfriend of Country Joe McDonald.

I used to have opera scores autographed by some very famous singers—Beverly Sills, Mirella Freni, Placido Domingo, Dame Joan Sutherland, Luciano Pavarotti—lots of others, I lost them during various moves from one apartment to another, and have none of them left.

That night, Ruth came over and we went to Tournesol, a fine, white-tablecloth French restaurant marooned in Long Island City.

Tournesol is the French word for "sunflower," because the sunflower moves during the day to face the sun wherever it is in the sky. I am a superfan of duck confit, and Tournesol makes some of the best duck confit in the United States.

As I recall, Ruth had a pounded steak with spicy green peppercorn sauce and loved it—in spite of the fact that she had to travel to Queens to have that dinner. Since she lives on Park Avenue at 61st Street, it was a very *au contraire* thing to do. Manhattanites seldom go to Queens except to get on planes at LaGuardia Airport or JFK Airport. I doubt she ever did it again; at least if she did, I wasn't there to see it happen.

Chapter Thirty-five

That evening there was a disturbing news item on the ABC Eyewitness News at about five thirty. A young fellow on a skateboard in Long Island City had crashed into an elderly Asian woman on the riverfront, knocked her down and then kicked her until she was unconscious—and stole her handbag.

There were several witnesses who heard the guy yelling at her to go back to China, so according to the news story, the cops were after him for an Asian Hate crime. If they caught him, he could be tried for a federal hate crime as well as a New York State one. Could be a long stretch in the slammer—maybe two slammers if there was a federal conviction. The video on the news made it look like the attacker was youngish and probably Black, with spikey hair and a long-sleeved checked shirt in red and black. No facial pictures, unfortunately.

I called Maggie and asked if she had seen the news. She had, and she found the article upsetting. After all, although she was considerably younger than the victim in the video, she was also physically smaller—easier to go after—and possibly with a handbag full of cash, given what she had been up to with the day spas.

"Looks like the bosses may not be your worst worry, given what's going on these days with the pandemic that the news says originated in China," I said.

She asked if I minded if she came over. Of course I said she would be welcome. The last thing anybody needs when they're scared is to be alone.

She showed up in minutes, given that she lives just across the street. She was white as a sheet when I opened the door.

"These kids who go after women—they're terrifying. No warning, no reason for doing what they do. They must be off their rockers."

I was having a scotch on the rocks, and offered her one, too. Nope, no alcohol. I offered to make some fresh coffee, and that sounded better to her. I have an electric percolator, and it makes coffee fast, so it was ready to drink in a minute or two. She wanted some sugar, no milk. I offered her a glass of champagne (I usually keep a bottle in the fridge in case somebody shows up and won't drink alcohol, but will drink the "soft" taste of champagne), but she declined.

"What if that turkey had come after me when I was leaving work at the May Ling Spa? First of all, I'd be in the hospital. Second, that asshole would have my handbag—which has my ID in it, my address, and my keys, not to mention a bunch of cash and a couple of credit cards." She looked really upset, and on the edge of tears.

I offered her a paper napkin to wipe her eyes. She sipped the coffee, and looked a little better.

"I'm okay," she said. "Nobody attacked me. I was just worried and scared. I lived in Manhattan for most of my grown-up life. Now I live in Queens. How strange is that? And I think I recognized that guy in the TV video of the mugging. I've seen him somewhere, no idea where, but somewhere near where I live. Maybe even in my building, although he looks like a homeless guy in the TV clip."

I asked her if it was okay to call Mike di Saronno and let him know how she was feeling. She nodded.

I told Mike she was at my place, having a cup of coffee.

"We have coffee here. Why not bring her over to my office? Either that, or I can take the subway and come to you. But it might be easier if you come here. We have some video that hasn't been seen on TV. We have some leads on who this guy might be. He does in fact live in Long Island City, if he's who we think he is. He's Black, tall, athletic, and seems to play basketball in his spare time. No record that we can find. Why would be attack that old lady? Probably saw her handbag and decided to grab it. The beating was probably just an opportunity that he took advantage of after she hit the pavement."

I said we'd head over right away.

"I'm gonna want Maggie to spend some time with one of our sketch artists, to see if we can get a sketch that we can send around to the precincts in Queens, and maybe give to the TV networks and newspapers.

"That gonna cause problems with somebody like Black Lives Matter if we accuse him of a crime just because he's a big Black thug?" Maggie asked. "And that woman was a totally unprotected victim. From what I can tell, she's not much bigger than me. I might be just his type."

When we got to Mike's office, his first bit of advice was to stay off the street at night, and to only go out when she was with at least one other person, preferably a guy, who might cause a potential attacker to think twice.

She looked at me.

"If I were you, I'd quit the day spa, just stay close to home. No reason at your age to be wandering around in the middle of the night on Vernon Boulevard. Some horny bastard who just got off in one of your spas would be just the right kind of suspect for us to be looking for." He mentioned that Maggie said she thought she recognized the guy.

"Could he have been a customer at one of the spas?" he asked.

She shook her head slowly. "I think I'd remember that. He was a big guy with a red shirt on. I think I would remember. Fairly sure I'd remember. Maybe he's a waiter. Maybe he's a pan-handler. I know there are some of what they call 'affordable' apartments in my building. Those places are open to Section 8 deals, so if I've seen him near where I live, he could actually be a neighbor."

Mike picked up the phone and said a few words to someone he dialed up. Shortly after that, a Latino-looking woman in what appeared to be her early twenties showed up at his door.

"Maggie, this is Kay. She's one of our best sketch artists. As it happens, she and Hugo are the same category of NYPD employees— civilian criminalists. Kay has been with us for several years, and she's a really talented sketch artist. If you don't mind, take a walk with Kay to her studio and let her do her magic for you. If you recognize the guy she sketches, we may have a winner here."

Kay was all smiles as they left. She had seen the TV video, she told Mike. "That could help," she said. "But I'll put it out of my mind when Maggie and I are talking."

After the two women left to go to Kay's studio, Mike and I talked a bit. "Why do you suppose she knocked on your door after she saw the news item on TV?"

"I think I'm a short-cut to you, truthfully," I said. "She trusts you, not me. She likes me and she's not afraid of me, but you're somebody she can trust completely, I think. You may be what psychologists call a 'father figure' for her."

"Maybe she just didn't want to be alone—and she knows you're part of the NYPD, too. Be careful how you judge why people do what they do. I doubt she just wandered out of her building and dead-headed for your building by accident. Maybe she got spooked just being outdoors and wanted to get indoors as fast as she could. You might have been the most convenient person to try. And remember she met me at your apartment, so if she does trust me, you really may be a shortcut to get to me. She probably wouldn't use her cellphone to call me, even though I'm fairly sure I gave her my business card at the Oyster Bar. Almost any cellphone can be tapped easily. I could have tapped it. Chuy could have tapped it. Some thug could have tapped it. No cellphone is safe all the time."

"One thing for sure," I said, feeling bright. "She's really spooked. I bet she's afraid of Chuy. He probably shoved her into the day spa position just trying to help someone in the family. He doesn't have a lot of relatives, as far as we know. No siblings, for instance."

After about an hour, Kay and Maggie came back, and Kay had her sketchbook under her arm. Sure enough, she had a sketch, and Maggie not only said that was the guy she remembered, but it was like Maggie knew him, too.

"Kay's job is to visualize what you tell her. So it's like any time she makes a sketch, she almost feels like she knows whoever you describe. It's what she does. Trust me."

The sketch certainly looked like the video clip from the TV news. Particularly the shirt.

Mike tapped some of the keys on his computer, and showed us a piece of video that hadn't been released to the media. The guy in Kay's sketch was a dead ringer for the guy on Mike's computer.

"I'd say we run this photo and see if we come up with a name. If we do, we should put together a lineup as soon as we can. Today if we can."

"I know where I saw the guy," Maggie said. "He was with Chuy. I think he was working for Chuy, maybe selling some product out on the street. I think he was hanging out around the Mister Softee truck on the river front."

"Looks like you did your job, Kay," Mike said. "Satisfied client here—and satisfied citizen there," he said, pointing at Maggie. "I'm gonna send this sketch to the Vernon-Jackson precinct now, right now, and if they know this guy, I'm gonna see if they can round him up." He stared at the sketch, and then said to Kay, "The guy in your sketch has a beard, or some scruff anyway, not really a beard. I don't recall seeing that on the video I've looked at. I think the guy in the video was clean shaven. Maybe a little scruffy, but not as much as on your sketch."

"I remembered him with a beard," Maggie said. "I remembered him with Chuy."

"Chuy is Maggie's son—family business," he said to Kay. "But we're going to have some problems with this beard/no beard stuff."

"Just erase the beard," Maggie said. "I was remembering it from the Mister Softee ice cream truck anyway, not from the TV video. That guy who runs that truck is there all day and all night. I bet he knows this guy, too. I bet he even knows his name."

Mike's computer buzzed, indicating a new message. It was from the Vernon-Jackson precinct. Sure enough, they knew the guy. "No record that we know of, but he's a local. We see him at Dominie's Hoek," Mike read aloud what the author wrote. Dominie's Hoek was a bar around the corner from the precinct house, an old Dutch name for the area that somebody picked up as a good name for a bar.

"See if you can pick him up for a lineup here in Manhattan this afternoon," Mike typed.

"Done," Mike again read aloud with what the correspondent in Long Island City responded. "We sent somebody over to the river front to look for him. He lives someplace close, but not right here. Maybe closer to the project over by the Queensboro Bridge. But he spends all his free time on the river front right near here. Near the ice cream truck. I think he may sell a dime pack here and there. Nothing big, nothing we'd nail him for, but not as clean as a baby's butt either."

The guy's name was Russell Einhorn—odd last name for a Black guy—and the guys in Long Island City were right—no record. He was an athlete, a student at La Guardia College, also in Long Island City. He lived in a dormitory-type building near the college, but with a real street address. No car; he was a walker—sometimes a skateboarder like on the TV clip. This wasn't the first time he'd run into somebody on the sidewalk. "Strictly speaking, skateboards aren't allowed on the sidewalks in New York City. They have four wheels; makes them a vehicle that needs to be on the asphalt, not on the sidewalk. We can book him for the skateboard and then bring him over to your office," the man from Long Island City told Mike.

Chapter Thirty-six

Mr. Einhorn was picked out of the lineup by Adelina Chao, the eighty-six-year-old woman who was attacked by the man on the skateboard. He was also picked out by Maggie, who knew him from the neighborhood where she lived, right near the river front across the street from the building where I live.

Mike di Saronno's team arrested Einhorn, charging him with assault and robbery, both as hate crimes. They also asked him about his last name. His real last name—the one he was born with—was Stafford. He changed it to Einhorn when he was a middle-schooler because his best friend was named Rick Einhorn. He filed a change of name with a friend of his father's who was a lawyer. It was his legal name.

He was, as we had thought, an enrolled student of La Guardia College, a two-year campus of the City University of New York (CUNY). His encounter with Ms. Chao had nothing to do with any other crime. Mr. Einhorn was unemployed. His GPA was nearly three point seven, which entitled him to a full scholarship for up to sixteen credits per semester, but he had no normal source of income, so he blocked and filled by mugging elderly people.

"Women for the most part carry a handbag, but they typically have less cash on them than men have," he said when he was asked how he chose his victims. "Men usually carry cash in one of their front pants pockets. They carry a wallet, with ID and sometimes credit cards in one of their back pants pockets." He admitted that although attacks on women were easier to accomplish, attacks on men were more likely to put cash in his pockets to buy food, school supplies and the other things he needed to sustain his life and everyday needs.

"My parents are both unemployed," he said. "I've always studied hard and made good grades, but I don't have enough money to buy food and books, much less to take the bus to get to class. I try not to hurt people, but sometimes I get so hungry that I do things that make me ashamed of myself." And then he started to cry and sob like a child.

Mike took a deep breath and I thought he was going to launch into a sermon—but I was wrong.

"If you were a cop, I'd be proud to call you brother, young man. I hope nothing bad comes of this day in your life." I could see Mike's eyes sparkling with tears and knew what he was thinking. He was thinking about Grace Kim and Ty Green—the kinds of good-hearted young people who wanted to spend their young lives helping people, however they needed help.

Mike stood up in the interrogation room. Everybody else started to stand up as well, and he motioned to them to sit back down. "I want everyone in the country to know that there are good people wherever you look in the United States. What does a good person who's always hungry do? Do they steal when they need food? Sometimes. It probably doesn't make them proud of themselves, but sometimes you gotta do what you gotta do."

He almost didn't stop talking, just kept on with the breath he had just taken. "What if you have a kid? If the kid's hungry, what stops you from swiping a few cans of soup from the supermarket?"

I patted Mike on the back and added my own few thoughts to what he had been tending toward.

"Russell," I said, "I think what Mike is trying to say is that when you need food, you need food. You do what you have to do to get it." I paused. "What you hope is that you don't have to tackle an old lady and steal her purse to get what you need."

"Are your grades as good as you implied? What's your overall GPA look like?" Mike asked.

"I'd say it's three point seven most of the time, sometimes three point eight."

"What makes it three point eight?"

"When I have an exam in math, the GPA moves up. I'm strong in math."

"What kind of math are you taking now?"

"Analytic geometry," Russell answered. "It's a kind of combination of algebra and geometry. The curves of geometry coincide with the equations of algebra. So it's part math and part art. Perfect. Next semester I'll be taking calculus, which is the study of how things change—like how a train's speed changes as it goes faster and faster. How long would it take a rocket to get past the Kármán. One of these days I'll be able to get into a four-year school, maybe even with a scholarship that would give me something to eat. I've applied to the old CUNY campus in Harlem. Fingers crossed."

"Why didn't you apply to MIT?" Mike responded.

"MIT? You kidding? I'm a Black kid from Queens. No money in the family. If I got in and they didn't pay the whole thing with scholarships, I might as well not have applied in the first place.

"On the other hand, if you got into MIT, you'd have grad school made in the shade, wouldn't you?"

"That'd be like flying weightless beyond the Kármán line, which is the fictitious line that demarcates Earth's gravitational pull and the part of space where there is no gravitational pull from Earth at all," Russell said. "Like the official line between our atmosphere and outer space."

"What if I told you I might be able to introduce you to somebody at MIT who could help you make that big brain of yours into something that might be worth a full ride scholarship?" Mike teased Russell. "Heck, if we could get that set up, you might be Dr. Einhorn one day, not just Mister Einhorn."

"That must be how you wave your wand and make things change magically," I said to Mike. "You probably know some MIT guys from your years in the department. A favor here, a favor there. Sometimes an active brain is like twenty-four-karat gold, right?"

"Right," Mike answered. "Absolutely right, and yes, I know a guy that knows a guy at MIT. If Russell here isn't a liar, we might be able to put him on the right road to where he wants to get—a mathematician with an idea of how to win a Nobel Prize one day."

"You remind me of Merlin, man," I said to Mike. "Do you get younger every year as you live backward? Merlin was born elderly, and aged backward, getting closer and closer to being a child every year," he said. "I think that was an invention of Sir Thomas Malory when he wrote his book on King Arthur, which was published about the same time that Richard III was killed in what got to be called the Battle of Bosworth Field. That battle was never fought and Bosworth Field was never found, but he turned out to have been buried in Leicester in what was originally a Franciscan chapel at the time of the battle where he was killed. Centuries later, it became a parking lot that was dug up at some point, and Richard III's body was found—about five hundred years after he died."

That's how Richard III's body was found, and was finally interred in Leicester Cathedral in about 2015. Of course, there would be no question of burying him in Westminster Abbey—not after what Shakespeare did to his reputation as an evil hunchback (he wasn't a hunchback, by the way).

King John, who is the least popular of the English monarchs, is buried in Worcester Cathedral, so Richard III might as well be buried in Leicester Cathedral, which has only been a cathedral since the diocese of Leicester was created by the Church of England in 1927. A cathedral is where a bishop's in residence. The word *cathedra* means "chair" in English. A bishop's throne (a throne is a chair, right?).

Chapter Thirty-seven

It's amazing how a police gumshoe like Mike di Saronno can become a hero-saint when he tries to help a series of potential criminals get into a series of good colleges. It's also amazing how a medieval monarch like Richard III can be the embodiment of evil under the Tudor playwright, William Shakespeare, and can then be canonized in a 1951 novel called *The Daughter of Time* by a writer who called herself Josephine Tey.

Her novel was about King Richard III and whether he was responsible for the infamous murder of the "Princes in the Tower." (Tey's answer was no, he wasn't even involved at little). The novel was named the greatest crime novel of all time by the British Crime Writers' Association. In 1995 it was named the fourth greatest crime novel of all time by the Mystery Writers of America.

The Daughter of Time also proved once and for all that Richard III was not a hunchback—not in any way, shape or form—a Tudor lie from beginning to end. Shakespeare and Sir Thomas More originated the idea that he was misshapen—might as well say he was shaped like a witch if you wanted to portray him like a warlock.

So there is the counter-story to the Royal Shakespeare Company and its famous actors who have been Rigoletto-like Richard III— Laurence Olivier, Kenneth Branagh, Alec Guinness and even Americans like Kevin Spacey and George C Scott. The real Richard III was probably short, but athletic and with a normal masculine body. He was nothing like his elder brother, Edward IV, who was about six foot four and maybe two hundred and five pounds. Edward got fatter and fatter as he got older and older, and had become morbidly obese by the time he died—not super-different from his great-grandson, Henry VIII, as a matter of fact.

But back to Mike di Saronno. He had pulled Tyrone Green out of the muck he was wading in as a potential criminal—and plopped him into the NYPD Police Academy, and into the John Jay College as a criminology student instead of a scummy member of a Mexican drug cartel. Then, when Tyrone was murdered, he did the same for Grace Kim, a former Madame in a small group of brothels masquerading as massage parlors (or "day spas"). Finally—and most successfully—he converted Chuy Acosta-Gonzalez's mother, Maggie Landover, from being a pimp/Madame to being a potential savior of smart kids with good grades who were being sucked under by the quicksand of prostitution and drugs.

Maggie went the whole nine yards after a couple of long talks with Mike, the highest-ranking detective in the NYPD, stationed at the Midtown West precinct, and reporting to the Police Commissioner himself. Maggie bit off the whole donut that Mike was offering. She had been the theoretical manager of the three day spas on Vernon Boulevard. Most people would have believed that the three spas were actually massage parlors—or even brothels, stocked primarily with Asian girls who had probably been smuggled into the United States, possibly across the southern border with Mexico, courtesy of Chuy, Maggie's son.

Mike had spent a good deal of time explaining to Maggie that paying for sex was illegal, but that paying for a massage was not illegal. If the massage includes a "happy ending," which is a somewhat polite name for a handjob or even a blowjob, then the sexual part may not be illegal, especially if it is included in the posted cost of a massage. It took a while for Maggie to soak up what Mike was saying, but Mike—who is a lawyer as well as a police detective—was vehement that what he was telling Maggie would keep her girls safe from the police. And he didn't want any money or other kind of compensation for helping make sure the girls were okay. The last thing he wanted was for Maggie's largely Korean girls to start being deported because of technical violations of vice laws from working in a massage parlor with naked men who wanted to be masturbated as part of a relaxing massage.

In the end, Maggie gave in, and started educating her girls that getting paid a fixed fee for a massage allowed the fixed fee to include some "extras" that might otherwise have been add-ons that might require a tip or extra payment. So if the posted price of a massage was forty dollars, that fee could be all-inclusive of whatever the service ended up including. And the cops, if they raided and started harassing the girls, would have a difficult—maybe impossible—time proving that something happened that would be a violation of the law.

But then Maggie apparently resigned from her work with the day spas. She had some savings, partly from a settlement with her ex-husband years earlier, and partly from jobs she had worked for the years before Chuy offered her a position where she could make more money by a long shot by helping undocumented girls sell their bodies for sex. She moved back inside her apartment, across the street from where I live near the East River and across from the Chrysler Building and the Secretariat Building of the United Nations. Real landmarks of Manhattan. Then she started interviewing for hostess positions at some of the fancier midtown restaurants. The fact that she had a recommendation from an NYPD detective didn't hurt.

Anyway, she found a job—weekends only, just Friday to Sunday—in an Asian Fusion restaurant next to Grand Central Terminal. Apparently, it was enough for her to get along. She was healthy and well-adjusted, and she owned her condominium without a mortgage, so she had some equity in her real estate holdings, probably worth the better part of four hundred thousand dollars if the property was put on the market. If it had been in Manhattan, it might have been closer to a million dollars.

Then her son Chuy came through, and offered her an office job with his consulting company, which was located on 3rd Avenue in the high 40s. That sweetened her situation a bit. Again, it wasn't full time, but he slipped her some extra here and there, for some voluntary work she did with their CPA and corporate lawyer. The business was legitimate, and dealt mostly with rental properties on the east side of Manhattan. It had been started by Chuy's father, Manuel Acosta-Gonzalez, as what they used to call a "candy store" in the days of the Mafia. Initially it started with a barber shop, but expanded to include take-out food stores and a few ethnic restaurants—mostly Chinese or Japanese, to match Maggie's Asian looks (and Chuy's).

Mike continued to help Maggie with any legal advice she needed. He was convinced that she wanted to be on the "straight and narrow," and was trustworthy in terms of being on the right side of the law. No knee-cappers to collect rents. No protection agreements that kept shopkeepers from being harassed by thugs who promised to "protect" stores from robberies and burglaries. "Straight and narrow" all the way, but she still slipped some cash to the girls who had worked for her at the Long Island City day spas. Some of those girls even got married, and moved to Chinese or Korean parts of New York City or New Jersey (like Newark, which had always had a substantial Asian population and a section with enough Chinese signage that it was called "Chinatown." Most of the girls managed to have jobs and children at the same time, and Mike helped several of them earn Green Cards that made them legitimate residents of the United States (as long as they paid their taxes, which they all did, often with Mike's help financially and in other ways as well).

Chuy alternated between his fancy mansion home in the Rancho Mirage area of California's desert resort district—and a smallish but probably expensive apartment in a tower near the United Nations. He also spent some time staying with his mom in her place in Long Island City. He was very proud of her insistence on being a law-abiding citizen with a cop detective as a good friend. He was also pleased that she tended to hang out with Ruth and me. As far as she was concerned, nobody was more respectable than Hugo, Ruth and Gabriele. She even went to the opera with Ruth occasionally—and said she enjoyed it, in spite of it being high-class and high-flying. She didn't go to the Monday night black tie events, but she did buy some nice-looking sleek dresses with Christian Louboutin high heels, so she would "fit in" when she went someplace fancy with Ruth or Gabriele (or both of them).

She also took Kung Fu lessons, and went through several colors of belts over a period of a year, ending up with a purple belt indicating Strength in the Kung Fu world. She decided not to try for a black belt—

she was too physically small. She felt like she could take care of herself if she could throw a grown man across the room, so it made her feel like she didn't have to worry about being attacked on the streets because of Asian Hate.

Chuy didn't approve of his mom taking Kung Fu lessons, and being able to protect herself. He was taller than Maggie, but not by much—and they looked like twins except for the difference in ages and gender. He liked being stronger than she was, which he got from lifting weights in the gym in his apartment building near the UN. He wasn't muscular, but he was lean and seemed confident of himself in public.

He bought her a red and yellow scarf that had a similarity to the Chinese flag, and told her that she should wear it when she was going out, to prevent thugs from trying to take advantage of her. Then she took a step that Chuy never expected. She converted to be a Catholic, which is how Chuy's dad raised him. She told him she wanted to go to church with him on Sundays—not that she was religious, but because she thought it was a good thing to do, and it was a real family activity in case she ever had a grandchild.

She actually asked Chuy if he liked girls or boys, which incensed him when she brought it up. He wanted his red and yellow scarf back—it was a Hermes scarf and he had paid what seemed like a fortune for it at Bergdorf Goodman. She tried to explain that she was just asking because it would be great to have a grandson or granddaughter, if he was okay with that. Of course, he would have to get married if he wanted to have a kid if he wanted that child to be legitimate, but when she said that, it made him even angrier, and he wadded up the scarf and stuck it in his backpack in a way that showed he didn't give a shit how it looked.

He did show up with his arm around a pretty Latin girl who it turned out was from Mexicali, which was where his father lived when he was waiting on getting his immigration papers and Green Card, so he could move across the border into the United States. Obviously it had worked for Manuel, but he was wealthy from the giddyup, because of his connections in Guadalajara and across the borders in Arizona and New Mexico, where there were no fences or border walls, and the wetbacks just walked across where they wanted to.

Chuy never did marry. He did have two kids from two different girls, both Latin-looking. They did go to church together from time to time, but Chuy felt like he was desecrating the church when they took his bastards there. They were baptized with Mexican godparents, and both made their First Communions after an appropriate amount of time in catechism classes. If Chuy is 20 in 2021, when did he have these kids?

Chuy wore a navy-blue suit with a white shirt and striped tie the days the two kids made their First Communions. He was clearly proud of them, in spite of their having been born on the wrong side of the blanket, so to speak. They were for sure his kids. Both of them carried his features, which was like saying they carried Maggie's features, too. Clearly Asian eyes, although with wavy black hair and tanned skin with fine features that looked about half Caucasian and half Mexican, still with those fascinating almond-shaped eyes.

Chapter Thirty-eight

Mike di Saronno wanted to get together to talk about what to do next. He was feeling closer than he had ever been to erasing the lines between cops and civilians.

"Do you mind if I stop by your apartment for a dirty vodka and some cheese and crackers?" he asked me. "It'd make sense to me if Gabriele and Ruth could join us, too. I like the way they think, just like I like the way you think."

I told him that I would invite Gabriele over for dinner, and see if he felt like shopping and cooking for the four of us. He shocked me when he said he'd like to bring his cousin, Dante, with him. If that was okay with us, he and Dante would both cook. Of course that was okay, and we agreed they could get started whenever they wanted to, but that dinner would be around six o'clock.

Ruth was overjoyed at the idea. After all, the people in my living room were some of her favorite people in the world. She was also someone who appreciated the types of food that Ora di Pranzo served. Gabriele said that he and Dante would close down the restaurant for the evening, since Dante would be taking the night off from the kitchen—so there wouldn't be an Executive Chef watching over things.

Mike arrived at four o'clock with a magnum of blended scotch and containers of guacamole and a bag of tortilla chips. Some of my favorite munchies, and for sure one of my favorite drinks. My dining table was aligned with the kitchen wall, next to a generous pass-through that took up most of the kitchen other than the deep and capacious pantry, which stretched back from the kitchen toward the balcony. So the table was next to the pantry wall.

I got out my mother's wedding dishes. If this wasn't a special enough occasion, I couldn't image what would be special enough. When I grew up, my mom's Lenox dishes meant a special evening. Those dishes were for Christmas and Thanksgiving—sometimes for a birthday, but not much more often than that. They were too fancy, with twenty-four-karat gold patterns on all the pieces (at least that's what my mom told me). My parents were married in 1943, during World War II. Obviously I wasn't there when they got married, but I had the pleasure of being part of two subsequent outdoor family weddings, both of which were similar to what I had been told about my parents' wedding day.

My Dad was a New Yorker, a Catholic, a Republican, and had been to school at Notre Dame, where he was, among other things, captain of the golf team. Years later, when he was seventy, he was still what they call a "scratch" golfer, meaning he had no handicap, was simply expected to score par no matter which golf course he was playing. He was a scary golf partner if you thought about winning—because it seldom happened.

My mother was a country girl, a drawling southerner, a Methodist, and a Democrat raised in a family that had a photo of Franklin Roosevelt over the kitchen table. On the other hand, as I found out many years later, my father's family rules included a prohibition against speaking that President's name.

The wedding was held in an empty lot next to where my grandparents lived. They owned the property and it was fashioned as a fairly formal French garden that was balanced against the house itself, to the left if you looked at it from the street.

My grandmother collected tuna fish cans all the time. She also collected broomsticks and shovel handles, both of which were in plentiful supply when it came to a wedding. The tuna fish cans were painted silver by hand and nailed to broomsticks or shovel handles, and pounded into the ground along the garden borders. Then there was a candle added, and a glass hurricane lamp that kept the candles, once lighted, from blowing out. It looked like a fairyland with all the candles flickering. At least that's the way I remember it from the two weddings I attended as an elementary school kid.

Of course, the wedding china had all been contributed by guests at my parents' wedding, many of whom arrived with fancy-wrapped boxes, almost all of which were wedding china, because that was what you did at that point in history. Foley's Department Store had a wedding registration service in Houston (the nearest big city). So the deal was, you went to Foley's, and found my mother's name in the wedding registry. Then you bought something that nobody else had already bought and took it to the wedding, where you put it on a special table at the front of the wedding garden

Nothing was delivered in advance. There was probably no such thing as UPS at that point—and there was fuel rationing for every purpose during the war anyway.

It turned out that my mom had a china service for ten people—as long as nothing was ever broken (which didn't work out perfectly over the years). That included sterling silver flatware that was in a Gorham pattern called "Chantilly" that was fairly common—which meant that extra flatware could be borrowed from relatives if and when it was needed. I don't recall ever borrowing flatware, although my Texas grandmother had the same silverware pattern that my mother chose—so it could have happened, I suppose.

I set the glass-topped table for five people (there were six tall-backed black leather chairs) with my mother's fancy wedding china, which I had inherited when my mom died—and with sterling silver flatware from my New York grandparents, which had the letter M engraved on each fork, knife, spoon, etc.

The flatware was smaller than one would expect next to my mom's gorgeous china, and there were more types of utensils than most families would have—or use. But that meant there were oyster forks, for instance, not to mention fancy serving pieces like lemon forks and pickle forks, which were seldom used, and not that evening. Of course it was the New York family flatware, which meant that oysters were not unheard of, since I was living in New York City. The Texas family wouldn't have known a fresh oyster if it walked in the front door.

Mike helped out the best he could, folding napkins and straightening placemats. I had several types of wine and water glasses, but not many that matched. Mike spaced the glasses out artistically. It was obvious that he came from a big Italian family the way he handled the fancy china and silver. I put silver candlesticks on the table, though I had no intention of lighting them. It was just part of the way I grew up. Candlesticks belonged on the dining table. Period.

Gabriele and Dante arrived next. Both of them admired the table setting, but spent their time unloading the groceries they had brought with them. It was a good thing they closed the restaurant, because they had cleaned out the kitchen, bringing whole branzino fish, as well as pounded chicken breasts that looked like they might become chicken parmigiana or chicken schnitzel of some kind. Lots of mozzarella and parmesan cheese (the parmesan on a smallish wheel, to be ground or grated or even shaved if you wanted big thin pieces).

A large cooler like you might take on a picnic was handled carefully, and when it was opened, it was clear why—it was a large circular *tiramisu*, a traditional Italian dessert that combines cocoa, fine-ground espresso, mascarpone cheese and tons of ladyfingers that make up the backbone of what looks like a cake before it's cut. The name means "wake me up," because it was rich and sweet and full of chocolate and coffee (both of which were rich with caffeine).

Gabriele whipped out three bottles of Barolo and three bottles of Barbaresco, two related northern Italian red wines, both made from Nebbiolo grapes. The Barolo wines are typically high in tannins, and aged carefully to coddle the tannins to the smooth, soft palate-pleasing taste that make Barolo wines the monarchs of the Italian wine industry.

In Italy, Barolo are "Sunday" wines, and Barbaresco wines are everyday wines—what you might call "hamburger wines" in New York. For me, I love them both.

I frequently can't afford to pay for a good Barolo, because they run to hundreds of dollars for a bottle, but I can usually scrape together the price of a fruity, wonderful Barbaresco, which is like a second cousin to Barolo. Anyway, I reached back into the rear of the pantry and pulled out a case of Montepulciano d'Abruzzo, which is an everyday wine made east of Rome in the center of the boot of Italy. It's a pleasing wine, easy to drink, easy to appreciate. It's also a wine that's frequently poured by the glass by a bartender. If you had to pay the per-glass price for a bottle, you'd be harder-put to buy the bottles.

There were big smiles all around the room when I put the box of Montepulciano d'Abruzzo on the pass-through from the kitchen. I popped a bottle open and poured quick tastes into five small whiskey glasses, since I didn't have any tasting glasses. Was it Barolo? Nope, it wasn't. It was Montepulciano d'Abruzzo; tasty, a little rough, but easy on the way down.

Ruth showed up last. We hadn't really expected her to be early to the dinner. She had two bouquets of flowers with her. I pulled out some vases—nothing fancy, more like old florist vases, with the occasional tall vase made to accommodate a dozen tall, showy gladioluses, which are actually members of the iris family, and originate in South Africa, as well as the coastal areas of Africa along the Mediterranean and the Indian Ocean African shores.

Ruth had mixed about a dozen glads in with the other flowers, some of which—including a few roses—had scents that wafted gently through the living room/dining room of my apartment. The name of gladiolus is a derivative of the Latin word for "sword" ("gladius," as in "gladiator"). Ruth sprang forward and arranged the flowers picturesquely and scattered the vases around the room, putting a tall clearly hand-made colorful ceramic vase featuring the tall gladioluses in the middle of the dining table, between two silver candlesticks that had once been on my grandparents' dining table in Mt Vernon, just north of New York City. My aunt used to kid us by saying that Mt Vernon is "next to one of the biggest cities in the world"—making it seem that Mt Vernon was in some sort of race for one of the largest cities in the United States.

Pretty soon there was the smell of olive oil warming in a skillet. Dante and Gabriele were both in the kitchen. Gabriele was cleaning the fish. I offered to help, but Gabriele didn't want an amateur handling the branzino.

Chapter Thirty-nine

Mike tapped on his wine glass with a spoon, to indicate that he wanted to make a toast. He scooted his chair back and stood up.

"It's a pleasure to be here with my favorite friends," he said, gesturing with his glass to each of us in turn, and then sipping the Montepulciano d'Abruzzo with a big smile. We clinked our glasses around the table, and swallowed a gulp of the tasty wine.

"I appreciate the fact that you all managed to fit this dinner into your schedules. I wouldn't be standing here without you all—especially Chef Dante, whom I don't see often—unfortunately.

"I want to thank everyone in the room for all the support and goodwill you have given me over the years. I want to tell you that I resigned from the NYPD today." He paused. "I'm planning to hang out my law shingle, as they say. I want to help some of the fine people I've met over the years."

There was an audible exhaling sound from around the table.

"New York won't be the same without you as the prime detective in the NYPD," I said. "What's the Commissioner going to do when he needs a team leader?"

Mike smiled good-naturedly. "No idea what the PC will think of all this, but I know he got my resignation letter this morning. But I haven't given you the punchline. Here's the surprise ending to my announcement—I'm hoping to go into a partnership with Maggie Landover. She's not the only person I respect enough to shake hands on a partnership, but she's the one I'd like to work with most. Why? She trusts me, just as I have learned to trust her. She cares about the people she works with, and when I tell her there are ways to keep her hookers out of trouble, she doesn't laugh at me—she listens to what I have to say.

"None of you is surprised that I've gotten increasingly bored with my NYPD work," he said. "We're a racially problematic society, and just trying to catch the bad guys isn't the best way to make New York a paradise on Earth. We have to figure out how to raise confident, ambitious Black and brown kids who know that they're not in any way inferior to White kids of their same age. Maggie understands that. Maggie's mixed-race and I would've never thought of her as weighed down by being part Asian—until recently.

"This goddamn COVID-19 pandemic has brought out the worst in people who live here. Look at what we've done. The White people who speak English as their first language are almost all vaccinated. The elderly are almost all vaccinated. If you're not elderly or White—or both—your likelihood of being vaccinated is way, way less.

"Black and brown adults don't trust our public health efforts. It's hard to blame them sometimes. They've gotten the bottom of the barrel for most of their lives. They're brought up in the projects, go to schools that no sane person would want to go to. Their parents aren't educated the way White parents are, and they don't have the kind of goals for their kids that White people have.

"I haven't ever gotten married," he said emphatically. "It's not because I don't like women, because I do. It's because I know that if I had children, they would be privileged in ways that their neighbors of color would never dream about. White kids assume they'll not only finish high school, they'll go to college. They'll live in their own houses or apartments, and when they're old enough to retire, they'll retire with enough money to live on. The Black families with kids don't have the same advantages. They grew up as second-class citizens and now they see themselves as second-class at best. It's a matter of expectations. Does your Black neighbor plan to move to some tree-lined street on Long Island? Do they expect their children to be doctors and teachers?"

There was a riot of sirens all of a sudden.

"Cops," Mike said. "When there's something bad going on, it's always the cops that get called in. Cops don't get to try to make things right. They get to chase down the people they think are wrong. I'm sick and tired of being a cop."

The sirens got louder and closer.

"That sounds like it's outside," I said, standing up and walking over to the balcony doors. I opened the doors and the sounds were louder, and there were voices yelling, mixed in with the sirens and doors slamming.

"I'm going downstairs to see what the crap is going on out there," I said. "The last time there was this kind of noise here, Maggie was standing on her balcony covered with blood. Somebody had tried to rape her and she slit his throat."

When I got to the street, it was obvious what was going on. The street was jammed with NYPD cars with lights flashing and sirens turned on. There were two ambulances edging their ways into the narrow side street that Maggie's building faced.

The worst had happened. Maggie Landover was dead. Somebody shot her.

Two of the cops pushed their way out the front door of the building, leading a short, pale man who was handcuffed and being pushed into the back seat of a police cruiser. It was Chuy Acosta-Gonzalez.

By the time I got back upstairs, they had CNN on the TV, and the cat was out of the bag. Not only was Maggie dead, but her son, Jesus, had been arrested. Two EMTs were rolling a cloth-covered stretcher to the back of one of the two ambos.

"Damnit," Mike yelled. "They've got Chuy in cuffs. He must have shot his own mother."

She killed his father, I thought. *The kid couldn't stop himself. What goes around comes around.* I went back in my mind to seeing Chuy playing catch in Cooperstown, and on seeing him getting autographs, and wearing his Pee Wee Reese jersey with the Number One on it.

It was obvious that Mike's announcement had been superseded by real events outside my building.

"This is exactly what I was talking about," Mike said. "What kind of family is it where the mother kills the father, and the son kills the mom?" He was gnashing his teeth, and stamping his feet on the floor. He picked up the bottle of scotch he had brought and poured about three fingers of the amber-colored liquid into a juice glass, and pulled a couple of ice cubes out of the icemaker in their freezer. "Timing is everything," he said. "I never even had a chance to talk to Maggie about my idea. Chuy got to her first."

With Mike no longer a member of the NYPD, the best information we could get in the public media was from CNN,

Indeed, according to CNN's reporting, Chuy Acosta-Gonzalez had been arrested for shooting his mother, Maggie Landover. He had been arraigned that same evening, and was being kept in the precinct jail pending another hearing on bail or remand to Riker's Island.

Chapter Forty

One of the reporters on CNN was standing in the street in front of Maggie's building. "This is looking like a family dispute of some kind—one of the most dangerous types of police calls." She was struggling to talk to the camera that was watching her. "It sounds like a woman was shot at close range, and the shooter may have been her son, but nobody's been allowed in the apartment. According to the concierge, her name was Maggie Landover, and her son had just gone upstairs to see her. I'm being told by several different people—neighbors, cops, that she was married to the son's father some years back, maybe divorced, maybe not. Broken home. According to the local police precinct, the victim was arrested for killing her ex-husband a few months back, but there were no charges brought, because she was acting in self-defense. Stabbed him with a kitchen knife when he was trying to rape her, according to what she said at the arraignment."

I tend not to trust reporters talking to a camera. They back and fill more than they talk about real facts, real police-type findings. Having worked with Mike for several years, I know how careful cops can be, and how tight-lipped they can be if they don't think you have any business asking questions.

The CNN reporter did a brief interview with one of the cops who had been on the scene.

"When we got to the apartment, the woman was dead. Somebody shot her in the head. She couldn't have survived more than a minute or two," the cop said. "The shooter said he was her son, and he was talking about how she had killed his father about six months earlier. The dad lived in California, according to what the son said, and had been visiting New York on business, ran into his ex-wife on the subway."

Later on, the reporter aired some more of the interview. "The shooter said his dad was wearing a surgical mask because of the pandemic, and he never said anything to the woman, but grabbed at her like he was going to assault her, and was trying to wrestle her handbag out of her hand. She yelled at him, but he didn't say anything.

"There were several witnesses on the train, and they said at a hearing that she was very loud about wanting him to keep his hands to himself. Some men who were on the train tried to pull him away, but apparently he never said anything at all, just grabbed her and tried to pull her toward him.

"She said afterward that she had no idea who he was. They had been married, but had not seen each other in more than twenty years. He was Catholic and didn't believe in divorce, so the fact that they hadn't seen each other in more than two decades made no difference at all to him." "What God has joined, let no man put asunder," was the phrase the Church used at the time. Marriage was permanent, no matter what.

I felt the same way, but I never tried to rape my wife. Would have been a piss-poor rapist anyway, more violent than sexy, which I gather is the rapist's way of looking at life anyway. Ugh.

After we had been married for well over twenty-five years, I moved from California to New York to open a new office for the company that I had founded and had been running for a long time. Because it was a Sports PR company, it was important that it have an office in New York, which was, after all, the media capital of the United States.

Hollywood was the land of movies, and increasingly of television, but what mattered at that time was the newspapers and the news departments of the television networks. Anyway, my wife stayed in California, in the house we owned together. I made sure she was taken care of in every way possible, and agreed to spend holidays like Christmas and the Fourth of July in California with her and the kids (who were grown and no longer in the house). And truth be told, companies that made royalty deals with sports figures were the point of my company, so

I was more interested in Nike and Reebok and sneaker endorsements than I was in basketball or track.

It never occurred to me to abandon my wife. She had a ruptured brain aneurysm eventually—just after she turned eighty—and her brain was damaged considerably by that. She ended up in a nursing home in a wheelchair, and often without knowing who she was. She was deeply demented and delusional, and frequently believed that the building she was in was a cruise ship that was going to sink.

"I can't swim," she would say to me, as though that would matter if the building sank into the Hudson River, which was just outside her window.

My wife died before the pandemic took over the United States. I was relieved when she died, but never remarried—or even considered dating. If I had felt like being married again, I might well have proposed to Ruth, who was always attractive to me, and who was one of my best friends. I had been married twice—once a short-term farce that was annulled quickly after the wedding, and then once with my wife, where we had five children. Only two grandchildren, both girls, and both with my same last name—Miller—because both of them were illegitimate, and took their mother's last name (which was the same as mine).

I always said, "three strikes and you're out," when it came to marriage. My first marriage had been more of a joke than a marriage, and had lasted less than three months before we both knew we had made a terrible mistake. Her father took over the legal details, filed for a divorce and later had the marriage annulled, so that legally it had never actually happened—we were both still single. I think in his mind that was to make sure I never made any claims on her estate, whatever it was worth. I was so happy never to see her again, that annulment or no, I would more quickly have killed myself with a jagged knife than I would have pursued her inheritance, if she ever had one. She was a drug addict. I wasn't, although I was always willing to have a scotch or two (still am, truth be told).

The real truth of the matter, because of the annulment, was that I was only legally married once, so I could have had a second swing of the marriage bat, so to speak. But I never did, and Ruth would have said "No" in a big way if I had asked her anyway. The most important woman in my life, eventually, was my second wife. We were married for nearly forty eight years before she died. Then I realized that my elder daughter had become the most important woman in my life, after I was widowed. Not the same thing as a wife, but at least as dear as a wife—just in a different way. Besides, one of my daughters had two kids of her own, and grandchildren are a special joy in life, as any grandparent knows.

I was never able to move back to California, where I had spent most of my life. I remain a big UCLA sports fan, and send a check to the UCLA sports department every year at around Christmas. I seldom have a chance to watch any UCLA sports games, because they're just not an important enough team to be broadcast nationally—unlike my dad's *alma mater*, Notre Dame, which always manages to get its football games televised week after week. Probably it's a major source of funding for Notre Dame's not-unimportant academic programs. My father's degree from Notre Dame was in Finance. It would be easy to tell the difference between his youth and my youth by the fact that my degree from UCLA was in Latin and Greek—a perfect degree in the 1960s, which got me a job in the book publishing industry and eventually into the Sports PR business. I had the privilege of meeting several big-name sports figures at UCLA, mostly in basketball during the John Wooden days, when he was known as the "Wizard of Westwood" due to his nearly unfailing successes with NCAA basketball wins.

Epilogue

Mike's planned partnership with Maggie was not his only shot at winning.

"I want to form a corporation with you, Gabriele and Ruth," he said to me, after he had time to realize that Maggie Landover was irreplaceable. "I'm not a cop anymore, and if I tried to withdraw my resignation, I'm sure the PC wouldn't accept the withdrawal. He's probably too happy to have me off his back to consider letting me back in the door."

I asked him what he intended to do about Chuy, who was clearly going to be a thorn in the side of whoever was prosecuting the young man for shooting his own mother. He didn't make much effort to distance himself from the deed.

"She was wearing a scarf I gave her that looked a lot like the flag of China," Chuy said when he was arraigned. "Red and yellow, and made by Hermes from Paris. That's how I knew it was her. That scarf. Nobody else would ever have worn it."

Being Latino and Catholic, Manuel never tried to divorce his wife when it turned out they didn't get along well. But they separated unofficially, and Maggie eventually petitioned for a divorce from her husband, which was granted by a Nevada court. She never considered herself remarried, and neither did he. Chuy was their only child, but he grew up solely in the home of his dad—a sprawling mansion on a three-acre lot with two huge swimming pools to help a sweating man (or his son) cool off in the desert sun.

Being the scion of a drug cartel family, Manuel traveled for business from time to time. On one of his trips to New York City, he found himself on a subway train headed toward a potential site of a new business operation in Queens—wearing a surgical mask, which was required on public transportation during the COVID-19 pandemic by the City of New York and the State of New York.

Who should he see on his subway car but his ex-wife, Maggie? She was easily recognizable, even with a surgical mask on. She was half Chinese, pretty as a picture, and slight, like a lot of Asian women. He sidled his way in her direction, still believing they were married. Like a lot of horny men, he had sex on his mind, and he went after her without ever saying a word to her. No "hello, how are you" or any other kind of talk. He had no idea that she wouldn't recognize him, since he had seen her and remembered her easily.

Anyway, he pounced on her like a rapist at night in Central Park, and the first connection he made was to put his hands on her breasts.

She slapped him and pushed him away, yelling something like "Get your hands off me, you scum!" He found it impossible that she didn't know who he was. They'd been married for decades—no divorce would ever have been effective, but neither of them had pursued one anyway, as far as he knew. She had, in fact, gotten a divorce, and had married a fairly elderly physician, Horace Landover, so her name was changed to Maggie Landover, although Manuel had no idea that had happened. Marriage was marriage in his mind. Nothing could break it, not even a separation from the Pope himself.

He refused to leave her alone, and when she got to her station, Vernon-Jackson in Queens, he exited the subway car behind her, realizing that this was his stop, too—and the potential location of a string of massage parlors that would be full of smuggled Asian girls who were ready to surrender themselves to anybody with a few bucks in his pocket. Sex wasn't a matter of morals to Manuel, it was two things: a matter of marriage and a matter of hormones. Both were active as he followed her to what turned out to be her apartment building.

He pushed his way into her apartment, and continued to force himself on her. She continued to yell at him, to the point where her neighbors called the concierge downstairs to complain about the noise. Then the concierge called the police, and sirens were coming around the corner in minutes.

The police heard the yells and screams when they got to the door, which was unlocked. They opened it and pushed their way in, just in time to see Manuel lurch and jerk his head while Maggie held a knife in her hand. It was obvious that the woman hadn't stabbed him, or otherwise tried to harm him. She was holding the knife still, like she was ready to use it, but wasn't trying to do that yet. The man slid his neck across the knife blade, and blood gushed out like an oil gusher spurting crude oil out the top of a rig.

The woman was covered in blood and had a terrified look on her face. She was still screaming at him to let her go. He still had his mask on, although it was sagging from the weight of the blood that was squirting from his neck.

Two of the cops pulled him away from the woman. She dropped the knife and he collapsed in a faint, probably from loss of blood. Four cops wrote similar reports on the incident, and an ambo took the man away, while the woman continued to scream and cry, running out onto her balcony over the street and shouting "Help me! Help me!"

Little did anyone know at that point that Gabriele and I were standing on the street in front of her apartment, observing Maggie as she screamed and dripped blood from her hair and hands. "I didn't do it!" she yelled. "He was raping me!" she yelled to the four cops who were in her apartment. All four would testify at the arraignment that the man appeared to be trying to assault her sexually.

His mask fell off, and she recognized him immediately.

"Manny! Manny! What are you doing here?" she yelled at the unconscious man on the floor, who was being loaded onto a stretcher and covered from head to foot with a yellow plastic cover. An EMT tried to find a pulse on the man.

Nothing. Dead on Arrival. They tried an electrical cardioversion (defibrillation), but there was no response. No breath. No pulse. They tried CPR, but there was no response to that either. They covered him up completely and rolled him out of the apartment.

"He was my husband!" she yelled to the four cops who were still in the apartment, looking pale and shaky.

"I haven't seen him in twenty years," she blurted out. "We have a kid, but I haven't seen him since he was about two years old," she was crying and talking at the same time. "I had no idea he was even in town. I didn't know it was him. He never said anything and he never took his mask off. He looked like a stranger to me. He lives someplace in California. What the fuck was he doing on my subway car?"

Then she knelt down on the floor and put her hands together in a prayer. "Forgive me, O Lord," she said. "I didn't mean to hurt him. I didn't know who he was."

About the Author

Joe Allen's first success in "trade" books (books for retail buyers) was *Sandcastles: The Splendors of Enchantment* (1981). His first mystery novel, *Rocky Point Road*, was published in 2015, followed by *The Monteverdi Manuscript: A Hugo Miller Mystery* in 2016. *The Hanging Man*, published December 1, 2018, is a second Hugo Miller Mystery, set largely in Manhattan. With characters including a murderous "gypsy" dwarf, a papal legate with an overactive Twitter account, a woman promoting canonization for a nineteenth century New Yorker, a long-dead gangster who may have left buried gold in the basement of a condemned building, the wife of a murdered man on the lam with her infant son, and a tribe of possibly mutant males who live in tunnels underground on the west side of NYC.

His novel about a sprawling New York family from the Eisenhower years to 2015, *Where All Past Years Are,* published September 1, 2018, is set largely on the west shore of Lake Champlain in New York near the Canadian border. *A More Perfect Union*, published early in 2019, is the third Hugo Miller mystery, following the fortunes of Eddie Hall, an African-American lawyer and politician whose intended same-sex marriage is cancelled by the murder of his intended on a sidewalk in SoHo.

Joe is currently working on another Hugo Miller mystery and a mystery, *Boom!* that starts with a deadly explosion at a fireworks factory in Arizona.

Joe is also the author of five nonfiction books, including *Effective Business Communications: A Practical Guide*. His *Systems in Actions: A Social and Managerial Approach* was used as a text in advanced problem-solving in several MBA programs, including the UCLA Anderson School of Management. He contributed chapters to two Aspatore (Thomson Reuters) books on investor relations.

Most of Joe's business career was with Bozell & Jacobs and then at Allen & Caron Inc., a consulting and investor relations firm he founded in 1981 in Irvine, California. Under his leadership, the company worked with clients in the UK, Ireland, France, Belgium, Sweden, Denmark, Italy, Greece, Germany, Poland, Switzerland, South Africa, Singapore, Australia, New Zealand, Brazil and Argentina, among other countries.

Joe served on the boards of several small companies, both publicly traded and privately held, was vice chairman of the United Way in Orange County, California, has written on a variety of topics for numerous leading magazines and newspapers, and has published interviews with financial luminaries on SeekingAlpha.com.

Joe studied Classical Languages and English Literature at UCLA in the 1960s, prior to becoming an editor of scholarly journals at scholarly journal publisher Sage Publications, and was then a marketing manager at Benziger Bruce & Glencoe, a college publishing subsidiary of Macmillan. He was married for 47 years. Now widowed, he has two children and two granddaughters.

Rocky Point Road

When his ex-wife drowns in a hot tub in California, Denis Rosa sets out to bury her and sell the house. He confronts her philandering history and her fixation on young Chicano boys and is the victim of a vicious attempted murder without ever knowing why. The house on the cliffside on Rocky Point Road holds a ghost, a hidden treasure of some kind, and decades of memories for the Rosa family. When Detective Sue Mason is assigned to the case, her son and his soon-to-be husband and two dogs move into the house with Denis to protect him from further attacks. Is it drug-related? The wife was alcoholic and smoked grass, but nothing hard. Denis confronts his ghosts as he finds himself attracted to Sue. The key to the plot is found when Denis slides off the edge of the cliff.

Chapter One – Rocky Point Road

The apartment was cluttered with art.

Denis Rosa's unfocussed appreciation of different styles ended up in a kind of warehouse approach to everything. There was a rubbing he'd bought in Cambodia, and a pair of late Ching-dynasty vases, probably not worth a lot. An early Chinese brazier or incense burner, coppery green on a Noguchi glass-top coffee table with his grandfather's crystal pipe ashtray that took two hands to pick up. Then an old Syrian inlaid wooden chair with bits of shiny mother-of-pearl diamond shapes here and there, a ragtag assortment of flat-weave kilim rugs, a Barcelona chair, a walnut harpsichord. His grandmother's heavy sterling candlesticks with Christmas red candles, an African table carved from a single ebony tree trunk and a mismatched assortment of African sculptures bought here and there; one a red-faced West African piece with monkey fur for hair. A dark, moody painting of Chief Joseph in television pixel patterns, a ghostly painting of shadowy figures on a bridge, an abstract oil of student riots in 1968 at the Gare du Nord, a couple of big academic nudes, a late impressionist picture of two people on the Staten Island ferry with the Brooklyn Bridge, a gaggle of Victorian tourist watercolors of Italian stereotypes (a cleric, a street musician, a woman with a big hat), two Persian miniatures of animals, a pair of impressive storytelling copperplate etchings from the 1960s, and five non-objective mystery pieces in bright colors by a well-known Irish artist. That's plus two dozen or so family photos scattered around the room, and seven or eight pieces of high-fired ceramic bas relief.

"What a fucking mess," he thought. "Why did I accumulate all this stuff?"

His wife had died and he was walking in circles with his back to the walls, looking from the walls toward the rooms, trying to make sense of something that didn't make sense no matter how you looked at it. He thought for a minute that he could just start hitting things, pick up that African ebony head shaped like a scythe and just hit the canvasses until they were all ripped and shredded. But like the temptation to throw her wedding ring in the river, the impulse subsided. Til death us do part. Death was here, and they were parted.

Why do you make a home after all? So it will be a place where you are comfortable, where you feel safe, where you can store all your pieces of string into a huge ball if you want. Then you pull away one of the foundation stones and what happens? Ashes, ashes, we all fall down.

"It's odd," he thought as he walked out the front door of the building, "how lucid I feel while I am nearly unhinged in the way I am thinking. Almost like I had taken some kind of designer drug that would make me high, but let me drive a car."

It was chilly outside and the sidewalks were wet. He scuffed through the puddles in the pedestrian mall that used to be Broadway, stopping to watch the lights dance across the buildings. A man on stilts with a tall red hat was handing out flyers for a comedy club, or maybe a nude club, and that man with white underwear and a cowboy hat was strumming a guitar for a group of people who were busily snapping cellphone pictures of him, and probably giving him money. How does he stay warm enough to play the guitar? How does his guitar stay in tune when it is so damp?

He turned onto 46th Street and headed for St. Mary the Virgin, hoping the door would not be locked. It was Sunday afternoon, so there was an even chance he could get in and smell the ghost of stale incense that constantly floated in the air. The door was, in fact, open when he pulled on it. There was to be evensong. Could he wait for that? He looked at his watch, which he had buckled on upside down, so he had to twist his wrist around and cock his head to read the clock face. 4:30. He scooted into a pew on the side. There was a scattering of people, a couple of ladies, a man who seemed to be dressed as a greyfriar with a rope around his waist, and a man with a young child walking the Stations of the Cross.

He stared at the beam that crossed above the old communion rail that formed a rood screen about 30 feet off the floor, with a life-size crucifix, and with six pendant, red glass altar lights in gold or brass fixtures at regular intervals across the span, swaying slightly from the motion of the earth, or the vibrations of the subways. The church couldn't get a permit for a crypt even though it was well over 150 years old because, basically, the idea of burying dead bodies under the theater district was too gross for the city to consider. And you can't dig very far in midtown without hitting something that makes the city run anyway.

Someone started to play the organ, stopped, and started over. If you play the organ you have to practice on an organ, he thought. Makes sense. Hard to have a full organ in your apartment, so you have to practice in a church. Well, evensong, after all, is only an hour or so away. Maybe that's it. The organist stopped again, and there was silence for half a minute, and then he started to play the Bach Toccata and Fugue in F Major.

Tony Perkins was speeding along a cliff edge in his little sports car yelling good-bye, John Sebastian, and singing along with the organ music on his radio. Odd the things that music makes you remember, he thought. "It's raining," Melina Mercouri had said shakily, staring out the window with half a pound of mascara on her magnificent burning eyes. Her husband would kill her, of course; that was the fate of Phaedra. But Tony Perkins had to drive his car off a cliff into the water with a randomly chosen Bach organ piece playing as he flew through the air toward the rocks.

His eyes filled with tears, remembering that time long ago when he could take Phaedra seriously. Hell, his wife had died out in California and he had so far felt no discernible emotion other than anger and a certain level of disorientation, even though he'd been alone when he got the call and could have cried. But crying is a communal thing, he thought. He'd cried fountains in the past; it wasn't that he was so macho that he couldn't cry.

"Yeah," he said, "I'm ok, I'll be ok. I'll get a flight right away, I'll, um, I'll call you later."

Sitting in the church listening to the organist practice made the knot in his stomach loosen up a bit, although he still felt on the edge of nausea. The slightly bitter sweetness in the air was restorative. In most churches you smelled candlewax, but in this church you smelled frankincense. They call it Smoky Mary's because they use so much incense it makes your eyes water if you sit in the front of the church. He knew to sit in the back on the side, and even so his throat sometimes coated with phlegm when the deacon came down the center aisle to read the gospel, and flung the censor back and forth, creating a cloud of gray-blue vaporized resin for the congregation to suck into their lungs.

He couldn't just sit there and wait.

He took out his cellphone and looked up an airline flight service, walked out the front of the church and booked a flight to LA Monday morning, getting in about noon. Yes, first class, upgrade with my miles; I'm not made out of money.

Bond 45 was dismantling the afternoon brunch. He waved at the maître d' and walked over to the long bar and ordered a vodka straight up, a little dirty, with olives. A drink would help. He asked the bartender for some roasted vegetables, too, cauliflower, string beans and eggplant.

You'd think something would be different when someone dies. Something would happen, people would not watch ballgames or something. But look around, he thought, just look around. Times Square is normal, even though Elissa drowned in the backyard hot tub on a sunny late afternoon at the south end of Santa Monica Bay.

The vodka had little bits of ice floating in it from having been shaken vigorously in a theatrical, over-the-head show that the bartender did. Show-off. Well, it's Times Square. It was deliciously cold, and there were three big olives. The salty olive juice took the edge off the alcohol, and he took a big loud slurp from the martini glass while it was sitting on the bar. He put his phone down on the bar and waved at the bartender, pointed at the restrooms, and mouthed Be Right Back.

Well, something was different. He had never felt like masturbating in a public restroom before. Just as he didn't destroy the paintings, though, he just peed, rinsed his hands, and went back to the bar.

The apartment was chilly because he had left the windows open. The vodka had cleared his head, and that businesslike avatar of his took over when something dislocating happened. He packed a few things, but didn't need to take much other than a suit, because he had plenty of clothes in the house in Palos Verdes.

He had to inject himself with a blood-thinner after a deep vein thrombosis years before, and if he waited until after he got on the plane because he did not have a membership in the right airline club, he did it in the head after he got seated in 4D on the aisle. He had never learned, after all those years, to just jab himself with the needle, had to push it into the fleshy part of his thigh and then push the plunger down. It seldom hurt, and frequently was almost sensationless, but there was a sense of dread when he pulled out an orange-wrapped syringe and wiped his thigh with an alcohol swab with his jeans around his calves. He threw the used syringe back in his cosmetics bag after the protective plastic sheath snapped up to protect anyone from getting stuck with the needle. And for some reason after he finished the shot, he felt more relaxed, as though he could fall asleep before the plane took off. There was still the minute coal-like bit of blood clot in a vein just below his left knee, and he had to be careful. He pulled on the doctor-prescribed, tight rubberized support stockings before he put on his jeans and thought what he always thought, that they were so tight he couldn't wear them. But he always managed to forget about them, and today was no different. He only had to wear them in the air, and it seemed like a penance.

The flight attendant gave him a screwdriver with an extra little bottle of vodka that he dumped into the drink. He reclined his chair a bit and stared out the window at the sky that was blue and glaring at the same time, left his eyes unable to focus momentarily when he looked back into the cabin. How could she drown? She was afraid of water because she was a bad swimmer, but you don't need to swim in a hot tub. Did she fall? Did she have a heart attack?

Theirs was not a standard-issue marriage, although they'd had children who had dutifully reproduced and given them grandchildren, so on Christmas Day they seemed Norman Rockwell-ish. They'd both been unhappily married before, and the scars from the previous experiences were deeper than they had thought and they were not able to achieve that easy trust and companionship that some enviable couples had. They didn't distrust each other, and they usually got along well. They shared some interests, notably baseball and classical music.

Things danced around in his head. A strong practical streak in him thought about what to do with the house, a house that meant even more clutter to deal with over and above the apartment that had driven him to the brink of despair the day before. He wanted "Simple Gifts" to be played. He would have her cremated as they had talked about, and he would scatter her ashes at sea. He saw himself dropping a lei of plumeria flowers onto the blackish blue choppy water of the Catalina Sound.

They loved each other, but they found after the children were grown that they couldn't get along without bickering, and he had moved to New York and opened a new office of the consulting business he had founded. He learned to cook because he did not want to eat at restaurants all the time, and she had taken up with a string of short-term boyfriends, some of whom tried to take up residence in the house with her, but she apparently drew the line at that. Backwards, right? He was supposed to be tomcatting and she was supposed to be cooking, but it didn't work out that way.

He wondered if one of the guys had been with her when she died. His business partner had not said anything other than that Elissa had been found by the gardener in the hot tub with the Jacuzzi function still running. She had apparently been there for a day or so. Ignoble to be all wrinkled and partially parboiled. The coroner had taken her, of course. He had not talked to the rest of the family; not a word. In centuries past, he thought, the women in the family would have cleaned her up and packed herbs around her in a plank-made coffin, basil and verbena and rosemary and mint, strong-smelling herbs.

The Monteverdi Manuscript (Hugo Miller Mystery 1)

The action revolves around the death of a famous musician, who hits the pavement outside Carnegie Hall from the window of his apartment seven stories up. He has recorded keyboard versions of a lost opera by Claudio Monteverdi, the man who "invented" opera. Set in New York, London and Venice, action includes a kidnapping, drug use, prostitution, LGBT characters, one character who comes back from the dead, and three classic New York detective characters led by Hugo Miller.

Where All Past Years Are (A Family Saga)

Starting on Thanksgiving Day 1954, the Chadwick family encounters wars, financial crashes, 9-11, and the Great Recession. As a family with a WASP history they discover the wider world that is America, marry across religious, racial and ethnic lines, live, love, laugh and celebrate Thanksgiving and Independence Day at the Old Home on the shore of Lake Champlain near the Canadian border in New York.

The love of husbands and wives, the closeness of relatives who are an increasingly rainbow-like group, the touching beauty of the Old Home on the Lake as some family members move back to the property into new cottages—all are major themes. Children running a three-legged race watch the young man, Gray Chadwick, drop to his knees to beg his pregnant girlfriend, Melissa, to marry him. Births, deaths, burials, 4th of July fireworks, boating and bass fishing, and the strengthening power of love lead to a final surprising and unexpected reunion of two branches of the family for the first time in over three hundred years.

A More Perfect Union (Hugo Miller Mystery 3)

Former ADA Eddie Hill, divorced African-American father of

two, plans to marry Jimmy van Gelsen, wealthy gay man who, like Eddie, has been unlucky in love. Eddie is injured in a car accident on the NY Thruway, and Jimmy is shot in the forehead, killing him instantly. Was it Eddie's gun? If so, with Eddie in the hospital upstate, who pulled the trigger? Hugo, Ruth and Gabriele sort through a thicket of clues—a stolen Bentley, a shabby vacation home on Antigua, a multimillion-dollar co-op in Greenwich Village with fabulous art. Major political demonstrations with thugs and tiki torches, reminiscent of the Charlottesville riots with protesters battling in the streets—one at a prayer vigil, one a "Million Woman March" down 5th Avenue, another outside the Copley Plaza in Boston. Eddie runs for Congress from a mixed-race district in Brooklyn. Jimmy's will left a fortune to Eddie, who doesn't want any of it. Is it a right vs left murder? A gay-bashing murder? A robbery gone wrong? The answers are close to home.

The HangingMan (Hugo Miller Mystery 2)

When wealthy investment banker Luigi's body is found hanging from the crossbars of the George Washington Bridge, it is immediately thought to be a Mafia hit. Is it? Not according to a Catholic bishop with a diplomatic errand from the Vatican and an out-of-control Twitter account. As the truth unfolds, the reader meets a mad dwarf who eats insects and small rodents, a long-dead candidate for canonization, a deceased gangster who owned The Cotton Club in Harlem, and a tribe of mis-shapen males whose lives have been spent in tunnels under Hell's Kitchen.

Explosions, whispers coming from walls, mysterious billionaires from Grand Cayman, Luigi's terrified young wife with a suckling baby at her breast, treasure-hunters looking for buried gold in the basement—provide a frightening backdrop to a mystery that literally goes deeper and deeper into Manhattan as the story develops.

Hugo Miller, Ruth the Sleuth, handsome Gabriele Cortese and stalwart NYPD detective Mike di Saronno pool their considerable resources to solve a series of crimes that may hark back as far as seventy-five or one hundred years.

Chapter One – The Hanging Man

Nobody wanted to go for a bike ride.

Too hot, too much traffic, what if you got a flat tire? I explained to each one I called that there is a bike path that goes all the way up the west side of Manhattan between the West Side Highway and the Hudson River. There are no places where you have to cross a street once you get on the path. It's paved and there are lots of people skating, running and biking on it all day every day, even when you'd assume most people would be at work. It's that kind of city. You don't have to worry about being by yourself and running into thugs.

Still, nobody would go with me. I really had my mind set on exploring that afternoon with a buddy. My trusty roommate, Carl, was, not unusually, out of town, up in Montreal. Finally I tried Gabriele Cortese, whom I had met as part of a murder investigation that I was partly involved in solving with my friend Mike di Saronno, a detective in the Midtown West Police Precinct. Gabriele was originally a suspect, but he had nothing to do with the crime. He was totally innocent.

Gabriele lives all the way in Brooklyn Heights, and I had no real hope he would be willing to schlep into town and then ride all the way up to Fort Washington Park, which was what I wanted to do. I had never seen the little red lighthouse that sits under the George Washington Bridge. Very few people have seen it, comparatively speaking, because you have to wander out under the bridge to see it. There are no vantage points in Manhattan where it is visible. One of those hidden treasures of New York—and there are a lot of those.

"*Ciao, Ugo,*" he said when he picked the phone up, clearly with a caller ID.

I told him what my idea was, and he said yes right away, without even thinking about it. Woo hoo! He said he was going to take the subway to Times Square, which is where I lived, because his bike folds up so he can carry it on the train. So there was no chance he would fink out after riding all the way from Brooklyn Heights. Perfect.

He's from the Isle of Capri, and speaks English with a slight

Italian lilt most of the time, but with pronounced "foreigner" grammar when the mood comes upon him, so to speak. He's startlingly handsome, and I have learned to be amused by the looks on faces and the craned necks when he walks into a room. He had also been a sex worker at one point.

Yes, the truth is that like most people, I find him handsome. We actually met because, although we were not exactly neighbors, I thought we were neighbors because, well, the area where I lived, which is the theater district in New York, is thick with sex workers. Even someone who looked like a movie star, as Gabriele does, would have fewer takers where he lives in Brooklyn Heights than where he used to hang out around Times Square, which is choked with hotels, bars and horny travelers. These days he is the respectable host of a white-tablecloth restaurant near Gramercy Park that he and his cousin, Dante, own together. Dante is the chef; Gabriele is the matinee idol. The food is to die for.

No, we aren't involved, and I don't see how that could ever change. When I first met him I thought he was trying to kill me. Fortunately I was mistaken. Maybe that's why we are close friends; we'd been to the mat together, so to speak. There's just too much clutter in our lives to toss it all aside and try to change everything in one swell foop. It's worth pointing out that I'm twenty years older than he is, which makes him young and me middle-aged. Okay, later middle-aged. Ok, senior. Besides, I have kids, even though I seldom see them because they live on the other side of the country, in La-La-Land. You know that old *New Yorker* cover that shows a New Yorker's view looking west? Well, way at the far side, before Japan. Nuff said.

I am very fortunate because I started a consulting company about twenty years ago, and was able to work there and increase the value of it, and then to sell it to a bigger company in the same business for an ongoing percentage of the profits. I have some duties there, but mostly I am on my own, with enough income to pay my bills, and a decent-sized – not princely – net worth.

And just to be clear, if I were going to throw everything over for someone, it would be Ruth. Luckily for me, she's happily married—so we are happily "friended" rather than anything else. She suspects that I'm gay even though she knows I would do her in a heartbeat (women like knowing that, especially when they think the stud is gay). Forget that, not in a heartbeat. I don't want her husband, Murray, coming after me with a cleaver – ugh! Ruth and I have known each other for decades, when she was working for a hedge fund manager who made a run for the mayoralty of New York (and lost). Before she married Murray we used to go to the theater together, or dinner sometimes, but we never so much as kissed romantically. It's still more or less the same – I am her regular "date" because Murray does not like opera, concerts, musicals or Shakespeare – and apparently he can snore pretty loud even in a sitting-up position. I like Murray; we're friends.

So there we were, starting out from my place at 48th Street and 8th Avenue at about one o'clock, heading for the GW Bridge on bicycles. It was Sunday and it was September, and it was still drippy summer humid, so we took bottled water in the saddlebags. Dehydration is not part of my plan for myself. It being hot, the population on the bike trail was not as heavy as it would be in better weather. On weekends in hot weather, by the way, the great and the good are not in town – they're still out east (in the Hamptons), or down the shore (the beachfront towns in New Jersey), or maybe at some lake upstate if they can't afford either of the first two places. Still, there were rollerbladers, runners, sweaty walkers, and helmeted bikers like Gabriele and me. We dismounted at the Boat Basin at 79th Street and polished off a full bottle of Poland Spring water each, then refilled the bottles from a water fountain next to the restaurant there. Then we were back at it, pedaling and staring at the people on parade.

Gabriele wanted to stop at Riverbank State Park, which is a place that could only happen in New York. It's a real park, like 30 acres of real park, built on top of, *literally on top of*, a sewage treatment plant. No it doesn't smell bad. The bridge was looming in front of us, but I still couldn't see the little red lighthouse. There is actually a kids' book called *The Little Red Lighthouse*. I saw one in a used bookstore one time, and actually that is what caused me to look it up in Wikipedia and decide it was being added to my bucket list. There is actually a Little Red Lighthouse swim every year, but the thought of submerging myself in the Hudson River with God knows what kind of vermin or ancient industrial toxins, is far too grim to consider.

I kept thinking we would see the lighthouse, but it is really obscured by the trees, and as you get closer, it is hidden on the river side of the huge aluminum-colored erector-set pylons that hold the bridge up. Originally the bridge was to have looked more like the Brooklyn Bridge, with the metal skeleton covered by stone or cement. They never got around to doing the all-clad chiseled stone exterior during the Depression because it was too expensive. But the distinctive girders filled with x-shaped struts have been admired over the decades by artists and architects almost universally. One famous French architect said it was the most beautiful bridge in the world, and that was while he was designing the General Assembly building at the United Nations. Finally there was a branch of the bike path to the left and the little red lighthouse was there in front of us, where the main path continued on north.

We walked up the cast-iron staircase inside the lighthouse to the lantern, which has been restored as a lighthouse, even though its light is ridiculously overwhelmed by the millions of lights on the bridge that towers over it. Needless to say, the lighthouse predated the bridge by more than 40 years, so there was a navigational purpose to it when it was built. We admired it, and then walked over toward the base of the bridge to see how the structure was raised that is the busiest vehicle bridge in the world.

Italians are very much into beautiful things, and Gabriele is no exception. He was very taken by the bridge itself, from the completely unaccustomed angle and viewpoint we had. The gigantism of the bridge is more evident from beneath it than it is driving across it. Like the Great Pyramid at Giza, the simplicity of its shape makes it look smaller than it is in real life. The bridge is basically what has been called an inverted arch where the suspension cables are the defining aspect of its appearance. He was busily taking photo after photo on his smartphone, looking across the river toward the stunning vista of the Palisades on the New Jersey side of the river.

I walked over to the pylons to look up, and started taking some cellphone photos myself. I have to admit that my distance vision, even with my glasses on, is not 20-20, especially when the lighting is not great, but as I looked up, I saw what I thought must have been a big bird's nest in a corner up about 60 or 70 feet. The sun was in front of me as I looked up, and it obscured the nest, which I thought must be the abode of bald eagles, because there are certainly bald eagles all over and their whole diet is fish. If you drive along the Hudson River on a cold winter day, you can see the bald eagles sitting on ice floes waiting for a foolish fish to be visible – and then they dive straight into the water and come up with a meal. I was determined to get a picture.

Then it moved. Or swayed. I thought maybe I was getting dizzy, and looked down, put my hand out to a tree to steady myself. When I looked back up, the nest was quite different looking from what I had thought before. The sunlight was very dazzling, almost blinding me so I couldn't make out anything for sure. I walked back over to the water's edge and grabbed Gabriele's arm.

"Come over here," I said. "There's something I can't really see very well, and I want to know what it is."

I pointed up inside the pylon and said, "I thought there was an eagle's nest up there, but now I don't think that's what it is. Can you see what I'm pointing at?"

He nodded and took out a pair of dark sunglasses from his backpack and put them on. "There are two large black birds. No, maybe three."

"Black? Are you sure? They must be crows. That's disappointing, I was hoping they were eagles."

"I can't tell what they're doing, but they're flapping their wings like they are trying to hold onto something," he said.

Just as he said that, the birds let go of what they were holding onto and flew up to a girder. What they were sitting on was a black lump that was actually swaying like a streetlight in a high wind.

Then without warning it started to fall, and as it fell we could both see that it was not a nest, but something with a black piece of cloth waving as it fell. As it fell, we both knew what it was. It was a body, a human body, and it had been hanging from a rope. It hit the ground with a squishy thud. Gabriele stared at it; I ran over to the lighthouse and interrupted a uniformed woman who obviously worked there.

"I'm sorry, miss, officer," I said. "There's an emergency over here." I ran ahead of her to where Gabriele was standing and as I ran up to him, he turned and vomited all over the ground. When the body hit the ground, the birds returned and started to eat again. It was also immediately obvious why the body had fallen – the head had become detached from the body and had landed a few feet away. There was a ferocious smell.

I thought the woman was going to faint, but she didn't. She called in an alarm to someone, and there were sirens almost immediately.

Gabriele, who has the darker skin of a Mediterranean, was as pale as a sheet. I walked him down the slight incline toward the lighthouse and sat him on a bench. I pushed his legs up so that the knees were bent in front of him.

"Put your head between your knees," I said in as authoritative a voice as I could summon while feeling fairly sure I was going to be sick myself. We had moved away from the sight and smell of the cadaver and the birds, and there were firemen in full regalia, and paramedics running by us toward the pylon. I sank down on the bench next to Gabriele and put my arm around his shoulder. I was still wearing my backpack and I reached inside and pulled out a fresh bottle of water, opened it, and handed it to him.

"Just a little. Don't drink much. It'll make you sick."

He sat up, sweaty but with his color returning. His hand shook as he lifted the bottle to his mouth.

"The Bridge is the most common location for suicide anywhere in the whole region," I said. "Although most people jump off into the river. Hanging yourself seems like a much worse way to die than just smacking into the water."

He looked at me quizzically. "Nobody would kill himself like that," he said.

There was a used-car lot melee of yellow crime scene tape being strung from every vertical to every other vertical, and two plain-clothes detectives arrived within minutes. One stopped and said, "You found the body?"

We nodded.

"Stay here," he said. "I'll be right back."

I did not feel faint, but I had the inevitable reaction after a tidal wave of adrenalin had rushed through my body: too weak to stand up, or to hold my head erect on my neck. I looked down at my legs, at the black-and-yellow bike pants and the cross-trainer shoes I chose to wear instead of bike shoes. I could feel myself shaking, especially my head and my jaw.

The detective came back. "OK if I ask you some questions?"

We told him the whole thing. How I thought it was eagles but couldn't see over the glare from the sunlight. The birds scattering, the fall. "I guess you saw how it all landed," I said. "Did he kill himself?"

"No way to tell. The M.E. will have to rule on that. Can you tell me how you happened to be here today?"

I told him that we came to see the lighthouse, rode our bikes. Gabriele said nothing, just stared at the ground between his feet. The detective asked to see identification. He took photos of the two driver's licenses with his cellphone, thanked us and handed each of us his card. Then he turned to walk off toward the pylon.

"Excuse me, detective?"

He turned back to me.

"I don't think we're going to be up to riding our bikes 140 blocks back to Times Square. Any chance you could give us a lift? We have two bikes with us."

"Wait here," he said. "I'll see what I can do."

I pulled out my smartphone and called Ruth.

"Hey, sweetie," she said.

"Hey yourself. I'm up at the GW Bridge, under it, actually. Gabriele and I found a dead body, or it found us. The cops are here. We need to be picked up, because we rode our bikes up here and we're both just wrecked, never make it back on the bikes. And I don't have an Uber account. Can you come and get us? We have two bikes, so it has to be a car with plenty of room in back, or a pickup or something like that."

"What do you mean, a body?"

"Can I tell you later? A body. A dead man, dead for a while, being eaten by birds. The cops are working on it. We just have to get out of here. Both of us are ready to blow our stomachs. Gabriele already did."

"Murray has an Escalade. I'll bring that. Where are you?"

"Fort Washington Park, near the little red lighthouse if you know where that is."

"I'll figure it out. Or GPS will figure it out. Be there as soon as I can get the car out of the garage and drive up there. I'm a sight, not gonna get pretty before I leave. A body! Cripes. You are a magnet for mayhem,

Hugo Miller."

Fools Playing Fools (Hugo Miller Mystery 4)

Ned Savage, the handsome young gay director of an Off-Broadway production of "Twelfth Night," has his head bashed in with a candlestick. This happened the day after Ned moved into a small apartment directly adjacent to the home of Hugo Miller in Long Island City.

Why was he already dying before he was bludgeoned? Easy, *Aspergillus*, a fungus that likes to grow on marijuana plants, and that had set off a deadly chain reaction in Ned's body.

Whodunnit? Why did gay Ned marry Siobhan, a woman with a romantic preference for women?

Twists and turns abound as the fools on the stage play the fools in the classic play.

Chapter One – Fools Playing Fools

When I heard the commotion in the hallway outside my door, I opened the door a crack and looked out. Cops, white-coated CSI workers. They were talking to each other, but it was so muffled that I couldn't understand what they were saying. I guessed someone had died.

We were in the middle of a thunderstorm, an almost every-afternoon phenomenon anywhere near the Hudson River or New York harbor in the sweltering summer humidity. Zeus was slinging thunderbolts right, left and center, and the giants were bowling in the sky, creating rolling peals of ear-splitting, bomb-like explosions. It was the kind of storm that throws boats onto dry land and smashes sailing vessels against rocks and piers. Fortunately, these summer storms usually come and go fairly quickly, and then the sun comes out to dry the streets and sidewalks.

The apartment the CSIs were filing into was occupied by a young man whom I had not met, mostly because he had just moved in. Because it was still summer, I was trying to keep windows open when it wasn't raining and frequently propped the front door to the apartment open with a small but heavy fake-marble lion statue I bought at the Metropolitan Museum some years back. A cross-draft is a blessing in a New York heat wave. So, I had seen the young man going back and forth when he moved in. Never said hello.

He was boyishly handsome with almost shocking rock-star hair of a chestnut-auburn color, a fashionably scruffy almost-beard, enormous dark eyes and the regulation Levis and black t-shirt but with black leather lace-up shoes. He had a problem with his right side, holding his right hand in a cupped position that was at odds with the angle of his arm, and he almost dragged his right leg when he walked but didn't use a cane and walked in a straight line. Looked like a long-term problem, not the consequence of a recent fall off a motorcycle.

He wore a headset and was clearly listening to music or a radio show, was smiling and occasionally laughing quietly. Not talking on the phone. He looked happy. I paid attention because for some reason I was surprised that someone who looked to be crippled was in such a good mood on moving day, which I surmised must have been difficult at best for him. I considered introducing myself, but he seemed to be busy, so I thought I'd wait.

Well, it turned out I missed my chance to say hello because when the CSIs arrived a couple of days later, he was dead. Couldn't possibly have been over thirty, maybe as young as twenty-five.

My name is Hugo Miller, and I'm mostly retired from a business I started that specializes in public relations for sports teams and players. But I am also a civilian criminalist with the NYPD—mostly an honorary designation that lets me work on cases assisting a detective I know in the Midtown North precinct of Manhattan, Mike di Saronno. I kinda fell into this because of a homicide case in Manhattan where I was potentially a witness of something relevant. That was several years back, and since then I've worked with Mike on four or five cases.

That's all well and good, but I live in an area of Queens called Long Island City that's on the East River directly across from the east end of 42nd Street and the United Nations. My Manhattan credentials don't carry much weight with the local cops. To be fair, I used to live in the Theater District on 48th Street—until I got priced out of Manhattan by skyrocketing rents. And although I continue to work with Mike when he calls me, I hadn't introduced myself to anyone at the 108th precinct that was a couple of long blocks up my street.

I called Mike, who poked around and told me what he found out. The victim was Ned Savage, twenty-seven, an Equity actor who had worked on Broadway and in smaller theaters in the area. Went to acting school in Los Angeles where he grew up but had lived in the Theater District for several years. He rented the studio apartment on my floor and told the leasing agent he would be living there alone. Apparently, someone had conked him over the head with a brass candlestick.

"Must have happened quickly," I said. "My apartment is directly next door, and I think we share a wall in my guest bedroom. I never heard anything, so there must not have been much of a scuffle."

He said he thought the detectives would be knocking on my door to ask me some questions since my apartment shares a wall with Mr. Savage's place. As it happens, though, my apartment is a large two-bedroom, and I sleep on the opposite side of my floorplan from the hall or that apartment.

"Still, I think if there had been people throwing things or yelling, I would have heard some noise," I told the detective who was now asking me questions. "And since it's been hot, I've been keeping the sliding glass door open to the balcony to catch some breeze." I showed him and his partner the living room, with the sliding door open, a screen door keeping bugs out, and balcony directly upstairs forming a ceiling that kept it mostly dry during rainstorms. "If the balcony in that apartment was open like mine, I would for sure have known what was going on."

They were there to get information, not to give it to me, so I didn't bother to ask them anything, because I knew they'd clam up if I did. Figured Mike could find out and let me know.

I don't trust coincidences, but Mike told me Ned had moved into the apartment next to me from a high-rise across the street from where I used to live on 48th Street. I'd been living in Long Island City for almost five years and when I heard that, I tried to remember if that building was even ready for occupancy when I moved away. Anyway, he had to be well-off to live in a new luxury building in that area, because rents were sky-high; through-the-roof ridiculous. When I moved out of the Theater District my rent was almost five times what it had been when I moved in ten years earlier.

"For sure I don't remember seeing him when I lived on 48th Street," I said. "I would have remembered. Very striking fellow. Combination of rock-star and person with disabilities. Like somebody who had fallen off a trapeze with no net, or been thrown from a horse jumping over a hedge."

Mike suggested it might be good if he and I could get together. It was almost mid-day so I suggested we meet for a quick lunch at Ariana, a hole-in-the-wall Afghan restaurant on 9th Avenue at about 49th Street that combined good food and cheap prices. He agreed.

To get from my place to Times Square is easy. Take the 7 train from my subway station, three stops—maybe eight minutes—and you're at Times Square, exiting onto 43rd Street. It was a warm day, no rain, so I could walk to Ariana in ten minutes. I took a quick shower, decided I didn't need to shave, and was on my way, tapping on my cellphone to retrieve text messages from relatives in California.

These days there is free WiFi on the subway platforms, so I stood and texted until the train pulled up, about three minutes after I got there. I was at Ariana before Mike, who only had to walk five blocks from his office. Go figure.

I'm fond of Mike, though we are not friends in a social sense. He lives right near where I used to live and before I met him professionally, I would see him in this and that restaurant or bar from time to time and never knew he was a cop. But I have a good memory for faces and after a couple of sightings, I recognized him, but we never were introduced or shook hands. So, when I did meet him, it was a shock that he was a police detective. Very normal-looking, Italian features, slightly bronze, even in the winter, good symmetrical features, hazel eyes, taller than normal but not as tall as me.

I grabbed the table in the front bay window so I could watch for Mike and stare at people who walked by. I am a born voyeur; there's nothing more fascinating than watching people, even if they're just walking by. It's a little like watching a fire in a fireplace, very calming and I can't take my eyes off the parade of people meandering or scurrying by.

Mike was all apologies for being late.

"You're not late. I was early. No prob."

He told me before he looked at the menu that he was going to be working on the Savage case. The guy had been directing a production of *Twelfth Night* at an off-Broadway theater just off 8th Avenue in the 40s. Talk was that he was a *wunderkind*, a young prodigy. The kind of charismatic genius that everybody loves, especially in show biz.

"He looked really young, almost like a kid."

"Maybe you're getting old, Hugo. I never met him, but his photos don't look like a kid to me." He told me some of the things the CSIs had found. First of all, Savage didn't seem to have any immediate family, or at least there were no entries on his computer or in an old address book. They packaged up a drawerful of manila envelopes with papers in them and took them to the lab to make copies. At that point there was no next of kin to notify.

Second, the apartment had not been ransacked. Savage's body was found on the floor between the coffee table and the front door. The cushions on the couch that was also a pullout bed were rumpled, so it appeared that he might have been sitting there before whatever transpired that left him on the floor. The candlestick that appeared to be the cause of his death was on the floor but closer to the door than the body. It had blood and bits of hair on the base, indicating it had been grabbed by the top. The wound was on the right side of Savage's head, indicating that if the person holding the candlestick was facing Savage, he or she was left-handed. If he or she was behind Savage, then the indication would be right-handed. The M.E. would have to make the determination as to where the assailant was standing or sitting.

Mike went on to say it seemed logical that I help him on this case if I had time. Since I had an official tie to the department, there would a modest paycheck attached to the assignment. Enough to cover expenses and maybe go out to eat—once.

"Got nothing but time, Mike," I said. "Okay if I talk to Ruth and Gabriele?"

He smiled a friendly grin and nodded vigorously.

I texted Ruth and Gabriele on my way to the subway to see if we could meet up that evening for a drink. "The game is afoot," is how I ended the texts. It's a quote from Sherlock Holmes, and it actually comes from what the Brits call "shooting." The "game" are the birds—grouse, whatever—the shooters are after. And they can be heard running around in the brush, so "the game is afoot." I always thought it had something to do with a game, like a game you play. Nope. Brits are different from Americans.

Yes and yes. We agreed to meet at Dominie's Hoek, a watering-hole on Vernon Boulevard about a block and a half from the subway station on the 7 line. It's an old Dutch name for the area from before the Brits took over in 1664. Kind of a silly operetta of a take-over. The Brits arrived in the harbor and signaled to the Dutch that they were going to lay siege to the city, which was then just a cluster around what we call Battery Park. The Dutch figured they were joking, said no, go away. Then the Brits signaled that if the Dutch resisted they would "sack" the city – in other words, burn it, steal everything they could find, and rape the women. Seemed like an over-reaction, so the citizens of New Amsterdam refused to defend the city from the English ships. They gave up, much to the chagrin of Peter Stuyvesant, who had been the director-general and autocrat of the colony of New Netherlands for eighteen years. He was known to history as Peg Leg Pete, because he lost a leg in a naval battle somewhere in the Caribbean. Even though he was no longer in charge, he hung around on his big estate on the East River and died in Manhattan in 1672, so it couldn't have been a terribly hostile time between the two Protestant powers. He was buried in St Mark's in the Bowery, which was built on the site of the Stuyvesant family chapel.

Anyway, Dominie's Hoek is a place where you can get a good drink and sit outside in warm weather in a garden-ish patio in the back. They make burgers and such. Mostly it's a noisy neighborhood bar where you can wave at people you recognize, even if you don't know their names. Just about everybody is in a good mood.

Gabriele was early and arrived downstairs at my building at about six. The concierge called up, and yes, of course, send him up. He rang the bell, and when I answered, he was gesturing at the yellow crime-scene tape that was all over the end of the hallway just feet from my door. I nodded and he came in.

"Kid just moved in a day or two ago. Young guy, apparently in the theater business, directing a Shakespeare play near Times Square."

"What happen?"

"Well, I guess that's what we'll be trying to find out. Mike is heading the investigation because the kid was working near Mike's precinct and used to live in that zombie Irish building on 8th Avenue, the tall, super-skinny one. You remember it?"

He nodded and hugged me. He's a hugger. He's from Capri, with a lot of relatives in Naples; not sure, it seems different from time to time. He and his cousin, Dante, have a popular white-tablecloth restaurant in downtown Manhattan called Ora di Pranzo ("dinnertime"). Heavenly food. Gabriele is one of those confident Italian guys who attracts every eye in every room he walks into. I always look at his hair, since I am thinning/balding myself, but remember how nice it was to have hair when mine was still brown. I met him because he was a person of interest in a fairly sordid homicide several years back. He didn't do it, and we found out who did do it. Gabriele and I have been fast friends ever since. He says he's in love with me, which I try to smile through, but secretly it pleases me. Myself, I'm a two-time loser, two ex-wives with assorted kids, all on the West Coast. Limited contact. Not interested in hooking up again, but if I were, I would be aiming at Ruth, not Gabriele.

I live on the tenth floor; nice view of the Chrysler Building and the UN. Also that crazy tall Trump building that's across from the UN. Since he was early, we had a very short snort of whisky at my apartment to get loosened up and then walked over to the bar to meet Ruth.

Ruth is a fashion plate for the modish set who are into "classic" looks. In Ruth's case, that means older Chanel clothing, nubby fabrics that approach Turkish toweling at times, kinda Joan Crawford shoulders sometimes, usually worn over fairly tight tailored jeans that made it clear she had Betty Grable legs. Ruth is comfortably well-off, a widow with some family issues – her husband's ex-wife and her own brothers. Her father was a rabbi, and Ruth was observant, at least at the important times of the year. "Acerbic" would describe her personality, but smiley and sweet on top of the film-noir attitudes. She was a picture in Chanel pink that evening, with pink and white Vans. Gotta love a woman in comfortable shoes. I read somewhere that an average woman in spiked heels exerted the same amount of pressure on the floor under the spike as a full-grown hippopotamus. Impressive.

She does good entrances and paused in the doorway at Dominie's Hoek to be silhouetted by the sun.

"You did that on purpose, didn't you?" I asked as I bussed her on both cheeks like a European.

"Did what?"

"Stood in the doorway with the sun behind you."

"Pish-tush," she said, pulled out a chair at one of the tables and sat down. She made me smile every time I saw her. I re-appreciated that she didn't carry three handbags, which is what a lot of New York women do. Men use pockets more, and women use pocketbooks, purses, or backpacks, sometimes all three.

So I briefed them on what Mike had told me about Ned Savage. "I guess there was no real evidence of any kind of tussle, so the assumption is that either he was surprised or he knew whoever it was that hit him and didn't feel in danger. Nothing yet on next of kin, or whether he had any close relatives."

"Did you say he was an actor?" Ruth asked.

"What I was told was that he was directing a production of a Shakespeare play," I said. "I think it was *Twelfth Night,* in some off-Broadway theater."

"WSR," she said. "West Side Rep. I'm on their mailing list. I've met him. He was Bottom in their *Midsummer Night's Dream* a year or so ago. Good looking, has a limp." She pulled out her cellphone and tapped on it. "Here," she said, flashing a picture of Savage. "Brings out the mother instinct in me," she smiled.

"Yeah, that's him," I said. "Small world?"

Gabriele grabbed the phone from Ruth and looked at it. "He come Ora di Pranzo maybe two times, *con amici. Parl' Italiano, ma bruto. È una brava persona.*" (*He brought his friends and spoke Italian, but not well. Good man.*)

I wouldn't say that's why I love both of them, because it's not. I've loved them for years on their own merits. But the fact that Ruth is involved in what seems like every arts charity in Manhattan and Gabriele owns a restaurant that you have to reserve a month in advance to hope to get in – it don't hoit, as they say. There I was, living next door to an apartment where a man was murdered a couple of days before, and both of my best friends knew him. Go figure. What? Eight million people living in the five boroughs? I live in Queens. Ruth lives in Manhattan. Gabriele lives in Brooklyn. All three of us turn out to know this one guy, and I had only seen him, never met him even though he lived next door.

I made a mental note to look up West Side Rep and see what I could find out. A waiter took our orders. Glass of red for me, glass of white for Ruth, dirty vodka for Gabriele. It felt good to be sitting with them on a warm summer day and to be working together on a puzzle. When I was a kid, my favorite thing was to work on jigsaw puzzles – big ones, lots of little pieces, lots of areas of color that look the same on the boxtop. You find all the edges you can find, and work your way in toward the middle. There's a lot more in the way of blind alleys and dead ends when you're dealing with a homicide—don't get me wrong—and it's a good deal more somber than trying to fit the pieces together in a picture of bright seas and sailboats.

Gabriele said that Savage had been to Ora di Pranzo at least twice, both times with a group of young people, probably actors or people he was working with. I asked if they were well-behaved. He said something noncommittal, like he didn't remember.

**FOR THE FULL INVENTORY
OF QUALITY BOOKS**:
http://www.roguephoenixpress.com

Rogue Phoenix Press
Representing Excellence in Publishing

**Quality trade paperbacks and downloads
in multiple formats,
in genres ranging from historical to contemporary romance, mystery
and science fiction.
Visit the website then bookmark it.
We add new titles**